RISING SON
THE ASCENSION OF CHIUN

GERALD WELCH

RISING SON
THE ASCENSION OF CHIUN

Gerald Welch

© 2024 Warren Murphy Media, LLC

All rights reserved including, but not limited to, the right to reproduce this book or any portion thereof, in any form or by any manner, with the exception of reviews or as commentary.

Requests for reproduction or interviews should be directed to destroyerbooks@gmail.com

Cover and other artwork by Gerald Welch

Published by Destroyer Books/Warren Murphy Media LLC

Edited by Devin Murphy

First public printing: June 2024

ISBN-13: 978-1-955850-33-9
ISBN-10: 1-955850-33-X

This is a work of fiction. All characters and events portrayed in this novel are either products of the author's imagination or are used fictitiously.

This book is dedicated to the
man behind the curtain,

Devin Murphy

who keeps the dream alive
without bending his elbow.

Thanks for everything you do,
both seen and unseen.

and to

Tim King

who lives in the coolest-sounding
city in America.

INVICTUS

Eon and Song

FOREWORD

MOLLY COCHRAN

This is the book that millions of *Destroyer* fans have been waiting for—the origin story of the legendary Master of Sinanju, Chiun.

In *Rising Son*, author (and *Destroyer* fanatic) Gerald Welch has captured the essence of the world's supreme practitioner of the art of combat in the years before he first appears in *Created, the Destroyer*, the first novel in the over-150-volume series begun by Warren Murphy and Richard Sapir. Since its beginnings, *The Destroyer* has grown into a global phenomenon, published in dozens of countries, with multiple spinoffs and a popular feature film, *Remo Williams: the Adventure Begins*.

The real adventure, though, begins not with Remo, who becomes the Destroyer, but with his teacher Chiun, an extraordinarily gifted child born into the poor Korean village of Sinanju, who shapes his destiny through his mind and skill to become the Master, and eventually the mentor to America's most secret—and lethal—weapon.

Please note that exquisite cover art of *Rising Son* is also the work of multi-talented Jerry Welch, who, like so many of us, fell under the spell of *The Destroyer* many years ago and has devoted much of his career to the series that brought the epic myth of Sinanju to life.

The myth is definitely alive in *Rising Son*. So turn the page, and begin an unforgettable journey into the adventure that created the adventure.

∼

Molly Cochran
June, 2024

In the village of Sinanju, for over five thousand years,
Masters past and present shape how the world appears.

By cliff and pillar, shadows thrown, the Master grieves, spirit worn.
In the morning calm, mentally battered, standing strong.

The villagers cry a silent Song, for their future gone,
The Master's son was lost, a foolish cost; his inner battle rages on.

He musters strength though a veil of pain.
His tears fall freely like autumn rain.

Every tear is a memory wept, an ancient cost, and a promise kept.

Through the thicket of his thoughts, and past the trees,
Runs the Master of Sinanju, above the leaves.

His traditions lay heavy, choking and grand.
He walks the path that fate demands.

He can't stop thinking of what could have been.

Then a voice from beyond, quite strange and clear,
Promises hope, despite his fears.

This tale of Sinanju, so deeply sown.
The story of a Master, no longer alone.

In each new breath and in each new song:
Witness the power of the Rising Son.

PROLOGUE

Life was always harsh in the small fishing village of Sinanju. Isolated between the cold waters of the West Korean Bay and the scattered mountain ranges that seemed to consolidate some of Asia's most brutal weather, the poor community would have long ago disappeared into obscurity, were it not for one thing: it was home to the most dangerous men who had ever tread the surface of the Earth—the mysterious Masters of Sinanju.

For Sinanju is more than a village, it is an art: it is a way of life and a tradition that has transcended human history. Over five thousand years ago, a Master of Sinanju was contracted in service to Atlantis, quelling an internal conflict that would have destroyed that fabled island's population long before its surrender to the depths of the ocean.

Centuries later, another Master single-handedly secured the throne of Pharaoh Thutmose III, ushering in a new era of Egyptian dominance, changing North Africa's political landscape for the next two thousand years.

Throughout the span of human history, the Masters of Sinanju had silently carved their symbol into the bedrock of history. Every world leader, from tribal chieftains, to pharaohs, and even young heirs who were poised to inherit the world, knew about the brightly-robed men from Korea. Their stories, rich in awe and tinted with a fear normally reserved for the old gods, were woven into the cultures of every corner of mankind.

The awe was earned. Masters of Sinanju possessed skills that defied human explanation. A Master of Sinanju could stand unflinching against waves of arrows as if the very air bent to their will, effortlessly plucking death from the skies. With a single strike of their explosive empty hands, they could reduce granite walls into rubble. Entire regiments fell beneath the unyielding wrath of the unarmed Korean Masters. Their stories were discounted by archeologists and historians as exploits of mythical demi-gods, as wish fulfillment for desperate peoples.

Indeed, a journey to the village would reveal an unremarkable scene, not unlike most fishing villages of its era. The villagers' huts, weathered and aged by the ceaseless onslaught of sea spray and frigid winds, stood closely together in humble clusters against stone cliff ridges for warmth.

The fishermen's faces were worn with lines as deep as the nets they cast. They congregated each dawn, casting skeptical eyes toward the vindictive skies and cursed the fickle tides. But every day, good or bad, they rewarded their attempts with drink and resignation for the next day.

Other villagers had their own purposes. The local trader had turned cheating into an art form. The Masters were aware of his actions, and even allowed his grift to a certain point. A bit of discord could liven up an otherwise uneventful village.

The elderly women of Sinanju, the widows and those who had never married, gathered in small groups, hiding in the Widows Hut near the village center where they could keep an eye on their neighbors, indulging in conspiracies worthy of the greatest spy novels and gossip sharper than a fish hook.

And *everyone* knew that in the long silences between the

clanging of anvil and metal in the blacksmith's forge, a different kind of heat was kindled — the desperate kind, found at the bottom of a bottle, or in the furtive touch of a woman who carried the scent of another man's trade.

We do not speak about the shaman, who holds secrets both sacred and profane.

Between seasons of desolation and profound tragedy, there were moments of great joy that strengthened the people of Sinanju. But despite its isolation, the village was not immune from repercussions of historical events, like the first world war.

In the Great War's haunting legacy, the world bore witness to how fragile historical borders and once-stalwart allies were. Millions upon millions of people had suffered and died. Ancient cultures had been altered or destroyed. Their identities lay shattered on the political upheaval that had surrounded them, and wiped off the modern map as though they had never existed.

The physical scars of battle served as enduring testaments to the veneer of 'civilization.' But it was the emotional scars, those private and invisible wounds that caused the most pain, casting a shadow long enough to be felt as far away as the village of Sinanju.

At the edge of the rugged cliffs at the edge of the village, a solitary figure sat in pensive meditation. The man had a thin, but taut build. He looked thirty, though he was decades older.

If asked, he would have proudly described himself first and foremost as Sinanju. He was an honored descendant of Dangun, the originator of the Korean race, and had experienced the dark side of the world of men far too many times.

He had sought wisdom from the scrolls of his ancestors and had meditated for three days, but he could not find answers. The peaceful reflection of the moon on the cold waters below betrayed his cluttered mind.

Nūk, the reigning Master of the House of Sinanju, was in conflict.

CHAPTER ONE

A few years earlier, Nūk had been approached by a foreign agent, who offered a small job to assassinate an Archduke from one of the smaller European countries, but Nūk had just lost his wife and was in mourning.

Nūk could tell by the starstruck look in the man's eyes that he was just making an excuse to travel to Sinanju, and Nūk did not trust flattering eyes. He took the man's gold coin and graciously thanked him for his time, but explained that he was not currently available for hire.

Because of Nūk's unwillingness, amateurs were hired, resulting in the largest outbreak of war that had ever been recorded in the scrolls of Sinanju.

Nūk only heard of the war later, after a small skirmish in the West Korean Bay. Four ships, none of which were equipped for battle, were fighting in the bay. The noise was not loud enough to reach the villagers' ears, but the sounds of gunfire were very familiar to Nūk.

He tugged on the cord attached to his chair and a bell pierced the family room.

Though he was asleep, Chiun heard the bell and bounced out

of his bed, quickly gathering his robes. He had never been called by the bell before. It was only used for official business.

Chiun entered the greeting room from the front door.

"All hail the Master of Sinanju," he said with a deep bow.

As always, his father was seated in a large monstrosity of carved teak wood, leather, and gaudy baubles, precisely centered in the greeting room. Originally carved by the Bughanum for a past Master that Chiun did not care to remember, it was later garishly adorned by the French.

The fact that the history of a chair was included in the scrolls was a perfect illustration of Chiun's disdain for them.

But somehow, it did not seem out of place. In fact, it resembled the house itself—a bizarre eclectic mixture of styles that, by themselves, were distinct, stylish and, perhaps even regal, but together, were blended into a brightly colored…noisy…thing, an architectural nightmare where each piece competed for dominance.

"Father?" Chiun greeted with a deep bow.

"Get your reception robes and meet me at the Horns," Nuk said.

Chiun left with a smile. He had never worn his diplomatic hanbok in public before. Unlike his father's passion for yellows and green, Chiun had chosen the brightest red that the stitch weaver offered. His father allowed the choice, despite the Chinese influence of the golden dragon which wrapped around his torso.

Chiun quickly joined his father at the edge of the cliff, beneath the towering stone monoliths that both welcomed and warned all that approached Sinanju. The cold, briny wind swept across the cliffs, carrying with it the echoes of turmoil from the bay below, but while most people would have arrived with many layers of furs and blankets, neither Chiun or his father seemed to feel the bite of the cold winds.

Their eyes, sharp and discerning, fixated on the chaotic

dance of the ships below. There were four vessels, locked in an awkward skirmish. Their movements, clumsy and uncoordinated, were more akin to an elephant ballet than a battle. The sound of gunfire, sporadic and ill-timed, punctuated the air in a symphony of desperation.

"Master Nūk," Chiun began, his voice carrying the weight of formality, "what unfolds before us?"

"We do not use the diplomatic voice between ourselves," Nūk instructed, his gaze never leaving the battle below.

"Apologies, father," Chiun said, adjusting his stance. "I must admit, I am confused. Are these not potential vassals?"

"Yes, but unfortunately, they arrived at the same time. Once they realized that the others were also there to hire us, they began fighting."

"They seem lost, confused even," Chiun observed, his eyes narrowing as he tried to make sense of the scene. The ships, like wounded creatures, lashed out in blind fury, their purpose obscured by their own ineptitude.

Nūk nodded. "This is no longer a group concerned about hiring Sinanju; it is a struggle for survival. Confusion and fear now captain each of those vessels."

Chiun watched as the largest ship, a Celtic cruiser adorned with a long brass figurehead of a scantily-clad woman attempted to assert dominance.

"The Celtic ship, it bears the image of Danu, but why is she… undressed?"

Nūk's lips curled into a half-smile. "Artists are like bad writers. They create only what they want others to see. The figurehead is less Danu, and more of the artist's own longings, most likely a mistress."

"I don't understand," Chiun said. "Are they not mocking one of their gods?"

"As you travel, you will quickly find that what people claim is not what they actually believe. The details themselves don't even matter," Nūk sighed. "Yesterday, she was called Danann. Today, they call her Danu. Tomorrow, they will likely give up and start calling her Mary as the rest of the West has done."

"But Sinanju is forever," Chiun said with a confident smile.

"Sinanju is forever," Nūk replied with his own grin.

They continued watching the futile battle until the sound of gunfire disappeared. After they had exhausted their ammunition, the ships chased each other in an awkward elliptical dance. The only ammunition they had now was the shouts and slurs of sailors as they hurled small objects at each other.

"Pathetic," Chiun said. "Our widows curse better than that."

"Much better," Nūk admitted.

With two ships already treading water, it looked like the Celtic ship would be the victor. Only the small, pearl-encrusted galley from Kalimantan remained. It was too small to be attacked directly by the figurehead, but also too slow to escape.

The Kalimantan captain steered his vessel towards the port side of the Celtic behemoth. The ship had been scarred with an earlier collision and the planks were damaged. It was a suicidal gambit. but the captain placed trust in his ship's sturdy brass bow. It boasted a falcon head, pointed toward the sky. It was not as large as the Celtic maiden, but was incredibly sharp.

The impact was not a clash of titans, or triumphant bellow of victory, only the whimper of rending wood and the tinny screams of men. The Kalimantan vessel pierced the Celtic ship's hull, but was now being dragged down with it. Men from both ships jumped overboard and tried to swim for shore.

"That was briefly amusing," Chiun said. "What happens now?"

Nūk's gaze fixed on the churning sea, watching the flotsam of ambition surrender to the bay.

"We wait. The sea will claim its due, but a few men may yet reach our shore. If they do, we will be here."

They stood together, master and apprentice, silent witnesses to the unforgiving nature of the sea. Fewer than a dozen men had reached the shore only to die soon after. Of that, only four were able to reach the stone steps to the Horns of Welcome.

The men were uncontrollably shivering from hypothermia before they reached the top. Their thin tan smocks indicated that they had escaped from the Kalimantan vessel. Their shriveled leather sandals had been no match for the Korean sea. Seeking the man at the top of the steps, one of the servants bowed himself to the frozen ground.

(*Please help!*) he nearly shouted in his native tongue.

(*Where is your master?*) Nūk asked, recognizing the Kalimantan tongue.

The man, a portrait of misery, pointed a trembling finger towards the bay where only a few floating timbers remained, and then quickly hid behind the sixty-foot-tall Horn of Welcome as protection from the wind. The men gathered together for warmth.

(*He lies at the bottom of your sea, lord. Please, mercy sir!*)

"Did you understand what he said?" Nūk asked.

"Of course, but aren't these men just servants?"

"Yes, but even servants have ears," Nūk said and turned to the man. (*Why have you come to Sinanju?*)

The man's eyes widened with recognition.

(*Sinanju! The world has gone insane! War has spread to every realm and it cannot be stopped! We were sent to obtain your help!*)

His voice trailed off, helpless against the ceaseless howling of the wind.

Nūk nodded and traced an invisible sigil in the air with his hand. The man nodded and told the others to follow Chiun.

"Take them to one of the empty huts in front. There are some old goat furs inside they can use for warmth. Start a fire and have the butcher bring them meat."

"Father?" Chiun asked, confused.

"These men will not survive if we don't hurry, and I have

many questions. Tell the butcher to prepare all of the scraps that were left over from yesterday's feast and feed these men. After they are warm and rested and their bellies are full, they will retrieve any valuables from the ships and salvage good pieces of wood for us. When they are finished, we will pay them so they may return to their country to explain what happened."

"It shall be done," Chiun said, motioning for the men to follow him.

(*Mercy upon you, sir! Many blessings!*) the Kalimantan servant said, clapping his hands together and smiling.

One of the servants died before making it to the hut. The other three carried him to the sea the next day to join their captain. After recovering from the cold, the men spent almost a week retrieving spoils and maps. It took another three days to break good pieces of wood from the ships. Nūk kept two of the larger pearl inlaid boards for himself and instructed the rest to be spread out among the villagers.

After they finished, Master Nūk provided them with a small boat and gave each man a handful of copper. He instructed them to send someone from their nation to return, but he never heard from them again.

Nūk soon began hearing of the many battles that embroiled the west of Europe, threatening to spill into Asia, Africa and had even reached the new lands of North America. It seemed that the world decided that they would take care of this growing war on their own and rely on their new weapons and countless soldiers. They would win this war by grinding blood and metal together.

The world had chosen a war without Sinanju.

Nūk stood alone by the Horns of Welcome, watching the distant horizon. The sea, vast and unforgiving, mirrored the uncertainty swirling within him. He looked at Chiun, a flicker of doubt clouding his face, and wondered if there would be a need for Sinanju in his son's world.

CHAPTER TWO

*H*is name was Chiun, and a gentle smile danced across his face as he looked into the mirror. Renowned for his lustrous, dark hair and immaculate appearance, today, he saw a newfound maturity in his eyes. Chiun studied himself in the mirror. He seemed to be a stranger in another man's clothes. There was a sheen to his eyes he hadn't possessed before. It was not arrogance, but something more—a weight unseen by those who did not know where to look.

He had just turned twenty-five and this was his first official day as the Apprentice Master of Sinanju. He ran a hand through his hair, feeling the dark strands of silk play between his fingers. He smoothed the black tunic that was draped over his frame, the fabric still imbued with the memory of a harder man, and a stark contrast to the bright red robes he was used to wearing.

It was more than just a tunic, it was an heirloom from his father's youth. The only touch of color was the gold threaded symbol of Sinanju, embroidered with painstaking detail over his heart. Its cool threads were a constant reminder of the responsibilities now resting upon his shoulders.

Chiun adjusted his center for the (*unnecessarily*) flowing

sleeves and flared leggings, each movement a balancing act. He had been so used to his own clothing that he had not expected the slight shifts in weight to matter as much as they did. Perhaps, he thought, that was the point. Satisfied with his appearance, Chiun exited his room and entered the central hall.

Every oddity and each disjointed decision about the central hall was the result of the Master at the time: a man who knew more about having children than architecture. His only claim to fame, beside adding two extra bedrooms to the house, was fathering the most children of any Master in the history of Sinanju.

The scrolls never forgave Wotan the Lover.

Masters of Sinanju are, of course, commanded to father one son, and highly suggested to have two. Most masters end their heritage at that point, including Nūk. After he was satisfied with Chiun's training, he allowed his wife Ji to have another son. Nūk named him Kwan, based on the name of a Qi chieftain who had recently doubled his tribute.

Kwan was the light of the house, his laughter a melody that lived in the bedroom closest to the kitchen, where his caretaker could more easily access him.

Exiting the central hall to the north, Chiun entered the small clearing that was used for meditation and practice. The area had been cleared of most of the trees and surrounded by a natural wall of Ginkgo and pine trees. Chiun had not used the area for practice since he was twelve. He looked at the familiar marks where his young hand had struck a tree stump too quickly, carelessly shattering the bark. It was still a familiar ache, and a reminder of the lessons learned through pain.

He bowed to the stump, thankful for its lesson, and began the early forms, his body was a fluid whipcrack, every precisely controlled movement honoring the masters who came before him.

An arm thrust, led into a twist around a scarred boulder. A

leap propelled into the air—not too high—by an imagined foe. In these moments of communion with the past, Chiun felt not just the weight of lineage, but the thrill of his own power taking shape within his body.

Forms that had begun as stiff, rote movements sung through the air as his body blended seamlessly from one move to the next.

Years earlier, his mother Ji had sat under the shade of one of the larger ginkgo trees, watching her little boy attack tree stumps. Chiun had begun late in Sinanju training. He was three when he was weaned and was not yet breathing correctly.

Chiun was picky about the little bright robes that Ji had brought him. He absolutely refused to wear pink or yellow. Once he put on a green robe similar to his father's and mid-lesson stripped it off. Ji teased Nūk that if Chiun never became a Master of Sinanju, he would make a great fashion designer.

"Mighty Chiun, Fashion Master of Sinanju!" she would shout, clapping as he pretended to strike a large stump with his fat little fists.

Chiun would then attempt a somersault, rolling toward her and leap into her arms.

Her eyes, he remembered. There was something about his mother's eyes that he did not see in any other Sinanju woman.

They were almost round.

In those eyes, Chiun saw love and he saw life. Those eyes sparkled with mirth as she wove tales of Sinanju's past for him, especially those concerning Chiun's father. Her voice, soft yet resonant, spoke of heroes and legends, imbuing Chiun with a sense of pride and purpose in his lineage.

The day after Chiun began breathing correctly, Ji had gently taken Chiun's hands and bowed, saying, "You carry our history and our soul in every breath you take, young master."

One of the smallest women in the village, Ji's eyes were a light green and their shape not of the village. This caused her great stress when she was younger. She was often taunted for her "weak western eyes", and when Nūk's father chose her to be his bride, Nūk was furious.

How was he expected to explain this to clients if they ever came to the village?

But his father had insisted and the wedding proceeded.

It was only after she gave birth to Chiun that Nūk began to see things differently. The way she lovingly attended to his son, the smile they both shared...something softened inside Nūk, and he began to pay attention to her as a person.

He discovered that Ji was a fair woman with a good heart and a sharp mind, charming and funny. He had been blind to what his father had seen. Where he had once only seen her as a maid and bedfellow, he now saw that she was appreciative of life and filled with laughter and joy.

Nūk began thinking of her as a proper wife, and on that day, he looked into her eyes and no longer noticed their shape. Once Nūk discovered who Ji really was, he fell in love with her unexpected charms.

The next time he saw his father, Nūk humbly thanked him for his wisdom.

Chiun was fourteen when he was old enough to first accompany his father on a diplomatic trip. Ji smiled and leaned over to give him a kiss on the cheek. Although he was technically too old for such a thing, Chiun did not mind.

She pulled the front of his hanbok tightly together, even though she knew that he would not be affected by cold on the trip.

His three-year-old brother Kwan squinted at Chiun's ceremonial robe.

"You look funny," he said, giggling.

Chiun tried to ignore him, but his recent studies on spacial awareness meant that he knew when Kwan stuck his tongue out at him, and each time he awkwardly danced behind Chiun to make fun of him.

"Be good and remain silent," Ji reminded Chiun. "This is a very important meeting."

"I will serve the Master with honor," Chiun said sharply, giving her a deep bow.

Nūk winked at Ji. Chiun looked cute, especially when he was pretending to be a Master.

"We're taking the coach to Seoul to meet with the Governor General," Nūk said. "We'll return in a few days."

"I will be happy to see you return," Ji said. "In your absence, I will be training Somi."

"The one who just got married?" Nūk asked.

"Her husband is not happy with her progress as a wife."

"I can have a talk with him if you want," Nūk said with a sharply raised eyebrow. "That tends to straighten things out."

Ji smiled at the thought. Somi's husband was known for his arrogance.

"If these lessons do not help, I will accept the offer," Ji said with a smile. "Somi has tried her best, but her mother died when she was young and her father was unable to properly train her. She is a shy girl, so we will meet in the mornings away from prying and gossip-hungry eyes."

"Just be careful," Nūk said. "Ice builds up strong in the morning, so don't go too early. And don't bother the shaman."

Kwan took the moment to speak up with what he called his 'angry eyes.'

"I want to ride with the ponies, too!" he said. "Chiun always gets to go!"

Nūk kneeled to Kwan's eye level.

"One day, you and I will ride the ponies for as long as you can stay awake," he promised.

Kwan's eyes opened wide with anticipation and joy as he

watched Nŭk's hands perform a complex dance in the air and then they suddenly swooped in, faster than his eyes could follow. Nŭk's left hand playfully pinched his nose, triggering a small nerve that sent tickles throughout his spine. Kwan fell to the floor laughing.

He then hopped up and gave Chiun a big hug.

"I love you, big brother!" he said, squeezing as hard as he could.

Chiun started to push him away, until he saw his father's eyebrow raise.

"I love you, too, little brother," Chiun said, almost believing it.

Kwan released his grip and pulled Chiun down to give him a big kiss on the cheek. Chiun had to concentrate on his breathing to remain perfectly still and only wiped the slobber off after Kwan turned away.

Nŭk slowly bowed to Ji, keeping his eyes fixated on her.

"Jalga nae salang," he whispered. *Goodbye, my love.*

Ji followed them to the door and tapped Chiun on the shoulder, silently handing him a honey rice cookie. Any form of sweet was a rare treat for a pupil of Sinanju and it caused Chiun's heartbeat to race in anticipation, something that Nŭk instantly noticed.

"If he is good, I will give the boy a small piece each day," Nŭk said, suddenly holding the cookie.

Ji lovingly blew a kiss to Chiun and waved goodbye. He smiled and gave her a hug and then raced ahead to his father, a blur of red against green, oblivious to the pain that lay ahead.

CHAPTER THREE

The rising sun painted the road to Seoul in bright, hopeful shades of gold. Every creak of the carriage, every rhythmic clop of the horse's hooves, vibrated through Chiun with anticipation. He barely paid attention to the familiar sights of his homeland as they passed, the stooped figures going to the fields, the call of seabirds along the rugged coast.

Chiun was only thinking of Seoul.

The trip was longer than he had remembered, so he nibbled on the rice ball he brought, wondering where his father had hidden the cookie his mother had made. They had traveled through the night so they could arrive in Seoul early the next morning. Chiun had managed to force himself to sleep, because this was not merely another trip to Seoul, which was already exciting enough.

This was an initiation, a rite of passage that would bind him to the long lineage of Sinanju. Today, he was not just Chiun, he was a participant in a legacy stretching back generations. Perhaps his father would write about this in the scrolls! And if he did, maybe he would mention that his son attended this important meeting! Chiun was doubly intent on impressing his father, lest his first entry in the scrolls would be a bad mention. Those masters who began with bad mentions never improved and Chiun was aiming to be the best of them all.

Well, maybe not better than Wang. The GREAT Wang, not Wang the lesser or the Wang who the Great Wang was named after. No one even paid attention to that Wang!

Seoul shimmered on the horizon, the heart of Korea itself! Chiun pressed his face against the carriage window, eager to see the grand shops and bustling markets that always filled him with wonder.

But as they took the road that would lead to the government building, Chiun's forehead wrinkled in confusion. Thinking he had never seen this part of Seoul before, his mouth almost opened in shock as he saw a large Japanese flag towering over a Korean Temple.

He had thought that by going toward the center of the town, he would be happier seeing the large pagodas and colorful crowds, but he couldn't forget seeing a Japanese flag planted in the very heart of Korea.

Then they entered the center of Seoul. Buildings unlike any Chiun had seen before, adorned with symbols that spoke of a foreign power, marred the familiar landscape. A knot of unease tightened in his stomach as they neared the city. The things he knew about Seoul were overshadowed by imposing buildings, each adorned with strange symbols. Disappointment pricked at his excitement. By the time they were a mile from the Government-General building, Chiun's excitement had already been extinguished.

As the smells of the city began to overtake those of the country, Nūk opened his eyes for the first time. His peripheral vision immediately captured his environment, mapping out the locations of all possible threats and then fell upon his son, who was grimacing as he looked out the window.

Chiun was currently in training to master each of his senses. He was currently concentrating on smell. The city's stench had hit him in waves, first small and putrid, then flooding his olfactory receptors with a noxious, unnatural mixture of spice and sewage.

He involuntarily gasped, and tried holding his breath, but his sense of smell only flared, opening him to even more localized smells: the decay of meat and sweat and damp wood, blinding him to everything else. The overwhelming odor of his surroundings almost overpowered him until he concentrated on his breathing.

Within a few minutes, he had regained control.

His father had noticed Chiun's struggle, but said nothing. He was proud that Chiun was able to manage it himself. Nūk's lips twitched almost imperceptibly — the closest he'd come to a smile in weeks.

Clearing his mind, Chiun looked around. The few Koreans that he saw were scurrying from place to place as if they did not belong in public.

"Why are you scowling?" Nūk asked.

"The Japanese stain our land."

"Do you mean those?" Nūk asked, pointing to the various Japanese ornamentals that adorned the larger buildings.

"Yes!" Chiun said sternly. "They do not belong here."

"This is an attempt to show power," Nūk explained. "Yesterday, it was the Chinese, today, it is the Japanese, but you must always remember: Sinanju is forever."

Chiun continued glaring out the window in disgust.

Nūk's brow wrinkled in concern.

"Why does this bother you?" he asked. "Are you Korean or Sinanju?"

"I am Sinanju," Chiun said proudly, returning his gaze to his father. "But Sinanju is Korea."

"Sinanju is *in* Korea," Nūk corrected. "You must never mistake the two."

"This still bothers me," Chiun admitted. "But I will not allow the Governor to see my disdain."

The carriage stopped in front of the Government-General building and they exited. The building showcased a mixture of neoclassical Western architectural elements with fixed motifs, reflecting Japan's imperial dominance.

The soldiers stationed at the front of the building were young Japanese men, highly disciplined and chosen for their loyalty to the emperor. They were accustomed to seeing dignitaries and high officials, yet the approach of the Korean visitors struck a chord of dread within them.

Their eyes were trained in the rigidity of military discipline, yet still buried in the myths of their homeland. Nūk and Chiun seemed to silently float across the ground, a movement so smooth and graceful that it whispered of the supernatural.

The soldiers tried to quell their shivers. They bowed deeply as the pair approached, clinching their eyes shut while remembering the tales told to them by their elders.

Koreans use dark magic.
Koreans can never be trusted.
Koreans are demons.
Never look an old Korean man in the eye.

After Nūk and Chiun passed, the soldiers returned to attention a quick glance to each other was all that was needed to silently agree to never mention this to anyone.

Chiun scowled as they entered. The inside of the Government building was just as bland as the outside. Someone had attempted to liven the place with runway carpeting and a few paintings, but it did not help.

Then they reached the hallway leading to the Governor General's office. It was fully carpeted and the dead concrete walls were covered with lightly-stained blossom wood and regally bordered paintings of the emperor.

The guards stationed outside the Governor's office were more lavishly adorned than those outside the building. Bright pins and strips of gold cloth, symbols of past glories and military experience held them to their stations. If they found Nūk and Chiun's walk unnerving, they kept it to themselves. With a grand flourish, one of the officers opened the door, allowing Nūk and Chiun to enter.

Windows, tall and imposing, framed the back of the large office. Filtered light passed through panes that danced across polished wooden floors. The furniture was a statement, highlighting a craftsmanship and artistry worthy enough to serve the emperor himself. Dark woods had been imported from distant lands and carved into shapes that pleased the eye, yet suggested strength and endurance.

Behind a desk that was as much a barricade as a piece of furniture, Governor-General Terauchi Masatake sat with the confident poise of an oak tree. His face was a mask of imperial intent, betraying no emotion that might reveal the thoughts churning behind his steely gaze.

Terauchi had received a phone call from Prime Minister Okuma Shigenobu the week prior. He was told to clear his schedule and prepare to receive a representative from a small Korean fishing village.

A man out of his time, Shigenobu was known for his Western-style dress, a choice that reflected his forward-thinking and openness to Western ideas, which was seen by some as an abandonment of Japanese heritage. But behind the façade was a man who clearly saw Japan as the next great world power.

"Perhaps I did not understand you," Terauchi said. "I am to clear my schedule — an entire day — for a fisherman?"

Prime Minister Shigenobu was not used to being questioned, even by his friend.

"Governor-General, your personal beliefs and the details of this meeting are irrelevant. You will concentrate on the emperor's satisfaction with this meeting."

Terauchi remained silent for a moment and tried to directly appeal to his long friendship with Shigenobu.

"Okuma," Terauchi almost whispered. "My friend, what are you not telling me? Korean fishermen are mud people. They drink fish water and eat with their fingers."

There was a pause as Shigenobu considered his words.

Terauchi heard a long sigh.

"I can only tell you that this village is not like the others. Its shadow stretches farther than you know. It is not safe to underestimate its significance."

"Very well," Terauchi said, begrudgingly.

The conversation had revealed only enough information to obtain Terauchi's acceptance. So, when the door to his office opened, Terauchi's initial irritation had given way to curiosity.

There were two Koreans, not one—a middle-aged man and a young boy. Instead of the muddy rags that he had imagined, both were adorned in some kind of ceremonial Korean robe. Though they might have been considered decorative in their home village, the robes were bright and gaudy. And what reason could justify bringing a child to a diplomatic meeting?

As they entered the office, Chiun's senses flared again. Freshly-applied stain and warehouse dust began to overwhelm him. He tried to center his breathing again, but it only got worse. He began to notice other scents and became lost in their haze: a whiff of mint, burnt tobacco, lemon.

This time, Nuk quickly placed a hand in the middle of Chiun's back and manipulated the nerves in his spine, blocking his ability to smell. Chiun quickly regained his composure and repressed a scowl as he looked around the room.

Terauchi, the cog in the imperial machine that ground down

Korea, sat in front of him as if he had a right to be in Seoul, much less Korea.

Chiun kept his hands in the sleeves of his robe, and he clenched his fists until his long nails began digging into his palms.

"You are early," Terauchi remarked as he motioned for them both to sit. His gaze lingered on their robes with obvious contempt.

"Sinanju is never late, Governor," Nūk said as he and Chiun took a seat.

Chiun's eyes flickered to the wooden train set displayed on the table at the side of the Governor's desk. There were six small cars, each handmade of teak, with tiny details carved out for the windows and the wheels. Chiun loved trains, but forced his attention back to the Governor.

Terauchi was looking at Nūk with disdain.

"I do not like my time being wasted, especially by fishermen. What is it you want?"

Chiun almost gasped and his eyes opened slightly in shock. No one had ever openly spoken to his father like that. Chiun took in a quick, silent breath to strengthen his center, ready for anything. Surely, his father would tear the tongue from this insolent Japanese man and raze this entire building!

Nūk merely leaned forward and smiled.

"We only seek that which has been promised to Sinanju," he said, handing a thick envelope to the governor.

Terauchi noted that it was sealed by the emperor's personal wax stamp. His hand darted out, snatching the envelope from Nūk's hand. Terauchi looked at the envelope and then at Nūk.

"You expect me to believe that this is real?" he asked.

"I expect you to listen to your emperor," Nūk suggested.

Terauchi's eyes narrowed as he looked more closely at the back of the envelope. The Imperial Seal was undeniably authentic. He grabbed a small knife and carefully broke the seal.

Inside was a short letter personally signed by the emperor. Its intentions were clear: the governor was ordered by the emperor to supply the village of Sinanju with monthly shipments of food and goods beginning immediately and lasting indefinitely. It sounded too good to be true. These people… these Koreans with their endless tricks could not be trusted. Yet, if true, the emperor's intent was clear.

A flicker of frustration crossed his features before settling back into a mask of impassiveness. He would follow the emperor's orders and supply the village, but only to the letter.

"How did you obtain this?"

"The emperor personally handed it to me."

"The emperor personally met with *you*?" Terauchi asked in disbelief. "I believe that to be a lie."

"That is not my concern," Nuk said.

Terauchi looked at the letter again, seeking any indication of forgery, but there was none. His fingers tightened until the paper began to crinkle. A vein pulsed in his temple and he finally loosened his grip. He had not taken this post to bow and scrape before a fisherman. He had come to Korea to subjugate, not serve.

Terauchi simmered in his seat and slapped the paper on his desk.

"A convoy shall be sent each month on the first," he said, his jaw muscles flinching uncontrollably. "But if I find this to be a forgery of any kind, the next shipment you see will be tanks and Imperial soldiers."

Nuk continued to display the calm smile he had entered with.

"Sinanju appreciates your compliance," he said and motioned for Chiun to follow him out.

. . .

They remained silent as they exited the office. The air of the Government-General building seemed to tighten around Chiun, a physical manifestation of the political and emotional tensions he had just witnessed. His expectations prior to arriving now seemed naïve. His father did not kill the Japanese Governor for his insults, but the dignity with which he carried himself filled Chiun with a profound sense of pride.

The carriage was waiting outside the building and the two quickly entered.

"That was not what you had expected?" Nūk asked after they began moving down the road.

"No," Chiun admitted.

"You think perhaps that I should have killed him?"

"Yes! He treated you like a Siamese beggar!"

"Am I a Siamese beggar?" Nūk asked.

"No," Chiun admitted. "But…"

"Then why do you feel the need to protest it?"

"I don't want anyone to think of you that way," Chiun said.

"How sharp is the edge of a lie?" Nūk asked.

"'A lie is only sharp to those who wish to cut themselves with it'," Chiun repeated from the scrolls.

"What defenses has Sinanju devised to protect you from words?" Nūk asked. "Much less words that are not true?"

Chiun thought long and hard.

"There is no defense," he said.

"Because there is no need for a defense. If a word comes from a man's mouth and you allow it to hurt you, who then has the real power?"

Chiun looked down. "The man."

"Besides," Nūk said, winking, "when do we kill for free?

"He speaks to you with no respect," Chiun said, a hint of youthful defiance tinting his words.

"And what does that tell you, that a man insulted me and

lives?" Nuk probed gently, encouraging his son to look deeper into the nuances of their interactions.

"This is something that I do not understand and I need to learn more," Chiun answered.

"This is your very first piece of wisdom," Nuk said. "Very good. Remember it."

As they returned to the village, Chiun clenched his fists, images of the Governor General's scornful face flashed before his eyes, a phantom wisp of pipe smoke clinging to the memory. The road home felt foreign, each bump of the carriage a reminder of the insults endured. But Chiun had maintained a composed demeanor throughout, a testament to his father's training.

Chiun's gaze wandered across the landscape, now viewing the familiar scenery through the lens of his newfound experiences. The verdant fields, a patchwork of labor and beauty, whispered stories of generations rooted in these lands. Most people were too busy working to notice the carriage pass, but those who did, gleefully bowed as they passed.

This may not be Sinanju, Chiun thought, but these were his people.

"Now that we have some time," Nuk said, grabbing his attention. "Let us think forward to the day when you are Master. I will be an old man looking to my son to lead our village into the future. Hungry, but hopeful eyes will look at you, with one question on their minds: Will he fulfill his duty as Master?"

Chiun looked down in thought for a moment and then he remembered the little wooden train set in the Governor-General's office.

"When I am master, I will build a great railroad that connects our village to the rest of the world!" he declared, motioning with his hands. "This will give us access to food and goods."

"That is a mighty ambition, indeed," Nuk replied. "But what

connects us to the rest of the world also connects the rest of the world to us. Our village is small and cannot handle an invasion of foreigners sniffing around our village for gold."

"Then maybe just one to Seoul and back," Chiun suggested with a smile. "I like trains."

"So, what would you do with this carriage or our horses? Should we feed them to the Mongols?"

Chiun's face warped in shock. The ponies were large and strong and majestic, the most beautiful beasts he had ever seen. He could not imagine anyone eating them, especially Mongols.

"Perhaps we should start small," Nūk suggested, "we could choose to travel by rail whenever possible and enjoy trains that way?"

"I suppose," Chiun said, defeated.

Nūk nodded. As the carriage rolled on, a shared silence enveloped father and son, and each became lost in their thoughts. The journey had been a pivotal moment for Chiun, a step closer to his destiny as Sinanju's future master. Yet, as the carriage moved on, a simple, childlike yearning surfaced within him, a reminder of the innocence not yet lost to the weight of his future duties.

"I still wish we could have a train," Chiun murmured.

Nūk's laughter, soft and understanding, filled the carriage.

CHAPTER FOUR

The next morning, Ji grabbed a bundle of laundry and headed for the bay, early enough to trespass on the morning fog, but not so early as to bother the shaman. Normally, she would have waited and washed clothes with the other women in the afternoon, when the day was warmer, but she had asked a young woman named Somi to meet her there.

Somi had just turned fifteen and had recently married one of the farm boys north of the village and was having a difficult time. Her mother died when she was three, and her father was unable to properly raise her.

Worse, her brown hair marked a visible impurity in her Sinanju blood and the village was not known for tolerance. Ji understood that feeling all too well. Had she not married Nūk, she herself would still be an outcast, most likely married to one of the fishermen, if at all.

While Ji's position as the wife of the master held no official title, she did have *some* influence with the other women. Somi's eyes held the same lonely shadows that once haunted her own. To weave her into the social fabric of Sinanju, Ji would first have to thread the needle with trust.

They would work on the other women later.

Ji's brow wrinkled in concern at the thought. How many other girls were like this that she didn't know about?

As she approached the western part of the bay, Ji was glad to see that most of the ice had already melted. Slipping on ice was one of the main dangers of working so close to the water. She scrubbed the surface of one of the flat table rocks that lined this section of the beach, before placing her laundry on a rock near the churning waters of the bay.

As Ji leaned over, a gull screeched overhead, echoing its morning call across the sky. The waters appeared to almost glow with a luminescent green in the early morning because of the bright moss draped across the stones.

Somi appeared from the north, carrying a small bundle of clothes. She was still a young woman, and, with the exception of her hair, quite beautiful. She wore a thick pink overcoat, with a small turban binding her hair tightly to her head. Ji had heard that her husband demanded that she wear her hair in a turban at all times so she would not embarrass him.

Her awkward walk was only partially due to the weight of the laundry. Ji could almost see the shame coiled in her belly: shame for her ignorance, shame for her hair, shame for being a burden. Somi carried her head low as she approached.

"Annyeong!" Ji said, smiling cordially.

Somi nodded back and forced a timid smile.

"Thank you for your help," she managed to say. "My husband says that I must learn to be a better wife. He is very upset with me."

"He will be singing your praise in no time!" Ji said, showing a smile that caused Somi to show a genuine smile of her own.

"Place your basket near that flat rock," Ji said, motioning to the one beside her. "How much do you know about washing clothes?"

"I do not…nothing," Somi admitted.

"It's easy," Ji said supportively. "First you just remove mud, fish bits, old food, then you rub the clothes together on the rock, then you rinse then clean. Do you have a drying line?"

"Yes, but it is very short."

"That is all it takes," Ji said. "Now, do what I do."

Ji offered her a thick old sponge to wipe the surface clean of debris. Her hands moved with practiced efficiency, with the rhythm of a familiar song.

"Sing with me," Ji urged. "It helps pace the cleaning and time goes by faster."

Somi bashfully bowed her head, but began singing along with Ji as soon as she recognized the words to *Sae Taryeong*.

> *Oh little bird, let's fly to where the pretty flowers bloom,*
> *Let's fly to where the clear streams flow.*
> *Oh little bird, let's fly to where the bright moon shines,*
> *Let's fly to where the cool breeze blows.*

USING the song for her tempo Somi struggled to follow, her brow furrowed in concentration. But after a while, each splash of water carried away Somi's anxieties, and she began to enjoy the song.

Somi began mimicking Ji's motions, separating each piece of clothing on the flat stone.

"See? This is easy," Ji said, encouraging her.

"Can you also show me how to be cheerful, even on the coldest days," Somi asked.

Ji laughed.

"My husband says that it is always better to be cold and cheerful than cold and grumpy!"

"How do you get the fish smell out?" Somi asked, embarrassed.

Ji smiled. "It's all in the wrist and a bit of patience. Here, let me show you."

As she leaned over, a shiver unrelated to the cold danced down Ji's spine. The rock beneath her foot gave way, twisting her ankle. Ji tried to regain her balance, but the emerald fingers of moss prevented her from gaining a solid foothold. She fell backwards toward the bay and her head struck one of the larger rocks between the stones. The sound of skull striking stone was sickeningly sharp.

Stunned by the impact, Ji was unable to stop her fall into the bay. The cold water filled her mouth before she was able to grab a breath. Her body, already numb from the cold, was helplessly carried away, when a strong hand reached for her, but it was too late. Ji was no longer able to hold her breath and the cold invaded her lungs. Her body began spasming for oxygen and she surrendered to the water's cold embrace.

"Aigo!" Somi screamed.

Without thinking, Somi jumped into the cold waters. She may not have known how to clean clothes, but she was an experienced swimmer. Somi ignored the cold shock as she entered the bay and grabbed Ji by the arm and pulled her limp body close, trying to hold her face above water.

Somi battled the icy current, her muscles screaming in protest. She managed to pull Ji back to the coastal rocks, but her strength was fading. She was not strong enough to pull her over the rocks.

She began to lose her grip on Ji's arm.

"Help!" she screamed, over and over.

The blacksmith was the first to hear her cry. The raw panic in her voice was not a sound he had ever heard from a human. The sound sent him running, abandoning his apron and tools along the way. Others arrived quickly after: first the fishmonger's wife, then the leather maker. Even Yena the teacher left her children to help.

Together, they pulled Ji from Somi's weakening grip and then pulled both women to shore. Gasps hung heavy in the air, punctuated by the nearby crashing of uncaring waves.

The leather maker noticed the light blue tint to Ji's skin.

"I'll get the shaman!" he said, dashing off.

Ji recognized several familiar faces as if in a dream and then smelled fresh stew. She smiled, from the intoxicating effects of oxygen deprivation. She could hear Kwan's giggles somewhere. She looked around for Nūk, but he was nowhere to be found.

Arms, rough and strong, carried her away from the bay to the fires in the village center. In the panic and rush, no one heard her last words.

"Jalga nae salang," she whispered. *Goodbye, my love.*

It only took the shaman a few moments to arrive. Panting like a beached fish, he lumbered to Ji, his round belly jiggling beneath his robes. The shaman took one look at Ji and motioned.

"Take her to the hut!" he yelled. "Hurry!"

The shaman followed behind the men, using an ancient chant, a blend of Korean and forgotten tongues, that vibrated through the air, matching the hum of the earth itself. His staff tapped a rhythm of urgency. His wife Hye met them at the door. She was Sinanju's mid-wife, and as such, was referred to as "Life-Giver."

Hye motioned for them to quickly bring Ji inside. She cleared off their table and the men placed Ji there.

"Out!" the shaman ordered. "Out!"

The men exited the hut, joining a group of women who had begun assembling outside.

The shaman acted first. Drowning was a daily threat in Sinanju where the waves were designed to steal your strength and pull you out to your death. Turning her to her side, he was able to force the water from Ji's lungs, while Hye began to care for the head wound.

With seasoned eyes, Hye shaved away a part of Ji's hair to clear the wound. Hye dipped her fingers into a bowl of earthy smelling mud, the dull color of ginseng, flecked with silvery shards of mugwort. With a practiced gentleness, she first cleaned the wound of blood and then spread the warm paste over the gash, firmly binding the wound together with her palm until the clay hardened.

Sweat beaded on the shaman's brow, a stark contrast to the icy pallor of Ji's skin. His lips moved in whispered chants, torn between the rhythm of life thrumming in his hands and the chilling silence between Ji's heartbeats. Though he managed to get Ji breathing again, he was worried. Her breaths were shallow and her heart beat was irregular.

She had been underwater for too long.

He applied a putrid poultice on her chin to help maintain her breathing. But after forty minutes, despite their best efforts, Ji remained still and unresponsive. Her spirit was slipping away. Hye opened the door to address the women who were still standing outside. Her smock was covered in blood and clay.

"How is she?" one woman asked, but Hye's teary eyes told the story.

"Someone will need to keep Kwan until the Master returns," Hye said quietly. "You will say *nothing* to him about his mother."

The women all began to turn toward the Master's House and Hye stopped them.

"We only need one," she insisted, seeking which woman would best be suited. Her eyes focused on someone who would be a familiar face.

"Yena, take Kwan to your home. Let him play with your children."

"Yes, Life-Giver," Yena said, hobbling toward the Master's Hut.

With the villagers' attention focused at the shaman's hut, no one noticed the trembling figure who remained at the bay. Somi weakly leaned against the flat rock covered in Ji's blood, tears flowing hot and salty down her cheeks.

Ostracized by her village, her family and even her husband, Somi had given up. When she was approached by Ji, she thought that she had found hope and kindness, only to witness her light extinguished. She was the Master's wife! What would he do to her when he returned?

The thought coiled in her chest, squeezing the air from her lungs. Her gaze swept across the village, its thatched roofs huddled together like whispering conspirators, waiting for the chance to blame her.

"Somi probably pushed her into the bay!" she imagined one woman scream.

"That's why she called Ji out so early, so no one could see her!" another said.

"That girl deserves what she is going to get!"

There was no pity lingering in the dark smoke curling from the huts, and no sympathy in the stillness of the moment, only accusations. Her young heart, once desperately yearning for acceptance, now lay a lifeless stone in her chest.

A sob, dry and rasping, escaped her lips, and with it, the last vestige of her struggle for survival. Somi turned towards the sun, its bright golden fingers mindlessly playing in the morning sky. The light showed her a truth she had long tried to bury.

A bittersweet smile, born of despair, flickered on her lips. Tearing the turban from her head, Somi released her long brown hair, feeling the rush of freedom as the strands flowed defiantly in the wind.

She removed her pink overcoat, holding it overhead, and the winds tore the fabric from her hands. It fluttered like a wounded bird before disappearing into the icy depths of the bay. The air immediately bit into her exposed arms and legs, causing her to involuntarily gasp for air.

This is the only way, she thought, *an escape from the shackles of a life not meant to be.*

Casting a final look at the unsympathetic sky, Somi whispered a farewell to the only woman who had ever shown her compassion. She took a single step backward and stretched out her arms and then slipped into the waves without making a sound.

The water embraced her in its frigid shroud, claiming her as its own. The sun, a silent and momentary witness, blinked away the memory of her struggle, leaving behind only the ripples that whispered her story into the indifferent vastness of the bay.

And then, even the ripples disappeared.

CHAPTER FIVE

Chiun and Nūk had reached the village path shortly after sunrise. As the Horns of Welcome appeared on the horizon, a wave of warmth washed over Chiun. The familiar scent of salt and fish drying on the racks — home, in all its comforting simplicity, brought comfort. The journey to Seoul, though necessary, felt like a distant dream, erased by the rhythms of Sinanju.

The carriage wheels creaked their familiar rhythm against the worn path, a lullaby against the chirping of birds in the swaying pines. The fields surrounding the village were a patchwork of green and gold. Weathered hands toiled in their timeless dance, a testament to the cycles of planting and harvest that had shaped Sinanju for generations. Chiun's gaze lingered on a group of children by the shore. Their carefree laughter echoed the memory of his own youthful escapades, momentarily pushing the Governor General and his ornate palace to the back of his mind.

But as the village grew closer, a flicker of unease tugged at Nūk. There was a subtle shift in the air, a stillness he couldn't quite place. Some of the usual faces were absent — Minji, always a fixture by the market with her baskets of herbs, was nowhere to be seen. Her cart was unattended. Other carts on the road were empty as well.

Then, as the curve of the bay came into view, a figure materialized from the side of the road. A young woman, hair unbound and eyes red-rimmed, tears swollen eyes, sprinted towards them like a windblown gull. It was Minji. Her voice, normally soft and gentle, rang with raw panic.

"Master Nūk! It is Mistress Ji…" her voice cracked, words tumbling out breathlessly. "Go to the shaman's hut!"

Nūk motioned for Chiun to follow him and they bolted into the distance, faster than any horse could have carried them. Nūk left Chiun behind in raw speed, knowing that he would arrive soon after.

Along the way, one villager appeared, then another, their faces contorted with an urgency Chiun had never seen. They were pale and frantic, causing Chiun's heart to lurch in his chest.

As they reached the edge of the village, the crowd thickened, a living wall of grief gathered at the front door of the shaman's hut. Tears and choked sobs filled the air. Nūk pushed through, Chiun close behind, carving a path through a wall of despair. The air in the shaman's hut was thick with incense and prayers, the flickering candlelight painting grotesque shadows on the walls.

Ji lay on a table, but Nūk had trouble finding her heartbeat. The shaman rushed out of the way and Nūk moved forward. His hands moved with a master's precision, backed by five thousand years of experience. He pressed vital points, listening to the rhythms of her body. Even though her breathing was shallow, it sounded as if air was not being allowed to flow through her body.

"What happened?" he demanded, keeping his focus on his wife.

"She slipped on one of the rocks in the bay and hit her head," the shaman said. "We quickly pulled her out of the sea, but…"

Nūk took everything into consideration. Perhaps there was still enough water in her lungs to restrict her breathing. He turned Ji to her side and with a moment of reluctance, placed the fingernails of his left hand into her spine, manipulating the Dragon Essences.

For just a moment, Ji seemed to come alive. Her eyes blindly opened and she began to regurgitate salt water and portions of the prior days' meal.

Chiun's eyes widened in hope. She was still alive!

He looked to his father, who was still focused on saving her.

Nūk laid her on her back and ignored the smells of death that clung to her body. He looked into her open eyes, seeking any connection to her inner lotus. Seeing no recognition, he slapped her sharply in the middle of the back and more liquid came out, but this time, he saw bubbles of blood.

He moved quickly, working on the nerves beneath her jaw, forcing her to cough.

The sound of voluntary breath, in and out, is a sign of life, Chiun reassured himself.

Ji continued to cough until no more liquid came out and Nūk stopped when her eyes closed. Anything else left inside was beyond his control. It was not the water that remained in her lungs, nor even the wound to her head. It was the lack of oxygen.

Chiun remained a respectful distance from his father, his mind racing with Sinanju teachings that revealed a truth he refused to accept. He had learned how to identify death and the dying when he was six, but he had never been taught with how to deal with it.

"Father," Chiun whispered, moving toward the door, his voice weak from grief. "I can't…"

"Stay!" Nūk commanded. "We will not leave your mother when she needs us the most!"

Chiun's eyes never left his mother's face, clinging to the dwindling hope that his father would work a miracle. His knees felt weak, as if the floor itself could crumble beneath him. He wanted to hide, to disappear, but something held him upright. He wanted to scream, to break the thick silence, but he knew that his father's focus was the only thing keeping his mother alive.

His father had never failed. He was the Master of Sinanju and Chiun pinned his hope on his father's vast experience. Tears began running down his face. A Master of Sinanju would never cry, Chiun thought, but his resolve began to melt with each passing moment.

Nūk placed his hand over Ji's diaphragm and pushed. Chiun heard the subtle crunch of bone as Nūk's hands attempted to get her to hyperventilate. Her body responded by thrashing about and Nūk allowed her hands to strike him while he concentrated on maximizing her air flow.

Tears burning his eyes, Chiun watched his mother's convulsing movements and knew that she was fighting for her life.

As Nūk moved to Ji's back, he slapped her with precise strikes, Chiun could hear the fracturing of each rib. Every blow felt like a betrayal, but Chiun knew that his father would not strike her so hard if there was any other way.

The shaman and his wife began whispering prayers to the old gods, using their most precious incense. Nūk joined them, whispering prayers from every nation he had ever visited, imploring each of their gods for help, but nothing changed.

Ji's vibrant face, once filled with laughter lines and the scent of spiced seaweed, was now a pale canvas of pain. The rhythmic rise and fall of her chest, a cruel illusion of life.

Nūk took a deep breath and his movements slowed. In the

stillness of the twilight, with the light of candles filling the room, he stepped back in defeat.

Recognizing that they no longer belonged, the shaman and his wife quietly exited their hut, immediately ushering the other villagers to their homes.

After they left, Nūk stood behind his wife and placed both of his hands on her head, whispering loving thanks to her for their time together.

"Ji-ah, my love, with each day we shared, you filled my life with light," Nūk said, with an unfamiliar strain in his voice. "As you journey to the ancestors, my soul clings to the echo of your laughter. Thank you, my heart, for our seasons of joy. We will meet again."

After a few moments, her breathing ceased and Nūk softly kissed her one last time.

In that quiet moment of surrender, a feeling of helplessness threatened to shatter Chiun, leaving him swallowed by an unending grief. A sob involuntarily escaped; it was the sound of a boy, not an assassin. He felt an advancing darkness from deep within.

He tried to look at his mother again, but was frightened when he could feel no connection. It was just another body lying before him.

Nūk knelt, his posture as straight as ever, yet the lines on his face seemed to deepen, etched by an anguish he could no longer physically hide. Nūk, the Master of Sinanju, was the epitome of strength and poise, but Nūk the *husband*, Nūk the *man*, mourned his wife's passing with quick, frantic gasps.

He gathered Chiun to him, tightly wrapping his arms around him. His lungs began to heave in grief, ignoring the established breathing patterns he had followed since infancy.

It was the first and only time that Chiun ever saw his father cry.

CHAPTER SIX

The day his mother died had been the worst day of Chiun's life. It took years to process his grief. Even now, eleven years later, as he readied for his first appearance as the Apprentice Master of Sinanju, Chiun hoped that she would have been proud of him. He grinned as he could almost hear her shame him for thinking otherwise.

He adjusted his new garment, and walked down the marble steps from the House of Many Woods. Below, the center of the village was alive with the happy sounds of traveling folk singers and the laughter of the villagers. His father had even allowed local tradesmen and close relatives to attend.

Laughter bounced off the walls of the village, a joyful echo against the steady rhythm of a folk singer's drum. The air was thick with the smells of smoked fish and roasting grain, a familiar scent that was only recognized once a year.

Barter Feast was the largest holiday on the Sinanju calendar. Each year, after the short harvest season when villagers had a little extra money, the entire village came together for a five-day feast. The celebrations first began thousands of years earlier, during a time of near famine. Everyone gathered all of their food to distribute to each family, and over the centuries it had grown into a small festival.

Each family set up a table or booth and filled it with personally-crafted wares. Some brought food, others hand-stitched clothing. A few even brought small toys for the children.

The feast would not have attracted the attention at any of the larger cities that Chiun had visited with his father, but Barter Feast was as much a part of the Sinanju community as gossip and smoked fish.

The tables and booths were consolidated within the path that was shaped as a trapezoid bisected by a vertical blade. The shape of the village of Sinanju was a map, as seen from the Horns. Initially, it was an oval path of wooden planks that were used as a sidewalk surrounding the village well, but after thousands of years of foot travel and upgrades to the well, the path had slowly transformed into the familiar trapezoid for which the village was known.

The center of the village was the beating heart of the Sinanju community. The melodies of traveling folk singers filled the air, creating a symphony of much-needed merriment. Villagers, local tradesmen, and even distant relatives who had journeyed from afar, all converged upon this vibrant scene.

Among the throng, the folk singers held a place of honor. Their weathered faces carried the experience of the songs themselves, a musical wisdom gleaned from years of wandering the land. Their rough-hewn voices, imbued with a raw emotion, resonated with the very soul of the village.

Their instruments were handcrafted from humble materials that resulted in their own distinct sounds, a magic all their own. They wove tales of love, loss, and resilience. As their notes soared into the sky, they painted pictures with sound, transporting the listeners to distant lands and reminded the villagers of good times.

The villagers swayed and clapped their hands in simple

dance forms, carefree and flowing, their faces reflecting their shared joy. The tradesmen, their faces worn from their journeys, found a moment of respite in the music, their weary bodies finding solace in the rhythm. Even the relatives, strangers to the village, yet drawn by the irresistible pull of the celebration, found themselves swept up in the jubilant wave of music and laughter.

Chiun walked around the village center, greeting people at each booth. With the exception of some of the relatives from Pyongyang, Chiun knew everyone present. He had grown up with these people.

As he began his trip around the booths, Chiun snuck a peak at the booth at the end of the second row. All he could see from this angle were the bright-colored flowers that seemed to explode from the booth.

"Look at you, wearing father's robes!" his little brother Kwan said, noting Chiun's apprentice robe.

Kwan's face had filled in with age and Chiun could almost see his mother. Especially in the soft smile that Chiun had always remembered.

"Father is very protective of his garments," Chiun noted, pulling at his collar. He leaned in, as if to reveal a large secret. "I even got to see some of his steamer trunks!"

"Father has too many steamer trunks!" Kwan said, laughing. "I know when he goes out for service that he needs clothing, but I have never seen a man with that much luggage!"

"This is somewhat itchy," Chiun admitted, pulling at his collar. "And old."

Kwan leaned forward and Chiun received his hug. While his face was over Kwan's shoulder, his eyes narrowed fiercely at Kwan's new wife Min-Jun. For some reason, Chiun could tell that she did not approve of him. Though some in the village were fearful or even jealous of the Master and his family, he could not pin down her motives.

When his brother stepped back, Min-jun gave a deep bow to Chiun.

"All hail the master," she said, her voice a touch too sweet.

A muscle twitched in her cheek as she bowed, the movement stiff and mechanical.

Chiun held up a hand, a flicker of unease settling behind his eyes.

"I am but the apprentice, but sister, you may still refer to me as 'brother' or 'Chiun.'"

"Of course I can," she said, crinkling her nose condescendingly.

A flicker of irritation crossed Min-Jun's face before she hid it. It was too small a gesture for anyone else to notice, but Chiun had seen it countless times in those who resented his presence.

"Slow down, you stupid kids!" Tae, the leather maker screamed from behind.

Chiun looked around and instantly found the reason why.

The fishmonger's son Choi was racing his friends around the stone pavements of the village center. Choi was the fastest boy his age, boasting long, curly hair, a rarity in the village. Unfortunately, his friend San had lost most of his baby fat over the summer and was running faster as a result.

Choi ducked through the wall surrounding the water pump, dashing through the center of the village, leaping over the small benches facing the main fire. The other boys raced around the benches, but San, with a newfound speed and confidence, followed Choi over the benches.

Choi turned around in disbelief when he saw that San was catching up to him, so he ducked into the blacksmith tent, exiting the side. The blacksmith just glared as the other children followed him.

Choi had only a moment before San would recognize which way he ran, so he turned west and tripped over a large crack in the sandstone path.

Before he could hit his head on one of the rocks, Chiun lunged forward and safely returned him to his feet.

"Master Chiun!" Choi said in fear as he recognized who had caught him. "Forgive me! I did not mean to run into you! We were just playing!"

Chiun smiled. He remembered mindlessly running around the village center as a child himself.

The other boys caught up and, seeing the situation, instantly stopped.

"The fault is not yours, young Choi," Chiun said, glancing at the broken sandstone path that surrounded the village center. Here and there, sections of deeper carvings hinted at its original beauty, but the path itself was little more than a weathered snapshot to the relentless passage of time.

"I fear French stone does not hold up well against Sinanju children," Chiun said. "But be mindful. There are many elders walking around and if they were to be hurt, this would be a different discussion."

The boys all quickly bowed to Chiun and ran away as they left, but then remembered what they had been told and began slowly walking to their homes, hoping that Chiun had not noticed.

The condition of the village path was not something that Chiun had really thought about before. It had always been worn and always had large cracks. But he realized that with his new title came new responsibilities and one day he would be responsible for the village upkeep.

…but not today.

Today, Chiun's smile and focus fell on one booth: a vibrant wooden stall at the end of the second row, filled with what looked like colorful flowers and, more importantly, the most beautiful girl in the village.

Eon had brought their family wares early, giving her extra time to set up their booth in a good spot at the end. She and her mother had worked diligently over the past month making artificial flowers from dyed feathers and tiny branches.

It took almost an hour to set everything up, but when she was done, Eon was surrounded by a halo of colors as if the Earth itself was highlighting her beauty. Eon was tall for a Korean girl. In fact, she was an inch taller than Chiun. Her raven-black hair was held back by a pair of delicate cloisonne butterfly pins, enabling the dark outline of her hair to accent her soft eyes.

Chiun had known Eon his entire life.

In fact, his earliest memories were playing with her when they were toddlers. Through the years, Chiun had played with other children, but he always returned to play with Eon.

One day, shortly after Chiun had turned eleven, something changed. He began noticing how pretty her lips were when she smiled and how soft her hands were when they briefly touched.

On that day, Chiun disappeared into her eyes.

They began courting when Chiun was fifteen, but was quickly stopped after being privately shamed by Nūk. For the next week, Chiun was worried that another of the village boys would try to win her hand, but he had nothing to worry about. All of the boys knew how Chiun felt about Eon and none of them were stupid enough to face his wrath.

"This is a very beautiful flower," Chiun said when he reached Eon's booth.

"My mother has trained me well," Eon said with a soft smile and small bow. She held up the flower she was working on and gave it to Chiun.

"I was speaking of you," Chiun said, accepting the flower.

Eon blushed and turned her face away.

Chiun loved the way that a few strands of her hair were tousled by the wind. Something stirred within him, and he could not help but quote poetry in celebration of her beauty.

. . .

I stand beside a flower
Its scent more lovely
Than the best perfumes gifted to Sinanju
Sweet and heady, its beauty is delicate...
Radiance falls on Sinanju

"Forgive me, Master Chiun," Eon said bashfully. "I am not worthy of Ung."

"To you, I am just Chiun, the same boy who allowed you to push him into the mud."

"No, Master," Eon asserted. "My mother has taught me the proper ways, and we honor the House of Sinanju."

"Your mother is a gracious and wise woman," Chiun replied. "And your father…"

Chiun stopped midsentence. He tried not to think about her father. Joon-Hu was one of the younger fishermen who had fallen into the terrible habits of the others. While fishing was difficult in the icy waters of the West Korean Bay, it was still possible. They proved this on the days they were sober.

"I…I respect my father," Eon managed, her voice barely above a whisper.

"Your father is an angry and lazy man who only cares about what he can drink," A voice boomed from behind, startling her.

Eon flinched and she dropped the delicate flower she had been holding.

Chiun and Eon turned to see Master Nūk standing by them. While his robe depicted a morning scene of the rising of a golden phoenix, he was not happy.

"I will speak with my son," Nūk said.

"Of course, Master Nūk," Eon said, lowering her face in

embarrassment.

Chiun cast a silent glance to Eon and followed his father. After they were far enough away where they could not be heard, Chiun spoke.

"Father, I have done nothing wrong," he said.

"You were about to," Nūk replied, his gaze remaining forward. "I noticed that your mother's ring was missing this morning."

"It is my right to give it to the girl I will marry."

"That is why I showed up. You did not even notice my approach!" Nūk said, shaming Chiun.

"I recognized your approach long before you spoke, father."

"And if my intent had been to attack instead of speak?" Nūk asked. "My son, this is why it is better to marry from the head and not the heart."

Chiun remained silent for the remainder of the walk. Anything he would have said at this point would have done nothing other than anger his father.

When they reached the House of Many Woods, Chiun stepped ahead and bowed, opening the door for his father. The warmth of the fireplace greeted them, along with the fresh scent of Chrysanthemum, which emanated from the marble bowl on the mantle.

Chiun of course, lived in the house, but like Kwan, the entire area below ground was off-limits, with the exception of Chiun's studies in the scroll room. Besides momentary glances inside the treasury room while following his father, the scroll room was the most detailed room that Chiun had been allowed to see below the common area.

The scroll room was carved out of the granite beneath the house, the walls pocketed out for storage. It smelled of old paper and worn leather, but despite the boring stories he was forced to memorize, Chiun had grown accustomed to the smell. It had become the aroma of home, of safety and time spent with his father.

But instead of a home, the House of Many Woods felt like a storage unit to Chiun. It was stacked with junk that would never have been kept if it had not been made from gold or gems. His father had many strengths, but he had a weakness for gaudy trinkets and shiny baubles, going so far as to nail colorful seashells to the front door.

An elderly Korean man in his eighties bowed as the two entered. His thick robe hid the frailty of his form and as he bowed, it seemed questionable if he possessed the strength to right himself again.

After Chiun shut the door and the breeze abated, the old man took a deep breath and his arms widened.

"All hail the Master of Sinanju, who sustains the village and faithfully keeps the code," he said in a raspy voice. After taking a deep breath, he continued. "Sovereign Lord of the House of Sinanju, our hearts cry a thousand greetings of love and adoration," he said, stopping again for a deep breath. "Joyous are we upon the return of he who graciously throttles the universe," after he finished, surprisingly, he stood upright.

Kong had been caretaker of the House of Many Woods for over sixty years. Chiun could tell that it would not be long before his son Pullyang would have to take over his duties.

"Kong," Nūk said with a mild nod. "You may retire for the day."

"Thank you, Master," Kong said with a deep bow before leaving.

Nūk took his seat and looked forward, and after he was confident that Kong had hobbled far enough away, Chiun knelt on the stool before him and bowed his head.

"Father, I seek a petition."

"Proceed," Nūk said, knowing what he was about to ask.

"As Apprentice Master, I am allowed to marry," Chiun said. "I wish to wed Eon."

"You seek Joon-Hu's daughter? The youngest of the drunk fishermen?"

"She is not her father," Chiun said in defense.

"Then put her aside for the moment. Why are you so determined to rush into marriage?" Nūk asked sadly. "You are young. You have the rest of your life to make this decision."

"Other boys in the village can marry at fifteen," Chiun said in a harsher tone than he intended. "All of the boys my age have been married for several years. They have their own huts and have begun to raise their children. Why are you determined not to give me the only thing I have ever asked of you?"

This was the first time Chiun had petitioned his father for something personal, so Nūk excused the barbed tone in his voice.

"I have taught you many things as a Master of Sinanju, but I have failed you as a father," Nūk said sadly. "The heart is foolish; it is fickle and selfish to the point that we exploit it as a weakness. It thinks only for itself, sometimes, just to spite knowledge."

"Is that not what love is meant to be?" Chiun asked with an infectious smile. "We train based on tradition, and we eat based on tradition. Are we also commanded to marry for tradition?"

"This is not about tradition; this is about *wisdom*. The girl you seek is tall…she is lanky. Her hips are not wide enough to bear you good children. Marry someone sensible and leave your fleshly desires for the many foreign women you will meet in your travels."

Chiun, unfazed, countered, "These are not fleshly desires, father, this is from my heart! Didn't you feel this way about mother?"

Nūk paused and momentarily lost eye contact with Chiun.

"Of course not," he said in a slightly subdued, but confident tone. "My father made sure that I would have a proper wife. He watched each of the girls that I cared for. One by one, he pointed out their weaknesses until I realized what was needed in a wife."

"Then you met mother?"

"No, my father chose for me."

Chiun's mouth silently opened.

"She was a good fit," Nūk said, defending his choice. "She understood what Masters of Sinanju must do from time to time when we are away and I grew to love her."

Chiun's throat tightened and he fought back tears.

"Father…is that the life you wish for *me*?"

Nūk paused for a moment and then leaned back in his seat.

"The young cannot see wisdom because it exists beyond the horizon of their experience. One day, you will understand."

Nūk raised both of his fists, stretching them far apart.

If Chiun had been one of the other boys in the village, he would have rolled his eyes. His father's favored teaching method was separating his fists to demonstrate the vast distance between two points.

"This is your life and this is your wife," Nūk said, motioning with each hand.

"That is not at all what I feel!" Chiun said, balling his own hands into fists and bringing them together. "I do not wish for any separation between Eon and myself!"

Nūk shook his head.

"My son, do you hear yourself? You sound like one of the widows! *'Poor Chiun, the lonely hearted Apprentice Master…'*" Nūk mocked. "And now you yell at your father? Do you see what she is doing to you?"

"This is important to me, father. I do not wish to marry for tradition."

"You are approaching the most perilous juncture in the life of a Master of Sinanju. Your focus must be unwavering in the coming years!"

"Father my focus remains…"

"Do you not remember the tale of Master Ti-Sung?" Nuk interrupted.

With a sense of dread, Chiun left his stool and dutifully assumed the lotus position, prepared for a lesson from the scrolls. The tale of Ti-Sung was a very familiar one, and regarded as a historical warning, referred to many times. He was the Master who served under King Cyrus, called the Elder, despite his ignorance and youth.

"Master Ti-Sung faltered because he heeded King Cyrus' advice, leaving himself vulnerable," Chiun said.

"Good. What was *the lesson* of Master Ti-Sung?" Nuk asked.

"Nod to every foolish thing that comes out of an emperor's mouth, but afterwards, do what you want. No client has ever complained about being alive, nor have any who died."

"That is correct," Nuk said, and Chiun began to stand.

"But that is *not* the lesson of Ti-Sung I wish to impart to you."

Chiun inwardly sighed, preparing himself for his father's deeper insights.

"Do you know why Master Ti-Sung's firstborn was not the next Master of Sinanju?"

Chiun fell silent, humbled by a gap in his knowledge.

"No, father," Chiun admitted. "I do not."

"That is because I wished to tell you this story when you were older, when you were ready for marriage, but I might as well tell you now. Master Ti-Sung was seventeen when he married. Like you, he chose to marry for love. He was not even an Apprentice when his wife gave birth to a son later that year. The boy was weak and he died. He had to make another baby."

Chiun's face squirmed. "It can still be a pleasurable thing."

"Not if it is done correctly!" Nuk stammered. "Do you ever listen to me?"

Nuk raised both of his fists again.

"This is pleasure and this is purpose!" he said of the distance between his fists. "Do you wish for your first born to be female?"

"No, father," Chiun said.

"Good. You may have a daughter later, if you want. They can be helpful to care for the home, but only after you have two sons. For that to happen, you have to follow the scrolls."

"And I will," Chiun insisted and then his face relaxed. "But I shall marry Eon father, whether it is today, or tomorrow, or next week, or next year."

Nūk lowered his face. He could order Chiun not to marry the girl, but that would only plant a seed of poison in their relationship.

"If you are determined to do this, I will give my blessing," Nūk said.

Chiun smiled, but then Nūk began wagging his finger. "but… your training will always come first. I will have to make it harsher to compensate for this weakness."

"As always, I welcome your training, father," Chiun said, knowing this was as good an offer as his father would ever grant.

Chiun stood and deeply bowed. "All hail the Master of Sinanju."

Nūk nodded and Chiun left to return to the annual barter and the girl he loved.

Where had he gone wrong?

CHAPTER SEVEN

Very early the next morning, when the predawn air was still shrouded in the waning night's cold, a lone figure stirred through the misty fog that blanketed the area, to begin his daily routine.

The shaman was a middle-aged man of some girth, but a youthful step. He was responsible for the morning rituals that began daily life in the village. Wearing his traditional white quilted jacket for warmth, he was usually the first of the villagers to rise.

Villagers wondered how he perfectly woke up every day just before sunrise. Some imagined that a crow came to his window and spoke a magical word to awake him. Others believed that he simply did not sleep.

The truth was that he relied on the alarm clock purchased by the previous shaman in one of his many travels. He was so impressed that he purchased eight of them, just in case. The shaman honestly did not know how they awoke prior to that clock, but he found the superstitious claims of the villagers amusing.

Over the centuries, the villagers had abandoned most of

their superstitions, but lighting the sunrise fires was still an important part of Sinanju culture. If the weather was bad, they would murmur that the shaman must have been late with the fires. If the harvest failed, they knew that the shaman had been late with multiple fires.

The villagers knew he was a doctor and, perhaps even a witch. He could speak with spirits and sometimes see the future. Some thought he was a minor djinn, bound to the village by a past master. Everything else was gossip and speculation.

The role was almost designed to be mysterious.

He reached the village center and began working with the smaller fire near the blacksmith's shelter. It had originally been placed in the back, near the leather worker's shop, but the fire kept going out. Placing it near the blacksmith's shelter provided a good barrier against the sea wind.

The shaman sprinkled some ash from a past fire and waved his hands, and the wood began to breathe a lively bright orange, springing to life with a roar larger than the wood suggested.

He moved on to the central fire pit and repeated the same steps.

The central pit was the largest of the three and lasted long into the morning. It was the communal fire where villagers gathered to share a morning meal mixed with stories, laughter and gossip. A large ring of wood benches surrounded the fire, but most villagers tried to sit on the south side where they could best feel the heat.

The last firepit was behind the large northwest wall that protected the water pump from most of the strong winds coming from the bay. This was the space reserved for the children, where they learned and played. The shaman could not help but notice their frightened stares when they looked toward him, but he did not try to dissuade their youthful imaginations. There is no simple way to explain to a child that you are not a demon.

The shaman's hands moved with a practiced ease, coaxing the flame to life. He spent a moment near the fire rubbing his hands together to warm himself before moving to the water pump. At first, he struggled against the cold iron handle, but then the water began to flow, first in gulps and spurts, and then a steady stream, into the basin that led down the concrete channel that took it to the bay.

He cupped a handful of water and brought it to his face. The water was icy against his fingers, and even colder on his face. He drank several handfuls, allowing the water to chill his insides before splashing it over his face again, chasing away any foggy remains from the night and returned to the fire.

When he was warm enough, he walked to the bay, a place of solitude for his morning rite. Once or twice, he had seen the familiar silhouette of Master Nūk, sitting on a weathered rock at the bay's edge. Their conversations were normally limited to a respectful nod exchanged between each other. Yet in that unspoken respect was a bond as old as the tides.

Today, he was surprised to see a figure standing at the edge of the bay. The boy Chiun, glowing orange in the morning light, stood near the edge of the bay. He had just been named Apprentice Master of Sinanju, which merely told the Shaman that he had survived training long enough to be titled.

Most villagers never spoke of it, but some children never lived long enough to obtain a title, much less a mention in the scrolls. Their bodies were silently buried in the field behind the House in an area called The Hallows.

Though it was not a part of his official duties, sometimes the shaman visited the Hallows to properly remember the children that Sinanju had forgotten. It reminded him of the cost involved in being the Master and helped him realize why there always had to be a second son.

In Sinanju, failure was unforgiveable. It was not an option, because failure meant starvation and death. The line of Masters had to always be seen as pure and strong.

For Sinanju is forever.

Chiun acknowledged the Shaman with a nod and stepped back to give him ample space.

As he did every day, the Shaman gently lowered himself at the point where the land and water met, bowing to the sea, accepting its salty mist as benediction. He closed his eyes and held his breath until it mingled with the bay. His senses expanded until he could feel the ocean's pulse, gaining a complete sense of the world around him.

He whispered his gratitude in the tongue of Dangun, the first Korean, with an ancient dialect and words unknown by modern man.

It was one of the few languages that Chiun did not understand, but recognizing the moment, Chiun bowed where he was and closed his eyes in shared reverence.

The shaman began his morning prayer in the strange tongue.

"To you, Great Spirits, who cradle this land and caress our sea, guardians of what is seen and unseen, hear my humble words," the Shaman began. "Protect our village as we tread the honored path of our ancestors. Let our deeds sing the harmony of the sky, earth, and water, as we trace the heritage woven by all those who walked before us. Strengthen the Master and Protect our village."

The shaman released his breath before acknowledging Chiun.

"What do you need?" he asked as both men stood to their feet.

"Your breathing technique…where did you learn it?" Chiun asked.

"We each have our own methods," the shaman replied coyly. "What may I do for you?"

"We have not officially spoken with each other," Chiun said.

"Master and Shaman only work together when necessary."

"But why?" Chiun asked.

"It has been the way of things for many centuries."

The Shaman grabbed some sand and rose to his feet, seemingly ignoring Chiun. His dusted fingers weaved back and forth, scattering it over his footprints as he returned to the village. Chiun followed closely behind. The Shaman noted that Chiun had not left any tracks in the wet sand.

"Hmmph" he said in admiration. The boy was further ahead in his training than he thought.

"Please, this will only take a moment," Chiun said and the shaman stopped.

"I will answer what I can," he said.

Chiun's mind raced with a dozen questions.

"Why can't the master and shaman speak to each other?"

The Shaman looked down before speaking.

"Have you heard of the Exiled Shaman?" he asked.

"No," Chiun admitted. "My history comes from our scrolls."

The shaman hesitated.

"Then this is something that you should ask your father."

"And I will, but I would like to hear what you have to say."

The shaman looked at Chiun in frustration, knowing that he would not leave without some kind of answer, so the shaman decided to tell him the truth.

"Fifteen centuries ago, the master and shaman had children at the same time," he explained. "This shaman was a shrewd and ambitious man. He was jealous of the master and conceived a plan to take over the line of Sinanju. The master was away when the children were born, so he would switch babies in the middle of the first night.

"After a week or so, when the mothers became familiar with their babies and claimed them as their own, the shaman would poison the natural son of Sinanju, who would die of a mysterious illness a few days later. Then, after the master returned, he would train the shaman's son in the art of Sinanju. When the shaman's son was fully trained, it would be revealed that he was of the shaman's line, bringing forth the first Master Shaman in Sinanju history."

"What happened?" Chiun asked with a sense of worry.

"The master returned home early to be with his newborn and discovered the deception, because he was familiar with his preborn son's heartbeat. The master saved his son and the shaman was exiled. His family was banned from ever holding a title in the village."

"I have never heard that story," Chiun said.

"The master brought in a new man to be Sinanju's shaman, a monk from the sacred temple of Mount Jiri—the source of all true shamans and my great ancestor."

"That does not explain why we can't talk," Chiun said. "Your family had no hand in it."

"After hearing the story, how can you still not see?" the shaman asked, disappointed. "The possibility for the office of shaman to betray Sinanju still exists."

"Perhaps, but shouldn't we be judged individually, by deeds, not blood?" Chiun asked. "Our histories scream of injustice. Why can't we learn from it?"

The shaman chuckled in disappointment. He would never tell Chiun — or anyone else — but shamans carried generational memories, passed from one shaman to another. He remembered the day his ancestor set foot in the village, wary of replacing another shaman. The master was a quiet man, full of anger and resentment. If he had not personally heard the call of the crows, he would not have stayed.

"Naivete is the first thing you will lose in your training, young master. Many before you shared the same thoughts, yet by the time they ascended, their ideals had been abandoned with their childhood toys."

Chiun paused for a moment, considering his next words.

"You failed my mother," he said, his voice low, but sharp. "But I could see the pain in your eyes as you tried to save her. Her passing meant something to you. You felt a personal failure for her death."

"Your mother was a good woman who died far too early."

The shaman brushed sand from his palms, silently wishing Chiun would drop the subject.

"We are both powerful men, each chained by our own traditions," Chiun said. "Have you ever considered that there might be a better way? What if breaking a tradition could lead to a brighter future for our village? Would you ever consider defying the old ways for the sake of progress?"

The shaman tilted his head in disbelief.

"How can you look at tradition as a chain? The accumulated wisdom of past masters has enabled the House of Sinanju to thrive over many thousands of years. Listen to the ghosts of your past and allow them to teach you their wisdoms."

Chiun slightly shuddered.

"The scrolls speak of past masters visiting during the life of a master. Are ghosts…real?"

"I believe that will be all for today, young master," the shaman said, walking off.

"Your name," Chiun called out. "What was your name before you became shaman?"

The shaman did not honor Chiun's question with a response, but continued to the village square. Chiun's mention of his mother was a bitter and painful memory.

As for his name?

The shaman had a name, but it was abandoned when he began apprenticing and he was never again referred to as anything other than 'shaman.' It was often said that those who grew up with him could not even remember who he was once after he took the office, as if the original shaman from three thousand years earlier had wiped his identity away.

It was such a strong reality that his own wife referred to him as shaman. When he was called to treat his mother on her deathbed, she did not recognize him. He watched with a crippling sorrow as she took her final breath, the warmth ebbing from her skin. When her heart stopped her eyes lost focus, leaving behind a porcelain effigy of the woman he once knew. He was forced by his brother to leave, so the family could grieve in private.

He stepped out into the bright and chilly village, and quickly reconnected to the flow of life in the village. The salt-laced breeze whispered through the trees, a timely comfort, but it was still not enough to fill the hole in his heart.

There was no one in the village who understood the privilege of possessing a name. With a name, you could have family, history, and connections. With a name, you could have friends. Even the Master could not understand, because even though he was referred to as 'the Master of Sinanju,' it was often used in conjunction with his name. He was an individual who lived an identifiable life, known for his individual actions, good or bad. But him?

He was just a shaman.

CHAPTER EIGHT

*L*ater in the morning as the villagers began to arrive for the second day of Barter, Nūk entered the crowd. He was dressed in his formal green robes. Opulent gold threads ran vertically down the garment, circling the fluted sleeves. Most villagers had never seen Nūk in this robe, so a hushed sense of anticipation settled over them as he stepped onto a small stand in the village center.

Typically, a marriage announcement for an Apprentice Master is a grand affair, complete with a lengthy speech given by the Reigning Master, extolling the virtues of the bride and groom, tying the families together in a poetic blend of history and aspiration, but Nūk's approach was a bit more subtle.

He held his hands up and the crowd quieted, awaiting his words.

"Apprentice Master Chiun will wed Eon," Nūk paused, letting each unbelievable word sink in. "She is the daughter of Joon-Hu, the drunk. The ceremony will be at high-sun, on the first of next month," Nūk said, his voice void of emotion or energy.

Finishing the mandatory details of the announcement, Nūk

stepped down, leaving a bewildering silence to engulf the villagers.

Eyes darted back and forth and mouths opened as they waited for the rest of the speech. After a short, awkward pause, a man in the crowd realized that Master Nūk had finished and began clapping. Confused, others followed suit.

Chiun looked at his father in disbelief. To allow their internal feud to be publicly portrayed, even in the slightest, was not something Chiun would have ever imagined. But then he realized it did not matter. He gripped Eon's hand and proudly led her to the stand.

Chiun passed his father after coming off the platform.

"Your excitement knows no bounds," Chiun whispered.

"Enjoy your moment," Nūk replied. "Remember, this is for love."

Nūk walked to the back of the crowd, leaving the remainder of the ceremony to his son.

Adorned in pristine white hanboks, Chiun and Eon ascended to the stand, their garments a symbolic blank canvas, awaiting the vivid brushstrokes of their future life together.

"All hail the Master of Sinanju," Chiun said, nodding to his father. He smiled at Eon while the villagers cheered for his father. After the applause died down, Chiun returned his gaze to the villagers. He had waited so long for this day. He would not allow his father to ruin it.

"As my father has so…eloquently stated, I have chosen Eon, the daughter of Joon-Hu as my bride. To those who know us well, this comes as no surprise."

A smattering of knowing smiles broke out among the villagers and they clapped. Even the boys who earlier wished to court Eon granted a reluctant smile.

"Consider this your formal invitation. Join us at high-sun, between the Horns of Welcome on the inaugural day of the coming month. There, my father, Master Nūk, the Reigning

Master of the House of Sinanju, will officiate our union and celebrate in a manner unparalleled in its grandeur."

Nūk returned Chiun's gaze with a warning frown.

"And," Chiun continued with a wide smile, "he has told me that he will personally invite a member of royalty to as a special guest to our feast!"

Chiun cast a sardonic smile toward his father, and the villagers cheered even louder.

Nūk shook his head and returned to the House of Many Woods. He would speak to his son later.

Typically, the father of the bride spoke next, but Eon looked around the crowd. Her father was not present. While Joon had certainly known of Chiun's intentions, he was obviously clueless about the timing of the announcement.

Eon looked to her mother, who had promised to find her father. Meeting her gaze, her mother silently shook her head and whispered, "No".

The crowd cheered, surrounding Chiun and Eon and calling for her father.

"Joon-Hu!" They shouted. "Joon-Hu! Joon-Hu!"

But after a few minutes, they realized that he was not there.

"To his house!" one man suggested and Eon felt a knot in her stomach.

"Do we really have to go?" she asked Chiun.

Her mother quickly rushed to the front of the crowd. It was apparent to all that she was embarrassed. Eon hid her face in Chiun's shoulder and his hand tightened around her shoulder.

"I'm so happy to finally leave his house, and his abuse," Eon said. "So why am I sad that he didn't show up?"

"Joon did not come home last night," her mother admitted to the crowd.

"He's probably drunk!" a villager from the back shouted and the villagers laughed.

"He's probably passed out at the dock!" another yelled.

The fishermen who were present looked at each other with a palpable tension carved on their faces. One of the men stepped forward and waved his hands to get the crowd's attention.

"Hey, everybody! Hey! I, uh…I was just there! Joon's not at the dock!" he said nervously. "I heard him say that he was travelling to Pyongyang for supplies."

The crowd laughed.

Everyone knew that Joon stayed at the dock most nights.

Their enthusiasm waned at the thought of travelling down the long and muddy path that led to the dock, especially on a cold and windy day, but the villagers loyally escorted Chiun and Eon eastward.

Eon's grip on Chiun's arm tightened. Her eyes began darting back and forth as if anticipating an approaching danger.

Chiun could feel her steps growing slower.

"What is wrong?" he asked softly.

"Despite your presence, I still fear him," Eon admitted, lowering her face to the ground, unable to meet Chiun's gaze.

She fought back the source of her tears, but her father had been beating her and her mother for so long that it seemed normal, even when he wasn't drunk. To this day, Eon believed that if Master Nūk had not intervened when she was eight, her father would have killed her that night.

Eon had accidentally knocked over an oil lamp in the middle of the night while trying to leave for the outhouse. The rug in the middle of the hut caught fire and the flames quickly spread. Eon woke both of her parents in time to escape, but once they were safely away outside, Joon lashed out.

Her mother tried to hold him back, but he pushed her down into the brush, picked Eon up with both hands and threw her to the ground, knocking the wind out of her little body. The flash of pain disoriented her and she laid dazed and helpless at his feet.

Joon brought his foot back to kick her in the head, but

suddenly found himself lying on the ground, looking up, directly into the eyes of Master Nūk.

"Is your child safe from the fire?" Master Nūk asked.

Joon was still drunk from the night before, but not drunk enough to do something stupid.

"She...saved us from the fire," Joon admitted.

"You have an odd way of showing appreciation," Nūk said, violently pulling Joon to his feet.

Joon felt a small pop in the lower part of his back and he was instantly sober.

Nūk raised his face in disgust.

"Your technique is weak," Nūk said, spitting on the ground in front of him.

Joon froze. His body was locked into place as Nūk walked behind him, leaning into his ear to whisper.

"I would be glad to demonstrate how to properly throw someone to the ground," Nūk offered. "It would not be enough to kill them, but it would leave the victim permanently crippled, suffering a life-long and incurable pain."

Joon's body instantly began to uncontrollably shiver and he gasped as his body gulped in a long overdue breath. Everyone knew that a Master could not kill a Sinanju villager, but Joon did not remember anything being said about crippling them.

"No, Master," Joon said, trembling. "Please, please don't."

"Pick your wife up," Nūk demanded. "Now."

"Yes, Master," Joon said with a subdued voice, running toward his wife. "I promise, it won't happen again."

He gently picked his wife up from the ground, and for a moment, thought about whispering a threat into her ear, but realized that Nūk would hear him.

"Your family may sleep in one of the newer huts," Nūk said. "It is close enough for me to hear...in case anyone needs my help."

"We give you many thanks, Master Nūk," Joon said, bowing deeply.

While there was peace during the time they lived at the bottom of the Master's hill, Joon chose a new hut further away and the beatings continued.

When she was sixteen, Joon listened as Eon rejected her fourth suitor, the youngest son of the village baker. Outside of the Master, the baker was one of the richest men in the village. Joon simmered in anger, but waited for the door to close before confronting her.

"What is wrong with this one?" he demanded.

"I do not love him," Eon explained.

"Love?" Joon laughed. "Who can afford to marry for love?"

"I am waiting for Chiun, father."

"Chiun?" Joon laughed.

"Chiun cannot marry until he is Apprentice Master," Eon's mother said in her defense.

"I know that!" Joon shouted. "You are going to wait a decade for the possibility of marrying him? What if he changes his mind? Do you realize that he travels the world with his father, bedding beautiful women everywhere they go?"

"He is not like that, father."

"You're sixteen…you know *nothing* about the world! All of your friends were married by fourteen, except for that sickly girl with the weird eye…"

"You mean Yuna?" Eon asked. "That is true, but Yuna found love, father."

"And now look at them, living in poverty behind the leather maker!" Joon said, mocking her. "That's right, Eon, even the sickly poor girl with the weird eye was married at fifteen! Do you expect me to pay for your food for the next decade? Do you know how much it costs to feed you?"

"I will eat less, father," Eon said, pleading.

Joon turned his back to Eon.

"I know that you don't believe me, but Chiun said..." Eon started to say, and something in Joon snapped.

He grabbed Eon by the throat, slamming her against the wooden wall.

"If you leave a mark, Chiun will know!" her mother intervened.

"Chiun?" Joon howled. "Chiun? Chiun! I am...so...*sick* of that name!"

Joon let go of Eon and she fell back against the wall, holding her throat.

"And you!" Joon shouted, turning to his wife. "Every time I try to punish that girl, you get in my way! I ought to..."

Joon paused and collected his thoughts. And then, for the first time in Eon's life, she saw her father smile. It scared her.

Joon stormed over to his wife.

"I bet he won't be looking for a mark on you!"

He punched his wife in the stomach and she doubled-over, collapsing to the floor.

"Mother!" Eon yelled, trying to intervene, but her father pushed her back into some rugs.

"Every time I hear that boy's name, every single time...I'm just going to take it out on your mother. This is your fault, Eon!" Joon said, rolling his wife over with a solid kick to the ribs.

She moaned and balled up into a fetal position.

"If I can't get to you," Joon said. "Then I'll just get to her!"

Eon sat back against the wall, crying with each kick and punch.

Then Eon felt a small pinch below her thumb and she returned to the present.

"Fear has roots deeper than a tree," Chiun said.

Eon remained looking forward. The memories were so fresh in her mind. When they passed the last hill and saw the dock, Eon felt a knot in her stomach.

"I just...you don't know," Eon said, wiping tears away.

"No harm shall ever come to you after this day," Chiun promised.

Eon's mother walked behind them, facing the same fear. Detecting the shivers in her steps, Chiun addressed her formally for the first time.

"You are also safe, mother," Chiun said. "This man's menace ends today."

"I do not wish to be a burden to you, Master," she said. "I only ask you to care for Eon."

"Within this family, I am to be called 'Chiun,' nothing more. And I protect my family."

"Thank you, Chiun," Eon's mother replied. "You are very gracious."

A warm glow of family settled in Chiun's chest, a sensation he had not felt since his mother's passing.

The crunching of gravel under the villagers' sandals seemed unusually loud. Wisps of cold sea breeze snaked through the crowd, causing even those accustomed to its icy bite to shudder. A flock of seagulls burst into the sky, their panicked cries mirroring the unease growing within Eon. As they reached the end of the muddy path, the crowd fell into an unnatural silence, remaining a respectful distance away as Chiun and Eon approached the dock.

The wooden cabin that served as the fishermen's storage hut was large and very well insulated. And while fishing supplies technically did exist inside, it had become more of a private sanctuary in the past few years, serving as a rustic hideaway from the pressures of wives and village duties.

The inside walls and floors were covered in multiple layers of furs and the sole window faced the village, serving as a lookout in case of any approaching visitors. The cabin was well stocked with many things including fish, jerky and drink. If someone looked carefully, they might even find the shelf that had been hidden for the shaman.

Chiun detected four people inside. Curtailing his anger, he stamped his foot on the edge of the dock, causing the cabin's foundation to sway in the cold waters.

Curses erupted from the inside and a fisherman angrily opened the door ready to fight, only to come face to face with a glaring Chiun. His anger drained as quickly as his bladder.

"Joon-Hu. Now," Chiun demanded, instantly waking the man from his drunken fog. His steely eyes gave them a warning that his voice did not reveal. "The rest of you will leave."

The fishermen roused the others and they scrambled from their hideout, embarrassed. Chiun heard one of the fishermen slapping Joon hard and telling him to wake up.

"You louse!" a plump lady in back screamed as she saw her husband exit the cabin. "You said you were leaving for supplies!"

"Those *are* supplies," he said in defense.

She chased him back up the path to the village.

After a moment, a tall man swaggered out of the hut and leaned against the door. His robe was muddy and tattered. Those close enough held their noses.

Eon looked away in embarrassment.

Despite the situation, Chiun followed the proper Sinanju wedding tradition and laid a wreath of pink and red plum blossoms, colors representing love and honor, at her father's feet.

Chiun turned his face away from the villagers to lock eyes with Joon. As one of the tallest men in the village, Joon towered over Chiun, but as their eyes connected, Joon felt very small.

"Joon of the house of Hu, I am Chiun, Apprentice Master for the House of Sinanju," Chiun said, keeping his voice deceptively gentle as his eyes narrowed in threat. "I am here to ask for your daughter's hand in marriage. In this, I pledge my heart and my future to her."

Joon swallowed hard, but could not keep from looking into Chiun's eyes.

"I shall protect her, feed her and keep her well," Chiun said, his voice becoming tinged with a cold resolve that was more of a threat than a promise. "We will bear children and carry on your…noble bloodline. I am honored to receive her mother into my family and my protection."

In one defining moment, Chiun had conveyed a clear message to Joon: not only would he protect Eon, but also shield her mother from any future harm he might wish to cause.

The traditional response was for the bride's father to demonstrate his power and show his future son-in-law that if he did not treat his daughter well, the groom would face his wrath. Overcome by the weight of the moment and the not-so-subtle threat from his future son-in-law, Joon's face lost all color. He turned and violently retched on the dock. His eyes rolled back in his head before collapsing on a rug inside.

The crowd behind Chiun laughed and Chiun publicly smiled in response, but internally was angry that he could not publicly punish this man.

Eon wrapped her arms around Chiun and gave him a strong and lasting hug.

"Thank you," she said. "Thank you so much."

Chiun looked at her and smiled.

The crowd grew still as Eon approached the cabin door. Traditionally, the father of the bride presented her hand to the groom, but she took one glance at her unconscious father and placed her own hand in Chiun's.

The couple raised their hands together and the crowd cheered.

CHAPTER NINE

Driven by the promise of an unparalleled wedding feast by his son, Nūk journeyed to Seoul to secure a favor of the Governor-General, Admiral Viscount Saitō Makoto.

At this time, Korea was still under Japanese colonial rule. The villagers of Sinanju seemed worried as the occupation grew, but Nūk reassured them that Korea had seen 'ruling nations' come and go. One puppet ruler was just as good as another, as long as they honored their commitment to Sinanju.

He reminded himself of his words as he entered Seoul. Remembering Chiun's reaction as a child, his eyes narrowed at the sight of Japanese flags fluttering atop local buildings. This time he did not see Koreans wandering the streets. The air in the city was tense.

Something was wrong.

Master Nūk had met the Governor-General many times and each time, it seemed harder to get a concession from him. Makoto was the third Governor-General sent by Japan, a thin man in his sixties, a man with weary, unfocused eyes. His flat mustache was the only personal flair he allowed, a fashion left-over from a political post thirty years earlier. After a life of stressful politics, Makoto looked twenty years older than he was.

The newly-appointed Korean guards standing outside happily bowed and opened the doors for Master Nūk.

Nūk headed straight to the Governor General's office, entering with a cursory bow. The office had been redecorated many times since Nūk's first visit.

Makoto used color as a weapon to demonstrate power. Strong red and gold angles, the colors of the Japanese Empire, framed the large room, growing smaller and smaller until they focused on the dark curtains behind Makoto's large teak desk. It was an indication to everyone in Korea: Makoto *was* Japan.

"Good morning," Makoto said in broken English.

"Governor General," Nūk acknowledged in perfect British English.

Nūk deliberately chose to converse in English because it was a language that Makoto struggled with.

"Please, have a seat," Makoto said, pointing to the chair in front of his large desk.

"My son is to be wed next month," Nūk said, accepting the seat.

"What does that have to do with the Japanese Empire?" Makoto asked mockingly, with the cold smile of a politician.

"We will need to prepare for a large wedding feast," Nūk said. "And that will involve your help."

"Large?" Makoto asked, rolling the numbers around in his head. "How large, exactly?"

"Large enough to satisfy our guests. We will be inviting the emperor, of course."

Makoto sat back in his seat with a look of disbelief. His wrinkled forehead pushed his hairline back even further.

"Who are you referencing?" Makoto asked in disbelief. "*Our* emperor?"

Nūk nodded.

"That is not possible," Makoto said, shaking his head. The diplomatic veneer of his voice abandoned. "The emperor is not someone to invite to your mud village."

"Indeed, it is unusual for an emperor to attend such events," Nūk said. "Yet it is not without precedent where Sinanju is concerned. I have shared tea with Emperor Yoshihito within the intimate walls of Fukiage Palace, discussing matters of state and the heart. His father, Emperor Mutsuhito, held Sinanju in great esteem for many reasons that I cannot disclose."

Nūk leaned forward in his seat to press his point.

"Each of your emperors understood the significance of The House of Sinanju. Hirohito has known of Sinanju since his early childhood."

"We...*no one* use's the emperors' proper names," Makoto said, clearly insulted.

"I do," Nūk replied. "I have been often told—*by your emperors*—that if the House needs anything, to just ask. So, I am asking you to invite Emperor Hirohito."

"I share the emperor's ear, but to even entertain such a request is preposterous."

Makoto tilted his head and scrunched his face.

"Do you hear how odd your request is?"

"I understand the audacity of the request," Nūk admitted. "But the emperor would be very upset were he to know of my request and realize that it was not sent. He would also be told who refused to send the request."

Makoto sat back and sighed. "Fine, the request will be sent tomorrow and..."

"No," Nūk insisted. "It will be sent now."

Makoto had hoped to conveniently forget the request once the Korean had left. He quickly weighed his options. On one hand, if he sent such a ridiculous request to the emperor and the Korean was lying, he might be questioned about his sanity. On the other, if he was telling the truth, Makoto would lose his post, and perhaps his head.

Makoto stared at the buzzer on his desk panel. Pressing it would call his secretary, who would do whatever he was ordered. He glanced back at Nūk and took a deep breath before pressing the buzzer.

A sharply-dressed Japanese officer entered the office and snapped to attention with a crisp salute.

"Sir?" he asked.

"Send a telegram to the emperor. Inform him that a Korean Master is re…"

"The Master of Sinanju," Nūk interjected.

The officer's posture remained rigid, but after hearing that the man seated in front of the Governor General was the Master of Sinanju, his eyes nervously darted toward Nūk, betraying a mixture of deep respect and personal fear.

The reputation of the Master of Sinanju was not lost on him, and his proximity to such a deadly legend was disconcerting. He returned his gaze to the Governor-General, who was casually writing instructions down.

Did he not know who was sitting in front of him?

"That *'the Master of Sinanju'* is requesting his presence for his son's wedding next month."

"At high-sun on the first of the month," Nūk added.

"That's 'noon' to us," Makoto said in a condescending tone.

"Yes sir!" the man said.

Before leaving, he saluted Makoto and then, with deep reverence, bowed deeply to Nūk.

Makoto's jaw tightened at the sight. He had never seen such a deep bow in his life. It left a bitter taste in his mouth that one of his own would give such deference to this fisherman.

"At least your soldiers are well-informed," Nūk said as the officer left.

"As long as they keep the peace in this backward country, I do not care. Is that all?"

"Wedding feast…Emperor Hirohito," Nūk repeated, standing to leave.

"Wait," Makoto called out and Nūk turned back. "I admit…I am puzzled."

"By what?"

"You claim to have a personal attachment with the Imperial line, but our emperors are not merely rulers, but divine symbols of our nation. To have been in the august presence of even *one* would be a lifetime honor, but…to claim to personally know *three* is unbelievable. May I ask as to the nature of your interactions?"

"You may ask," Nūk said as he once again turned to leave.

Makoto stood and his eyes narrowed.

"This position is not an honorable one," he said. "To serve in your putrid land holds no allure for me, but it is that very stench that drew me here. We both know of the eternal wedge that exists between us, established between the first Japanese Warrior and the first Korean Warrior. But while there was a beginning, be assured that we are planning for your end."

"Sinanju is forever," Nūk replied and walked away.

Makoto silently watched Nūk as he casually left the office. Never before had he harbored such hatred for a single individual.

CHAPTER TEN

Though his steps were furtive, they made no sound as they ascended the steps to the House of Many Woods. Chiun walked quickly through the house until he found his father in the scroll room. He was organizing some of the older scrolls that Chiun had not yet seen.

He gave a quick and mechanical bow to his father.

"Hirohito?" Chiun asked, bewildered. "Why would you tarnish my wedding with a Japanese Emperor?"

"Because my son made the mistake of telling everyone in the village that I would be inviting royalty."

"I was referring to Emperor Sunjong! I would even consider Prajadhipok of Siam...but a *Japanese* emperor?"

Nūk looked more concerned about his son's outburst than the topic he raised.

"You will remember your place," Nūk said and Chiun leaned back on his heels.

"Apologies, father. This is...very important to me."

"That is the only reason I made the effort that I did. Otherwise, I would have left you without any royal guest. As for Prajadhipok? That man will never step foot in this village."

"What did he do?" Chiun asked.

It was rare to see a glint of anger from his father.

"There are some scrolls that you will not see until you become master," Nūk said.

Chiun's face twisted in defeat.

"Don't worry," Nūk reassured him. "Hirohito will be the only one allowed in the village."

"So be it," Chiun conceded. "But I think the shaman should closely watch him to make sure that he doesn't steal anything."

"Some would say that a god blessing your wedding should be considered a great favor," Nūk said, returning the cloth covering the scrolls. "What does your betrothed think?"

"I have not told her," Chiun said. "I do not want to worry her about such things."

"Then tell her father, Joon. I am sure he will enjoy the emperor's company."

Chiun then realized what his father meant. Special wedding guests sat by the father of the bride and his eyes opened wide.

"What will we do? The man can barely stay awake long enough to drink!"

"The royal we, or you and I?" Nūk asked. "You have made it clear that I have overstepped my hand several times, so I will allow my wise son to address the specifics."

Chiun closed his eyes in thought.

"Hirohito knows nothing of our traditions. Perhaps he can sit by me," Chiun suggested.

"Then where would I sit?" Nūk asked. "You will not sit me beside that drunk. Besides, everyone in Sinanju is familiar with our wedding traditions and it would look like you are honoring Hirohito above myself. You wouldn't do that, would you?"

Chiun began thinking of the seating arrangement as a chess board, measuring dignity with presence and matching social status against royalty and realized that in all of it, he was the pawn.

"I just need time to think about it," Chiun said, providing a quick bow before leaving.

Nūk returned the bow with a hidden grin.

Chiun's mind was racing as he approached Eon's hut. He had to come up with a solution before discussing it with her, but no matter how he tried to rearrange the seating in his mind, he could see no way out other than removing Eon from the center and he was not going to do that.

I could just threaten her father, Chiun thought, struggling for a solution. *Yes, that would be easy. I would destroy all of his alcohol, and make a few spinal nerve adjustments prior to the ceremony to ensure that he was fully conscious...but what if Eon noticed her father was strangely coherent?*

No, if he was fully aware of his surroundings, the lout would likely soil himself from the pressure of being seated next to an emperor.

Chiun was still juggling his thoughts when he reached Joon's hut. After their old hut burned a few years earlier, Nūk had given them one of the large new huts, but her father had not properly maintained it. Pieces of timber that were damaged in the past two storms had not been patched, revealing small holes, and the roof only showed modest attempts at repair. Thankfully, Eon did not have to live here much longer.

The door opened as Chiun approached and Eon's mother greeted him with a bow and a wide smile.

"Chiun!" she almost cheered, motioning for him to enter. "Go in, it's cold today," she said, before remembering who she was speaking to.

"Thank you, mother," Chiun said.

"Forgive me, but I must gather a few things," she said. "Please, make yourself at home!"

"Be well, mother," Chiun said with a small bow as she left.

The inside of the hut was brighter than the last time he had visited. The windows were no longer covered by ragged furs and he could tell that the floors had been recently cleaned.

Thankfully, there was no sign of Eon's father, Joon. His padded seat remained clumped and dirty in the corner.

An aroma of sweets filled the house and, even though he could not partake of them, Chiun had learned to consume them by smell alone. Eon stood at the end of the hut, in a small kitchen area. She was busy with something, her arms working on practiced autopilot.

"Let me guess...dasik, fresh yugwa and...rice cakes?" Chiun asked her.

"Special rice cakes with one drop of honey, made specially for a Master of Sinanju," Eon said.

The pressures of seating arrangements and emperors faded away as their eyes locked. Eon rushed to greet him. Her smile filled his senses and they bowed in greeting. For the briefest of moments, their cheeks brushed each other. Within that slice of time, where everything in a Master of Sinanju's purview froze — arrows and bullets, and even love — Chiun clung to the feeling of her cheek as it bashfully retreated.

As she pulled away, Chiun glanced longingly at her lips and allowed himself a moment to consider their taste...sweeter than any rice cake, and equally as forbidden. Chiun felt his body fill with an urgency that sought to control his breathing and forced himself back. If he did not have control over his blood pressure, his own cheeks would have flushed bright red.

"Is everything okay?" Eon asked. "You looked worried when you entered."

"It is nothing that I cannot handle," Chiun said.

"If we are to be wed, the first promise we must make to each other is honesty," Eon said. "I am to be your wife, the mother of your children, but I am also your confidant. Look! I have two ears," she said with a smile that could shatter granite.

Chiun surrendered with a grin.

"You are right," he admitted. "I need to prepare my mind as well as my heart that we will be one."

Though he did not pace, per se, Chiun took his time to sit.

"In the coming years, we will face many things together, including serious political matters. The fate of the village will depend on my decisions. I will lean strongly on you during those times. Then, there are decisions like this," Chiun said, slightly embarrassed. "It is the seating arrangement for our wedding."

"I do not understand," Eon said.

Chiun started to speak, but turned as he heard aggressive stomps approaching the hut.

"Didn't I tell you that we don't have money for fancy foods?" a voice thundered from outside.

Joon slammed the door open, looking for his wife. The rage in his face melted as he came nose-to-nose with Chiun.

"Perhaps my earlier 'suggestion' to you was not clear, because you were drunk. I will not make the same mistake twice," Chiun said.

He placed one fingernail on Joon's sternum and Joon turned, emptying his stomach until it held no more alcohol. Before he could collapse into his own vomit, Chiun grabbed him by the back of his shirt and punched a finger in his spine, forcing him to breathe deeply until he overcame the alcoholic poison in his system.

"On my way over, I had considered neutering you so that you could no longer contaminate this world with your stupidity. Your sole good seed stands behind me and in every possible way that you can imagine, she is under my protection."

"Y-y-yes, Master," Joon said. "Forgive me."

"Our wedding will be held in mere weeks. The Emperor of Japan will be seated to your right."

"The...the..." Joon stuttered at the thought. "The what?"

"The Emperor of Japan," Chiun repeated. "If you choose to dishonor us...dishonor *Sinanju* in front of royalty, the wedding will end with a fatherless bride."

"I can…I *will* show honor," Joon promised.

Chiun turned to Eon trying to show a small grin.

"We will continue our conversation tomorrow, my love," he said and left.

CHAPTER ELEVEN

*E*mperor Hirohito sat quietly perched on the Chrysanthemum Throne, his crimson robes lifelessly spilled over his tired frame. His face, youthful but pale, bore the weight of an Empire teetering on the brink. The once-bright eyes, the windows to a curious and intellectual soul, were now clouded with a weariness that seemed to seep into the very bones of the throne room itself.

The Chrysanthemum Crest on his shoulder glinted faintly in the filtered light, as inert as the jade bead rosary he absently fingered. Another interminable day stretched before him, full of false praise and numbing reports.

The throne room, a symphony of dark, polished wood and muted gold, exuded an air of austere elegance. Tatami mats, immaculately woven from rice straw, stretched across the floor, their geometric precision adding to the sense of order and control. Shoji screens, translucent paper stretched over wooden frames, adorned the walls, their delicate rice paper depicting scenes of serene landscapes and mythical creatures. The air, thick with the cloying scent of incense hung heavy in the air, an oily balm smothering the whispers of discontent, a memory of tedious temples and stifled prayers.

His Privy Council, a collection of grim-faced men in starched military uniforms and somber suits, occupied the floor before him. Each man, a titan of industry or member of the Imperial military, sat perfectly upright, their silence a testament to the gravity of the situation.

The stillness in the chamber hummed with unspoken anxieties, restrained by the emperor's very presence, their anxious glances a silent plea for direction in the face of mounting crises.

Hirohito mindlessly traced the delicate veins of an ornate flower cloisonné vase. Each meticulously crafted petal seemed to mock the hollowness that he felt within. He yearned for the days of his youth, dissecting starfish on the sun-drenched shores of Hayama, the pungent scent of saltwater still clinging to his nostrils like a phantom limb. Now, he was a glorified prisoner in a gilded cage, his every move dictated by an ancient tradition, and judged by the insatiable demands of his advisors.

A cough, dry and rasping, cut through the silence. Marquis Kido, the Emperor's closest confidante, leaned forward, his weathered face etched with concern. "Your Majesty," he rasped, his voice a low rumble in the hushed chamber, "the Foreign Minister awaits your audience. The Americans… they wish to meet next week."

Hirohito sighed, the sound a weary exhalation that seemed to echo the anxieties of the nation. He straightened his posture, forcing a flicker of the imperial majesty that seemed to be perpetually on loan.

"Very well," he said, his voice regaining its practiced formality. "Call for the foreign minister. Perhaps America will provide the storm my reign so desperately needs."

One by one, the Privy Council droned on, each providing a sterile defense of their stances, each of their voices a respectful, monotonous hum punctuated by the clinking of teacups and the rustling of starched silk.

Hiro had heard it all and seen it all. The Americans would not bow to his throne, nor his policies or requests and the two nations repeated the same conditions over and over. Boredom had coiled itself around his spirit, suffocating the man beneath the title.

He had even lost the love of his evening walks in the colorful gardens outside. Meticulously pruned and arranged in dazzling patterns, they no longer offered solace, their sterile perfection merely another wall in his gilded cage.

Then a hush fell over the chamber, and Hirohito saw the Councilors bowing in unison as a messenger, clad in austere indigo, approached the throne. This was a ceremonial messenger, one Hiro had not seen in many years. His crimson silk scarf, the only splash of color against his muted attire, whispered of mystery. He knelt before the emperor, his head bowed low.

He held a scroll in his outstretched hand.

"Your Majesty," his voice resonating in artificial grandeur, "a missive from Master Nūk of Sinanju."

A tremor, almost imperceptible, ran through the emperor. For a fleeting moment, the murmurs of the council faded, replaced by the muted gold of his father's private chamber, and a young prince with eyes filled with wonder. The clang of shattered steel, the soft whisper of Korean, the promise of a friendship forged in a stolen moment.

Unbeknownst to the council, the emperor was deeply enamored with Sinanju. When he was ten years old and still called 'Hiro', the young prince had a fateful meeting that would forever link their destinies.

Hiro's father had invited the master to his private chamber, the rarest of honors. Unlike the public throne room that most people were aware of, the emperor's private chamber was a sanctuary of refined Japanese aesthetics. The walls displayed subtle artistry rather than the overt opulence of the throne room. It was a place that Hiro was told to avoid, but when he heard that the mythical Master of Sinanju had sought an audience with his father, Hiro had to see him.

Hiro had a perfect hiding spot. He found out when he was four that the curtains to the right of his father's throne were thick enough to hide him within its fold, and large enough to even sit if needed. He often hid within the curtain when he wanted to listen in on his father's conversations.

So, before the master was scheduled to arrive, Hiro tucked himself within the folds of the curtain and waited. He soon heard a door and quieted his breathing. He heard what sounded like several guards telling someone to stand here and wait for his father.

After the guards left and the door closed, Nūk spoke.

"Greetings, young Prince Hirohito," he said. "My name is Nūk. I am the Master of Sinanju."

"How did you see me?" Hiro asked, jumping out from the curtain. "No one can see me there!"

"No one but a Master of Sinanju," Nūk replied in perfect Japanese keigo, bowing slightly. "I not only saw you, I heard your rapid heartbeat and could even smell the cherry blossoms that were placed on your hofuku after they were cleaned."

To make the prince feel comfortable, Nūk had chosen to speak with the formality of the emperor's ancient patterns, each syllable articulated with the weight of centuries of tradition.

Hiro smiled as if he was meeting one of the characters in the books he loved so much.

"I am called Hiro among my friends," Hiro said. "I think we would make good friends."

Then Hiro tilted his head and squinted his eyes.

"Some people say that you're not real," he said.

"And yet, here I stand," Nūk replied, extending his arms.

"No, that is not what I meant. They say you are an illusionist, and have no real combat skills."

"Your father believes otherwise, or I would not be here."

"Prove it," Hiro said.

Nūk grinned and thought for something that would not be dangerous, but would entertain a ten-year-old.

"How many swords do you have?" Nūk asked.

"Every sword in Japan belongs to my father and myself," Hiro proudly replied.

"Do you have one I can see?" Nūk asked. "A good one?"

"Of course, I do!" Hiro said and ran away.

After a minute, Hiro returned with a guard, holding an ornate sword. It was small and obviously designed for Hiro. The guard was not happy.

"I cannot allow you a sword in the presence of the Prince of the Path," the guard said sternly.

"Give him the sword!" Hiro yelled, and the guard reluctantly handed it to Nūk.

Nūk accepted the sword with a slight bow.

"Now leave us alone!" Hiro shouted and the guard bowed, walking out backwards, keeping his eyes trained on Nūk.

"What do you think of my sword?" Hiro asked expectantly.

As soon as he held the sword, Nūk had sensed the profound weight distribution, noting its nearly-perfect balance. Despite being a small sword, the swordsmith had not spared on quality. Allowing the light to dance across the steel, Nūk observed the intricate patterns in the metal. He identified the unmistakable art of a master swordsmith.

"Good," Nūk noted. "This is very good."

As he tilted the sword, his eyes almost microscopically dissected the swirling patterns that extended the length of the sword. While most people just accepted the pattern as an artistic remnant, Nūk recognized the purpose of the patterns. They were the result of a complex mixture of high and low carbon steel, folding into each other countless times, each layer granting the blade additional resilience and strength.

Nūk turned and thrust the sword into the air. Despite the speed with which he struck, the sword made no sound in Nūk's hands. For a Japanese blade, Nūk was impressed.

He handed the sword carefully to Hiro.

"This sword was made by someone who knows their craft very well," Nūk said.

"My father has the finest swordsmiths in all of Asia," Hiro said proudly. "Only the Spanish come close to our steel and that's because they cheat."

"It is a fine sword," Nūk admitted.

"How strong are you? Can you bend it?" Hiro asked. "It's made of super steel!"

"I can do better than that, young prince," Master Nūk leaned in, whispering as if revealing a great secret. "I can shatter it with one fingernail."

"What? No way! That's impossible!" the young prince cried.

Master Nūk spread his fingers, revealing long and sharp looking fingernails. They reminded Hiro of the false golden fingernails of the Siamese, except they were real.

"Show me!" Hiro shouted in excitement and disbelief.

"If I do, your father will have to make you another," Nūk said, taking a step back and placing both hands in front of himself.

"I have six swords," Hiro said.

"Then throw your sword at me," Nūk said. "As hard as you can."

"I don't want to hurt you," Hiro said cautiously.

"If you can hurt me with a sword, I do not deserve to see your father," Nūk said, smiling.

"Okay, but I'm going to throw it really hard!" Hiro warned.

Nūk nodded, accepting the challenge.

Holding the sword behind him for a moment, Hiro leaned forward, throwing the sword at Nūk with all his strength.

Nūk saw the sword approach. The path was erratic, but thrown with admirable force for a ten-year-old. He allowed the sword to move as far away from Hiro as possible until the very last possible moment, and then, with one fingernail, met the very tip of the sword.

At a microscopic level, the kinetic energy of Nūk's fingernail spread throughout the sword, instantly shattering the bond between each fold and each layer. Unable to withstand such a devastating kinetic transfer, the blade exploded into a small ring of metal shards. Tiny grains of metal sparked, forming a small fireworks display. Some of the shards had shattered so quickly that they left a mystic blue vapor in the immediate area.

Hiro's eyes widened in shock. He saw the sword hurling towards Master Nūk. Then it seemed to explode into dust.

When he looked back, Nūk was holding the hilt.

"Can you show me how to do that?" Hiro asked.

"That is for Sinanju alone," Nūk explained.

"How do I become Sinanju?"

"Your fate is tied to the strong empirical line of your nation. You have a long and great life ahead of you."

"If I can't learn Sinanju, then I will learn to speak Sinanju!" Hiro shouted.

"Then you shall be a friend to Sinanju," Nūk said, smiling.

Excited with his new friend, Hiro bowed before Nūk.

"I swear on my life as the next emperor of Japan, that I will learn Korean and that I will be a friend to Sinanju!"

Nūk returned the bow and then heard footprints.

"To the curtain, quickly," Nūk said. "It's your father."

Hiro turned to run to the curtains, but first, he bowed deeply to Nūk.

Safely behind the curtains, he watched as his father, Emperor Yoshihito, entered the chamber. Master Nūk's face had reverted to the same honorific face that everyone seemed to make when meeting his father.

Hiro tried to silently sit within the folds of the curtain so he could listen, but something stiff in his outside jacket pocket prevented him from bending over. When he found out what it was, he smiled.

Somehow, Master Nūk had placed the hilt inside his pocket without his knowledge. Hiro almost squealed in delight.

Hiro had honored his promise and honed his Korean language skills over the years. He grabbed the missive from the messenger and he motioned to the Privy Council to be silent. The symbol for Sinanju was stamped on the scroll in gold wax. This was an official summons, a formality to be acknowledged, a thread in the intricate tapestry of imperial obligations.

If it had been from anyone else, whether individual or government, it would have been seen as an insult to ask for the emperor's presence on a specific date and at a specific location, because the emperor did not answer to man.

But his face radiated a long-lost smile as he read calligraphy as fine as spider silk written by the hand of Master Nūk himself. The emperor arose, his crimson robes flowing like a river of defiance against the stagnant air.

"Inform Master Nūk," he told the messenger, his voice resonating with a newfound vibrancy, "that the Emperor of Japan shall grace his son's wedding with his presence. Prepare the Imperial barge, for we set course for Sinanju on the first. We have a wedding to attend!"

The pronouncement wasn't merely a statement of travel, it was a declaration of power from the Emperor of Japan, a casting off of the shackles of office and a reunion with a piece of himself long thought lost.

But even as the emperor remembered that magical moment, a glacial silence draped over the Privy Council. The room, usually a portrait of stoicism, transformed into a canvas of barely concealed dread.

Hirohito stepped down from the throne, wordlessly passing the council, and briskly walked to his residence. His crimson train became an unfurled banner against the grey monotony of his court.

On this day, Emperor Michinomiya Hirohito had glimpsed a path out of his gilded cage, and a spark of life was rekindled by the whisper of an old memory and the promise of a new adventure. The preparations would take weeks, but he would make it work. For the first time in many years, a butterfly danced inside the Chrysanthemum Throne.

CHAPTER TWELVE

After the emperor left, the throne room seemed to dim. The members of the Privy Council stared at each other in disbelief, their faces ashen with fear. The American threat was no longer important. A much more dire situation required their attention.

Marquis Kido Koichi presided over the meetings. A confidante to the emperor and a veteran of the political arena, Kido's words often steered the course of discussions. His seniority was undisputed, but it was from the trust placed in him by the emperor that granted him authority.

Prime Minister Hamaguchi Osachi held a position of immense responsibility. Though technically a subordinate to Kido in matters of court hierarchy, his role as the head of government afforded him a significant degree of influence.

Admiral Yamamoto Isoroku, Chief of the Naval Staff, commanded respect due to his military prowess. His authority in matters of defense and naval strategy was unparalleled. His opinions mostly carried weight among those who favored a more aggressive stance in international affairs.

Baron Makino Nobuaki, former ambassador to London and

now Minister of the Imperial Household, brought a unique perspective to the council. His expertise in foreign affairs and his nuanced understanding of Western politics made him an invaluable asset.

Count Yasuoka Masaatsu, President of the House of Peers, represented the aristocratic legacy of Japan. His authority was rooted in tradition and the social hierarchy of the Empire. His influence was more ceremonial than practical, but in matters of imperial protocol and tradition, his word was law.

Every man in the council was a pillar of Japan, and they navigated the complexities of power with a single, shared goal: the preservation and expansion of the Empire, even when their visions for that future diverged.

One of the reasons the Japanese Empire was so feared was because of its broad range of contingency plans. Their military strategies were complex and thorough. Enemies had to take into account multiple possibilities whenever addressing Japan's intent.

But Japan had made no plan for a tiny Korean fishing village.

Sinanju was a village of legend and myth. It was rumored to shift and blend with the terrain like a chameleon. One day, it would be seen as a bustling market, full of cheerful people, the next, it was a ghost town, vanishing into the mist…or so the stories went.

And their Emperor had voluntarily chosen to walk into the mouth of the dragon.

Kido leaned forward, his brow creased in concern.

"While the emperor's well-being is paramount," he began, his voice tight, "we must consider the potential political fallout of such a risky venture."

Prime Minister Hamaguchi chewed on his lip.

"The people revere the emperor. If any harm were to befall him…" he said, leaving the unspoken implication heavy in the air.

The room fell quiet as a messenger boy appeared. Dressed in white silk, he quickly entered, bowed to Admiral Yamamoto and handed him a slip of paper.

Yamamoto grabbed the paper from his hands and the boy scrambled from the room.

"What is it?" Hamaguchi asked.

Yamamoto spat on the polished floor, his fury barely contained.

"The emperor has demanded the use of the Haemaekkori for the trip to Sinanju. The ship is only ceremonial—it is completely unarmed!"

As he spoke, Yamamoto's hand instinctively went to the hilt of his ceremonial sword—a subtle but clear sign of his escalating frustration.

"Worse," Yamamoto continued. "He will only allow the Imperial Guard to escort him!"

"Very odd," Baron Makino murmured. "Does anyone know if there even *is* a wedding?"

"Gentlemen!" Kido said, trying to calm the room. "The emperor has made his decision, but as guardians of the Empire, we need to make ours as well."

Their cigarette smoke curdled across the table, as heavy as their dread.

Kido's eyes had become dark pits in a mask of worry. There was no sound but the rasp of Hamaguchi's breath as he chewed his lip, his eyes flicking between his peers.

Whispers began morphing into groans as fear claimed control of the meeting.

Panic coiled in Masaatsu's gut. As the only person present who had directly spoken with the Master of Sinanju, he knew that Sinanju was not a myth nor a fisherman's yarn. Blood and whispers followed behind every action the Master made.

He cleared his throat.

"I believe that we are missing the larger picture. Let us say that the emperor is correct, and there is a wedding. The real danger is if any gesture…or any word from the emperor that might cause the Master of Sinanju to take offense. If that happens, his retaliation would be focused on this chamber."

Urgency filled the room as a cold shiver ran through each man as they envisioned their heads rolling on the floor in pools of their own blood.

"We all know what is at stake," Baron Makino said. "We cannot treat Sinanju as we would any other country. There is a reason they have no diplomats."

For the first time in council history, the members started talking over each other until Admiral Yamamoto stood and slammed his fist on the table. His voice shook with a barely contained panic.

"Are you mad? We can't sit around and discuss nuances!"

Then he turned to Kido, grilling him with his eyes.

"Intelligence, Kido-san!" he shouted at the council leader. "We need eyes and ears in Sinanju!"

Silence descended as no one volunteered. It was one thing to realize that this had become a game of survival; it was another to be directly associated with a conspiracy against the Master of Sinanju.

Hamaguchi thought for a moment and then raised his chin.

"I know what we can do," he said. "But I will need absolute discretion from each of you."

Councilmembers' heads began bouncing like Japanese bobbleheads.

"We need Kasuo Shimada."

The council looked down at the table, their enthusiasm instantly dashed. Kasuo was the captain of the Imperial Guards Division. While the guards' primary mission was defending the emperor, lately they had also been known to unofficially take care of certain embarrassing problems outside of their mandate, things both unsanctioned and lethal.

To mention his name in mixed political company in such a manner carried an air of shame.

"It makes sense," Baron Makino said. "He is with the emperor any time he travels."

Kido nodded his head in thought.

"If he was dressed in proper rags, perhaps with dirt on his face, he could infiltrate the village."

"The boy is a fop!" Admiral Yamamoto jeered. "He would be discovered immediately!"

"He leads the Division!" Hamaguchi replied. "That is not a ceremonial position."

"Ask his uncle how much he paid for that uniform," Yamamoto replied.

The tension in the council chamber thickened, the air becoming a blend of desperation and skepticism. Hamaguchi's proposal, while bold, illuminated the direness of their situation, forcing them to consider options they would have previously dismissed out of hand.

The idea of deploying a man more accustomed to the comforts of high society than the rigors of espionage was dangerous. But what other option did they have?

Hamaguchi, undeterred by the murmurs of doubt, pressed on, his voice a steady beacon.

"Shimada has trained with the Division, even if his appointment is a ceremonial one."

"Should he fail, his actions would be disavowed," Baron Makino said. "Shimada would be considered a rogue. But, should he succeed, we will all share in his fortunes."

The room fell into a contemplative silence.

Admiral Yamamoto finally nodded, albeit reluctantly.

Kido acknowledged the point with a grim nod.

"Then let us make preparations," Kido said, giving the council's official sanction. "Shimada will need to be thoroughly briefed."

The council members, rallied by Kido's resolve, began to discuss logistics, support, and contingencies, the initial shock of their decision giving way to the focused urgency of planning. In this moment, they were unified—not just by fear, but by a shared determination to protect the status quo.

CHAPTER THIRTEEN

The man who entered Kasuo Shimada's office moved with an odd, hurried gait, his steps quick and uncertain. Kasuo recognized his face, thin and pale, haunted by a nagging familiarity. The man's superior rank was betrayed by his age, yet there was an urgency in his manner that demanded immediate attention.

He bowed quickly, his name lost in a mumble.

"What can I do for you, Major?" Kasuo asked.

"Captain, I bear a message from the Privy Council," the major lisped.

He presented an envelope with a wax seal and backed out of the room, his departure as brisk as his entrance.

Kasuo took the envelope with a raised eyebrow. Instead of breaking the seal, he sliced it open with a practiced flick and began to read the short note from inside.

Kasuo glanced up from the letter, his gaze settling on the man sprawled casually across his office couch. "That was Nakano, right? Hamaguchi's man?"

Kage Morituri lounged across the couch with an air of calculated detachment. He was the newly appointed sergeant of the Imperial Guards Division. His military suit, custom-tailored, hung loosely on his slender frame, contrasting sharply with the depth of maturity that his eyes suggested. He favored a short, but thick beard, as black as any Kasuo had ever seen.

He made no attempt to conceal his boredom.

"Yes," Kage confirmed, his voice a low rumble of disdain. "Always lurking in the shadows of greater men."

"We've been summoned to Hamaguchi's home. Have you heard anything about this?"

Kage's chuckle was dry as dust.

"With Hamaguchi? It's either a banquet or a bloodbath."

"Then we'll bring a fork *and* a dagger," Kasuo said.

A chuckle was the closest thing to a laugh Kasuo had ever heard from Kage. Though it had been several years since he became Kasuo's blood guardian, Kage was almost as enigmatic as he had been the day they met.

"How old did you say you were?" Kasuo asked.

"Older than Nakano's great-great grandfather," Kage replied. "I do not remember in years."

"And you said you were born in…where was it, again?"

"Kemet," Kage corrected. "The land you now refer to as 'Egypt.'"

"You understand how crazy that sounds, right?"

Kage's reply was tinged with the sorrow of countless ages.

"For some, time is a pond, captain. For others, it is an ocean."

"I know that you can't lie to me, but I still can't wrap my head around it."

"It would be much easier if I could just tell you that I was born thirty years ago."

Though his blood oath with Kasuo prohibited him from lying, there were still things that Kage could not tell Kasuo. He could not reveal the nature of his being, nor who he was before being turned.

Kage was once a simple shepherd named Akhen, the

youngest of four brothers. He did not remember the exact date of his birth, but it was at a time when Egypt was ruled by the Persians. He specifically remembered his father cursing King Darius on a daily basis.

Their modest plot of land lay close enough to the Nile to grow their own food and draw water. In the mornings, Akhen could even see the morning light reflecting off Giza's pyramids. He had often wished to see them up close, but Persian policies severely restricted travel for ordinary Egyptians, trapping him in distant admiration.

The Persians were well aware of the pyramids' symbolic might, and refused to maintain their grandeur. The Pyramid of Menkaure had already showed signs of neglect before the Persian conquest, its limestone casing stripped in places from centuries of opportunistic looting, which only worsened under Persian rule.

These monoliths stood as silent witnesses to the erosion of Kemet's glory, waiting to awake when the Pharoah returned. The air, though still rich with the scent of the life-giving Nile, now carried an unseasonable chill. Persian patrols were a constant reminder of subjugation, and a stark contrast to tales of a golden age spoken of by Akhen's father in a low, reverential hum—a lament of the Empire's decay.

As night deepened, Akhen led his flock back under a blanket of stars. But as he counted his sheep, he realized with a sinking heart that some were missing. The disappearances continued, night after night, until a dozen of his sheep were missing. Akhen's father, his face etched with lines of worry and disbelief, accused him of negligence.

"Why aren't you watching them more closely?" he admonished. "Our ancestors kept our flock safe from wolves for hundreds of years, only for you to fail?"

"Father, I have never seen a wolf in the area," Akhen said in self-defense.

"Maybe I trusted you with too large a parcel of land," his father said in disdain. "Perhaps you are not ready for such a responsibility."

"I will spend the next few nights in the field watching for wolves, father," Akhen promised. "If I find any, I will bring you their pelts."

"Words are easy to speak," his father said, holding his chin high. "Let me see your actions!"

Reluctantly, Akhen agreed to guard the flock under the cloak of night, armed with nothing but a lantern and a short sword. But as the moon climbed, his eyelids grew heavy, and the landscape blurred into the realm of sleep.

He awoke in the middle of the night to a chilling presence. A tall man, robed in the darkness of the night itself, stood over him.

"What are you doing out here by yourself, boy?" the man asked, his voice as cold as the north winds.

"I watch over these sheep," Akhen stammered, aware of just how vulnerable he was. "A wolf preys upon them."

"There are no wolves out here," the man replied, stepping closer.

It was still dark, but Akhen could have sworn the man had no eyes, just pits of black where his eyes should have been.

"There is another kind of beast that lurks out here, though," the man said and lunged for Akhen's throat.

Akhen recoiled, but the man moved inhumanly fast. With a strength that belied his lean frame, he seized Akhen's arms, exposing his neck. At first, there was no pain. Akhen only felt the superhuman arms holding him in place. But Akhen clearly felt the sharp sting of the man's elongated teeth as they pierced the skin of his throat. Then he felt a burning sensation, as if a fever had flooded his body, scorching his blood from within.

Then Akhen lost consciousness.

He awoke to the most severe headache he had ever experienced in his young life and found himself trapped inside a small wooden coffin. His breathing became shallow and he began to panic. Akhen repeatedly struck the top of the wood. It easily splintered and sand quickly filled the void.

He turned his head to grab a breath, but the sand was everywhere. With a surge of sudden strength, Akhen clawed his way through the earth, emerging into the harsh light of day.

The man he had seen before awaited him, his features now clear in the cruel sun light. He was not as tall as he had earlier appeared, and his skin was actually lighter than his father's.

"It was a nice death ceremony," the man playfully said. "You would have appreciated it. Your family spent good money to bury you with a proper provision for eternity."

Akhen looked around, still confused.

"I am Zalmoxis," the man said, offering his hand.

He effortlessly pulled Akhen from the sand. Akhen looked around, disoriented and trembling, when the reality of his transformation dawned on him. Though he looked no different than he had the week earlier, his body felt different...changed, as if it was no longer his body.

The agony that had been burning through his veins had diminished. His skin was now dull and unfeeling, but he felt strong...stronger than at any time in his life. He felt the cool spiritual touch of something ancient and terrifying coiled around his heart.

"Why...did you do this to me?" he whispered, the familiar landscape of his ancestors' burial grounds now looking alien, and even menacing.

Zalmoxis's smile widened.

"Because, young Akhen, even Empires must evolve. And like Kemet itself, you were destined to rise from the ashes of your former self. Welcome to eternity."

Looking over the last two dozen centuries, it had certainly felt like eternity. Kage had lived many lifetimes, losing friends and lovers until he mentally broke. He began taking out his frustrations on whatever population he was near, until he traveled to a sacred temple in a Korean mountain called Mount Jiri.

Because of its altitude, the temple was hidden from view. It was filled with people like him, some gifted with great abilities, others possessing a genius mind unsuited for society, and some just odd—but all were mindful to the mission of peace.

For the first time in his life, he had found that peace. Not only was it a stable society, the people were not afraid of his immortality. They fed him and trained him in ways to keep the hunger at bay. He remained at peace for almost eight hundred years, until an outsider visited the temple wishing to speak with him.

That man was Kasuo's father. He had brought evidence of Kage's spree of murders, but instead of turning him in to the local authorities, he came with a proposal: kill the four people on the list he had brought, and Kage would be given all the evidence to destroy and live out the rest of eternity in the temple.

Kage tried to think of an alternative, but ultimately agreed to the man's terms.

But four victims then turned into eight and then twelve, and it got to the point that Kage could no longer feel peace even within the temple. That is when he decided that, if he was going to violate his oath, he would only do so one more time.

He snuck into Kasuo's father's hotel room and waited. As soon as the man stepped inside the room, Kage killed him, praying for his soul even as he snapped the man's neck. Kage closed his eyes and hoped that he would have the opportunity to cleanse his soul after this one last kill.

But the gods are fickle.

As the man collapsed lifelessly to the floor, Kage heard a shout from behind.

"Father!" a young Kasuo yelled in shock.

His eyes grew large and, without thinking, he attacked Kage. Kasuo's attack was mindless and clumsy, not a real threat, but Kage's heart sank. He had killed a man in front of his son, a mortal sin.

Kage quickly subdued Kasuo to stop his thrashing and knelt before the boy.

"Every life is sacred, even your father's," Kage admitted. "I swear that I shall atone for my sin."

Kasuo held his cracked ribs as he wept next to his father's body. The man was crazy!

"We do not yet know each other," Kage said. "But I will make a blood oath to you: For taking the life of your father, I shall protect yours until I die. You will not suffer injury from any man or by any weapon while I am near you. This I swear."

Kage grabbed Kasuo's hand as if to shake it. Kasuo tried to pull away, but Kage's grip was iron. Kage pulled out a small dagger and placed it between their grasped hands and twisted.

"We are joined together in blood," he said, holding Kasuo's eye contact.

Bound by ancient laws older than the blood running through his veins, Kage pulled the dagger out.

Kasuo, still traumatized by his father's death, screamed.

Their blood mixed as Kage squeezed, and blood began dripping on the floor. Kage tore off a piece of Kasuo's white shirt and tightly wrapped his hand to stop the bleeding.

After wiping the blood off his own hand, Kage showed no sign of ever being cut.

"We must go," Kage said. "Your screams have no doubt alerted your neighbors."

Kasuo's voice was thick with rage and grief.

"I'm not going anywhere with you!" he thundered, his figure rigid in rage.

Kage's response was quiet, almost a whisper, burdened with an eternity of regret.

"I know that no apology can undo what has been done, but my duty to protect you is now bound by blood. If I must first incapacitate you to carry you out, I will."

His eyes, reflecting centuries of sorrow, did not waver from Kasuo's.

Understanding the futility of arguing and driven by a desperate need to escape the echo of his father's death, Kasuo tensed, ready to fight. But before he could react, Kage moved with a speed that belied his calm demeanor. He lifted Kasuo effortlessly, not in aggression but in an almost protective embrace, and he leapt from the window, carrying Kasuo with one arm, the night air madly rushing past them as they descended.

Landing softly despite the four-story height, Kage placed Kasuo gently on his feet at the shadowed edge of the docks, the distant lights reflecting off the water.

"Time is short, and though your trust in me is shattered, my vow remains. Let us find safety first, then you can find answers," Kage urged, his tone blending urgency with an underlying pledge of guardianship.

Kasuo's voice cracked as he staggered back, his face a mask of anguish and rage.

"Just leave me alone!" he shouted.

His body weakened by emotional exhaustion, Kasuo slumped against the railing, his body tense as he struggled to reconcile the protector he now had with the killer of his father.

Kage stood a few steps away, his expression unreadable. The moonlight cast long shadows across his face, highlighting the eternal sorrow etched into his features. He took a slow, deliberate breath before speaking, his voice low and steady.

"I cannot undo the past, nor can I erase the pain I have caused. But under the weight of my sins, I offer protection and service. It is all I have to give," Kage said, his eyes never leaving Kasuo.

This pause allowed Kasuo to absorb the gravity of Kage's words, reflecting on the complexity of his feelings—anger, betrayal, and an unexpected sense of safety.

"Go away!" Kasuo yelled.

Kasuo calmed down later that evening. Kage explained everything that had happened, and apologized for the death of his father. It took weeks for Kasuo to fully comprehend the situation, but when he did, Kasuo knew this: He now had a guardian angel.

∼

"Kage?" Kasuo asked, repeating himself. "Kage! Did you hear me?"

Kage awoke from his reverie and caught Kasuo's eyes.

"I said, we are supposed to dress in civilian clothes, but that doesn't mean any of that French cape stuff you like."

"My taste for fashion is timeless," Kage insisted. "But I will not embarrass you."

"Then let's get ready," Kasuo said. "Dinner is at seven."

They arrived at Hamaguchi's home fifteen minutes early. The outside was quite modest, reflecting both the prime minister's personal values and his subtle disapproval of the increasingly extravagant tastes of the Imperial Court.

Hamaguchi's butler opened the door and Kasuo entered with the confidence of a man who had never been told 'no.' A proud Japanese man of moderate height and build, he was a refined soldier. Even in civilian clothes, everything about him spoke of discipline.

Despite his posh title as captain of the Imperial Guards Division, Kasuo's real talents were in the social arena, where he wielded his charm and perceived prowess like a weapon.

Kage stood silently at his side, dressed in a subtle green

sweater and black trousers. He scanned the room, evaluating each person. Sensing no risk, he stepped back into the parlor.

Hamaguchi gestured for Kasuo to sit. The stark simplicity of the room was a jarring contrast to the lavishness Kasuo was accustomed to, causing a flicker of disdain to cross his face. The council members, observing this, exchanged subtle looks—their initial concerns about his suitability validated.

As soon as Kasuo sat, Hamaguchi spoke.

"Captain Shimada, we need your help in a very delicate matter. The emperor has made a rather…impulsive decision. As his advisors, it is our duty to ensure his safety." His eyes narrowed. "This will require…the ultimate discretion."

Kasuo raised a perfectly shaped eyebrow.

"Enlighten me," he said, leaning back.

The plan was outlined with deliberate detail — the need for covert infiltration, and the mission to gather as much intelligence as possible to assess the threat level of Sinanju. Kasuo listened, feigning rapt attention. While the words registered, the underlying danger seemed merely a thrilling story rather than a real threat.

Admiral Yamamoto, ever blunt, voiced the unspoken doubt. "Look, Shimada, you're good at parades and charming the ladies, but this is different. Are you sure you're up for this?"

Kasuo scoffed. "Admiral, I only train with the best. My men are loyal to the last breath. This backwater village will be no challenge." His arrogance masked a twinge of excitement. Finally, something with stakes higher than a social faux pas.

Kido leaned forward, his tone deceptively gentle.

"We recognize your skills, Captain, but we also understand that certain arrangements were made by your uncle regarding your position. This will be your chance to prove yourself worthy of the title."

The barb landed.

It was a sore spot Kasuo usually ignored, but the thinly veiled challenge stung. He replied with a tight smile.

"Consider my abilities at your disposal. The council will be impressed."

Hamaguchi stood, a signal of dismissal. "Sergeant?"

Before Kasuo could object, Kage materialized from the shadows, silently bowing to the council. Despite his plain clothes, and the studied attempt to appear inconspicuous, his presence emanated a quiet menace.

"Sergeant Kage," Hamaguchi's voice held a hint of warning, "You will ensure Captain Shimada successfully completes this mission. And that his… indiscretions remain discreet."

Kage bowed again.

"As you wish, Prime Minister."

The butler escorted them out and Hamaguchi watched them leave through the window.

"They are going to fail," he said.

CHAPTER FOURTEEN

The Horns of Welcome loomed above the cliffs ahead, two ancient weathered monoliths, tall enough to be visible miles away. They were carved thousands of years ago, the world's first official landmark, serving to caution all ships that they approached the village of Sinanju.

The emperor's personal barge, the Haemaekkori (*Sunborn Wings*) sliced through the West Korean Sea like a whisper from the divine. Carved from the heartwood of ancient Hinoki Cypress trees, the Haemaekkori radiated an ethereal glow. Its hull, polished to a mirror sheen, captured the light, each grain of wood whispering tales of countless seasons. Ancient. Unbreakable.

But no iron marred its sacred skin. It was held together by intricate wood joinery, secrets whispered from master to apprentice across many generations. Where ever it traveled, it carried the hopes and dreams of the Empire, etched in the language of wood and wind. And in its Shikoku amethyst eyes, it held the promise of enlightenment, a guiding light in the twilight of an uncertain era.

Seeing the mammoth stone titans, the captain immediately turned to the direction of the stone horns.

Waiting at the front of the vessel, Emperor Hirohito stood with binoculars. Hiro wore his formal red sokutai. Its layers and pleated trousers helped protect him from the bitter winds of the bay.

"The Horns of Welcome," he said, smiling in recognition of something he had only read about in books.

Kasuo stepped closer and bowed his head to whisper.

"Heika," he said apologetically, "the proper translation is 'Horns of Warning.'"

"Only to those who bear ill will," the emperor corrected, keeping his eyes focused ahead.

Nūk and Chiun waited between the fifty-foot stone towers. Chiun thought he had been mentally prepared for the emperor's arrival, but everything inside of him resisted the idea of a Japanese emperor on Sinanju soil.

"He brings the finest of his ships, the Haemaekkori," Nūk said in recognition. "You should be honored."

"Every inch of that ship is a lie," Chiun murmured.

"But how beautiful some lies can be," Nūk replied.

"The ship means nothing," Chiun said. "It's the man who matters."

"Come, let us receive our guest," Nūk said and motioned for Chiun to follow him down the stone steps to the beach.

The Haemaekkori approached cautiously, mindful of the coast. It dipped and rose with the gentle swell of the bay as it neared. Each oar, a single length of polished hinoki, splashed in unison as the boatmen, clad in flowing robes the color of moonlight, dipped them into the water. Their strokes were a ritualistic poetry, and precise in their motion.

Finally, with a sigh that spoke of ancient oceans, the Haemaekkori settled gently against the sand, its keel kissing the earth as if kneeling in reverence. Two anchors dropped at the back and a plank was extended.

The first person down the ramp was Captain Kasuo. He took quick glances around the beach, seeing no one other than the two brightly robed Koreans standing at the base of the steps.

Hirohito had been warned about the smell even before the ship anchored, but as he stepped on the beach, he proudly took in a deep breath of the sour, smoky air.

"This is Sinanju air!" he said proudly, smiling to Kasuo.

The guards crinkled their noses, but said nothing.

"He brought soldiers," Chiun said quietly. "I thought he was coming alone?"

"Did you think he would row the ship himself?" Nūk asked with a chuckle.

"Soldiers are not used for rowing," Chiun pointed out.

"So you fear a handful of poorly-trained soldiers?"

"Of course not," Chiun said. "But this is a violation of his word."

"If you had been paying attention, you would realize that the soldiers were commanded to remain with the ship," Nūk said. "Listen with your ears and not your prejudices."

Hirohito turned to Kasuo. He snapped to attention.

"Under no circumstances will any of you enter this village," the emperor said with a sternness previously unheard. "Our occupation ends outside this village," he said, motioning with his hand. "This is hallowed ground and until my return, your duty will be to protect this beach."

Kasuo stepped forward and kneeled before the emperor.

"Tenno Heika, your men worry for your safety," he nervously replied. "There are rumors that this is a village of assassins. What kinds of dangers exist on the other side of that ridge?"

"The most extreme kinds in the world," Hirohito said proudly. "This is why my protection is ensured."

"We rule over these people, sometimes…in an unkind

manner," Kasuo gently pushed back. "There will be no one to protect you. If even one of these Koreans have ill will toward you…" the general paused and leaned close to his emperor. "Heika, please allow eight of your best men to accompany you."

Hirohito glared at Kasuo as if he was an idiot.

"Eight men? Captain, this entire Butai could not defend me should the Master of Sinanju wish my death," Hirohito said, irritated. "I will not hear of this again."

"Yes, Heika!" Kasuo said, bowing deeply.

He took a moment to privately contemplate how brave the emperor was for entering a village of assassins on his own. Kasuo had always personally seen the emperor as soft and coddled, but he had to admit that he was not brave enough to step foot in a place such as this by himself.

Kasuo turned around and started yelling at his soldiers, scolding them for questioning their emperor. He led the soldiers back to the boat. Two men were stationed at the end of the plank.

Hirohito held out his hands and his assistant handed him a small, but ornate chest. It was made of a deeply stained burl wood, bordered by gold and encrusted with gems. Hirohito nodded and the man retreated to the ship. He placed the box inside one of the many folds of his robe.

Hirohito walked toward the stone stairs and smiled when he saw Nūk and the magical memories from his youth returned. Master Nūk looked older than when Hirohito last saw him. His hair was in a different style; it was shorter now, and showed strands of gray, but he wore a similar hanbok and carried the same youthful joy in his eyes.

Nūk bowed deeply.

"Welcome to the village of Sinanju, honored Emperor."

"The honor is truly mine," the emperor replied and returned Nūk's bow.

Chiun stood behind his father, wearing a black silk robe.

Embossed gold dragons wrapped around his torso. His hazel-green eyes almost disappeared beneath the large black hat that covered his head.

"Emperor Hirohito, may I introduce my son Chiun. It is for his wedding you were invited."

"His eyes remind me of you," Hirohito said, bowing slightly. "Master Chiun, you will be happy to know that my men have been commanded to remain at the ship."

Chiun returned the bow.

"These Japanese occupy our land," Chiun said to his father in Korean. "Why must we pretend to honor them?"

"The Japanese Empire honors Sinanju, young Master," Hirohito replied in an almost perfect Sinanju dialect.

Chiun's eyes did not betray his surprise.

"You occupy Korean soil," Chiun said bitterly.

"Forgive the boy," Nūk said. "His young mind is still filled with nationalistic fever."

"His concerns are neither misguided nor trivial," Hirohito admitted. "Know that my quarrel is not with you, great Apprentice Master, nor with your distinguished father. It is with those who would plunder both of our lands."

Chiun's eyes softened. The emperor's voice, devoid of the usual imperial haughtiness, resonated with an unexpected truth. How could this man, occupying his homeland, truly hold any genuine regard for their safety?

"Let us continue," Nūk said, leading the way back, leaving Chiun to walk aside Hirohito.

"Though I consider Sinanju a realm apart from—and even above—Korea, I am not blind to the fact that it lies within Korean territory. Any menace to Korea imperils Sinanju," Hirohito confided, leaning toward Chiun. "I would rather forsake my imperial throne than endanger your revered village. You have the emperor's word that, under my reign, Korea—and

Sinanju in particular—will be safeguarded as diligently as any part of Japan itself."

Chiun allowed his body to relax. He had not considered that the occupation was a way to protect Korea.

"Your men do not seem to know this," Chiun said. "They treat our people like dogs."

"Apologies, but it is a necessary trouble," Hirohito said, embarrassed. "None below my highest advisors can be allowed to know about this, young Master, but the time will soon come when both Japan and Korea will face a great threat," Hirohito said. "And if Japan falls, Korea will be next."

"The Bear or the Dragon?" Nūk asked, referring to the Soviet Union and China.

Hirohito's brow furrowed in worry.

"The bear sleeps for now, but we are watching. We have cornered the dragon and if necessary, we are prepared to break their teeth, but sadly, I refer to another," Hirohito said. "A new predator circles this world, and its iron wings cast a dark new shadow upon all of Asia. This threat emerges from the West: the Eagle."

"We must speak of this," Nūk said seriously.

"Later," Hirohito insisted. "This is a day for celebration."

Nūk nodded, but was determined to find out about this new threat. Many nations had used the symbol of an eagle to represent themselves throughout history. Perhaps it was Germany. Nūk had been warned by too many people that the Germans had begun rebuilding their military in violation of their surrender agreement and Nūk did not want to see a repeat of the Great War.

As they ascended the crest separating the jungle from the village, Sinanju shimmered like a dragon's scale beneath the setting sun. Smoky tendrils curled from tiny rooftops with the sharp tang of kimchi and the musky weight of five thousand years of history.

"Behold, Sinanju," Nūk said.

Hiro involuntarily held his breath, taking in the sight of the promised land and a deep peace settled within.

"It is…I am speechless."

He bowed to the ground, placing both palms down, making contact with the earth.

"I am blessed to be on Sinanju ground," he said, taking a moment to let it sink in.

Chiun stood awkwardly beside him, not knowing what to do. After a moment, the emperor returned to his feet.

"May I present your wedding gift?" Hirohito asked. "I realize that some of the villagers might not be easy with my presence and I wish to avoid a pretentious showing."

"Of course."

Hirohito reached inside his robe and extracted the small wooden chest.

Chiun sincerely bowed as he received the gift. It was his first gift from a foreign ruler and it felt like a defining moment in his new life as Apprentice Master. He looked at the gilded chest and smiled. He had, of course, heard about such things, and even seen them in the House of Many Woods, but to be given one and actually hold it, was something else.

"I speak for my betrothed when I say that we are honored by your gift," Chiun said. "May I open it?"

"Of course," Hirohito said. "What is inside is far more valuable than what is outside."

Chiun unlatched the front of the chest in anticipation. It was obviously not heavy enough to be gold, unless it was a small medallion. Perhaps it could be a large ruby, or…

It was a small sword hilt.

If not for the ornate craftsmanship, Chiun would have believed it was made for a child. The blade had been totally shattered, leaving only the tiniest bits of foundational metal inside.

"It is a perfect gift," Nūk said, smiling knowingly.

"I am honored, but…I do not understand," Chiun said, confused.

"Allow your father to explain," Hirohito said.

Nūk told the story to Chiun about a bored prince who did not believe in magic until Nūk showed him. Chiun glanced at Hirohito with a new understanding.

Hirohito smiled as he heard the story retold.

"May your father's magic become your own," Hirohito said, with a slight bow.

Chiun allowed himself a moment of vulnerability before regaining his composure and forcing it back. He ignored his father's grin.

CHAPTER FIFTEEN

While most people correctly assumed that Kasuo Shimada had received his military post because of his uncle's financial gifts, he looked at it as being drafted into the Japanese military. Kasuo had inherited his mother's property and finances after she died at childbirth, but was unable to spend any of it until he reached the age of eighteen.

And when he did, he lost his anchor on life. Drugs, sex and parties filled his days and by the time he reached nineteen, he almost looked thirty. Emaciated and weak, his father could stomach it no longer.

Even though Kasuo was legally an adult, his father had high privileges in the Empire. He cut Kasuo's access to his funds and had him appointed to a ceremonial role in the Japanese military. To be captain of the Imperial Guard Division was the ultimate white elephant—a post that you could not quit without directly insulting the throne.

He quickly found out that Admiral Yamamoto was the man pulling the strings for his father from the inside. What his father thought was a safe job was, in fact, a political nightmare.

Yamamoto had already threatened to imprison him on charges of treason more than once.

So, when Yamamoto called for Kasuo to meet him at a small teahouse nestled in the shady underworld of Kiba port, Kasuo was compelled to comply.

Once he entered the poorly-lit shack, Kasuo immediately caught the heavy smell of fish, sweat, and something else that he couldn't quite place. Yamamoto was hunched over a chipped cup of tea in the back, where it was even darker. The admiral, usually a picture of military composure, looked like a hunted animal. It was not the place where someone of his stature would normally be seen.

Yamamoto looked up past the brim of his hat and saw Kasuo and Kage approaching. He did not know why, but Yamamoto always had a small edge of fear whenever Kage was close.

"This meeting is supposed to between you and me," Yamamoto muttered.

"Sgt. Kage is a part of any mission I have," Captain Kasuo said. "You can trust him."

"Dear boy, I do not trust my mother," Yamamoto said bitterly. "The things I have lived through do not leave room for the luxury. I will only say that if I hear of our conversation from lips other than yours, I will personally give the eulogy at your memorial without shedding a tear."

Kage silently grinned at the threat.

"Understood," Kasuo said, remaining calm.

Though he and the admiral never really liked each other, Kasuo had never before heard such a savage edge in his voice.

"A bandit robbed me at gunpoint this morning while I was at a stop sign," Yamamoto explained uncomfortably. "He was a young man with multiple tattoos running up and down his arms and neck. It looked like a…red snake twisting through barbed wire.

"He trained his pistol on my wife the entire time,

demanding that we hand over our money and valuables. The money was not really a problem, nor was my beloved wife's necklace. But he stole my father's watch. I want it returned and the thief dealt with. I do not want that man to live another day."

"Such tattoos are rare," Kage said. "This will not take long."

"Thank you," Yamamoto said to Kasuo, ignoring Kage. "I knew that you would understand."

He palmed a gold coin to Kasuo while shaking his hand and quickly left the restaurant.

It only took Kage two days to find the *Thorns of the Snake*'s location. They were a new gang housed in one of the poorer docks in Kiba and had amassed money and power from their fast, terroristic attacks. Everyone in the area knew of the abandoned dock they had recently claimed. It was quickly favored by ships with questionable cargo.

Kasuo would never have dared to travel to the port by himself, especially late at night, but Kage reassured him that he would be safe. They drove past several ports until they reached an isolated dock in the south that matched the description Kage was given.

It was a small dock with several layers of worn and chipped paint, eerily quiet and lit only by two street lamps. The small building at the end of the pier was new, obviously built with recently-acquired money. The smell of fish and burnt oil combined into its own noxious stench.

"This is the place," Kage said.

"What's your plan?" Kasuo asked as they exited the car.

"I am going to ask them to return it," Kage said honestly.

There were more than a dozen men standing on the pier, drinking and laughing. Each wore a black leather vest with a red snake on the back.

"Wait back there," Kage said sternly.

Kasuo did not protest. He quietly shuffled behind a small

stack of crates and found a small gap from where he could watch.

Kage walked over to the gang. Even though the aged and warped planks had creaked beneath Kasuo's cautious steps, Kage's feet made no sound.

As the men saw his approach, they stopped talking and spread out to maximize their presence. The leader of the gang walked toward Kage and smiled. Like the others, his arms and face were tattooed.

"Are you lost, midget?"

Kage noticed that he was wearing the watch they were looking for. The others, wielding chains and steel bars, silently fell in closely behind him.

"I want that watch back," Kage said, nodding to the man's wrist.

"But I *like* this watch," the leader taunted, showing it off to his friends.

They ooohed and aaahed in mockery, but maintained their eye contact with Kage.

Then, the largest man Kasuo had ever seen stepped out from the back. He was twice Kage's size and carried a thick chain and a deadly smile. Taking one last drag of his cigarette, he tossed it away and approached Kage. Even though he was shielded behind crates, Kasuo took an instinctive half step back.

Kage did not wait for the man to reach him. With a speed associated more with animals than humans, Kage tore the chain from the man's hand, twisted it around his neck and used his body like a large, ancient slingshot. The man grabbed his neck to try and free himself, but merely trapped his fingers inside the chain. He lost consciousness on the third swing.

When he had achieved enough momentum, Kage let go. The large man's head detached, but his body found its mark, colliding into the center of the gang, with enough speed to break bones. The men who were able to run, did so.

The leader turned and ran to the back of one of the older dock buildings and mounted a horse that he kept for a quick escape. Though slower than police cars, the horse was far more maneuverable and could easily escape through areas cars could not access.

Then he had an idea: instead of running away, he would charge Kage, trampling him to death. His horse protested, but he turned the animal toward Kage and kicked its ribs.

Seeing the approaching half-ton animal approach, Kage stood his ground. He waited until the last moment and grabbed the beast by its neck. He flipped it over his head, slamming its body to the ground. The sound of so many bones breaking at the same time caused a deep, primordial fear in Kasuo. The leader had been hurled from the horse on impact and his body struck the wall. The back of his skull left a dark red streak as he fell.

Kage walked over to him.

The leader pulled out a pistol and began blindly firing. The bullets emptied into Kage's body. As Kage got closer, the street light highlighted his face. His skin was pulled tightly to his skull, blanched into a pasty offset to the large patches of black where his eyes should have been.

Though he was dying from a mortal wound, the leader gasped in terror.

The remaining gang members reappeared with .45 caliber courage and opened fire from behind, but Kage ignored them. The leader's face was quickly covered by blood spatter as the bullets passed through Kage's body.

"The watch," Kage demanded.

The leader's last mortal act was removing the watch before collapsing.

Kasuo watched from a distance as the remaining gang members exhausted their ammo into Kage's body. He knew they were hitting him, because he could see small spots of blood as they exited the opposite side of his body.

But other than small jerky reactions and the occasional grunt, Kage did not fall. In fact, he did not even slow down. The gang members screamed as he tore into them. At first, Kasuo thought he was seeing things. It looked like Kage tore the arm from one of the gang members and tossed it into the water, but he began to understand that his eyes were not lying to him when he saw a leg and then a head splash into the water.

After the last gang member had fallen, Kage collapsed among the bodies and Kasuo thought that he had died from his many wounds. He rushed over to see if there was anything he could do. But as gruesome as it was seeing the gang members being dismembered, it did not prepare Kasuo for the aftermath.

The air held a strange, coppery sweetness that made his stomach churn. And just as he reached the spot where Kage had fell, he noticed wet, crunchy sounds, and a low growl that sent a shiver down his spine.

Kage was eating the gang members.

Kasuo must have passed out, because the next thing he remembered was waking up in his apartment. They never spoke of that moment again.

THE MORNING after the Haemaekkori had landed at Sinanju, Kasuo was awoken by one of the Imperial Guard.

"Apologies, Captain, but Sgt. Kage seems to have left the ship in the middle of the night," the guard said. "We shouted for him to return, but he ignored us. Do you wish us to find him?"

Kasuo acted upset, but any actual distress was a result of lack of sleep. Kage's disappearance was part of their plan to infiltrate the village.

"Under no circumstances will *anyone* leave this ship!" Kasuo shouted. "The emperor ordered us to remain with the Haemaekkori! I am responsible for the guard and shall find him myself! No one will speak a word of this until my return!"

"Yes, sir!" the guard said, sharply saluting.

Kasuo scratched his head and yawned as he dressed. Why did all plans start so early?

Kasuo grabbed an extra jacket and walked north, following the coastline. The cold mist bit into his protective coat and he hoped that he would not have much farther to go.

Kage told him they would meet north of the village, but he did not tell Kasuo how far to walk north. His body was not suited for outdoor exploration, and even for Korea, this had been a barbaric winter. It was well over ten minutes before he found Kage calmly sitting on a large stone serenely meditating in the moonlight.

While Kasuo had brought an extra coat for warmth, Kage wore a simple dark blue robe trimmed in thin white bands. His lower arms and shins were exposed to the biting winds. Even with a padded hood, the gale bit at Kasuo's ears, but Kage seemed unaffected by the cold.

"Follow me, captain," Kage said, motioning for Kasuo to follow him. "I found a way into the village."

They traveled a kilometer from the coastline, stopping behind a hill large enough to dull the wind. Kasuo rubbed his hands together, thankful for the reprieve.

Kage motioned for him to be quiet as they sat behind some thick brush.

Kasuo looked through the branches and noticed a peddler huddled near a small campfire.

"Stay," Kage whispered.

Kasuo watched as he silently approached the sleeping man. Though he knew what was about to happen and wanted to avert his eyes from the impending kill, Kasuo's was frozen as he watched the man's last moments of life.

Kage pounced on the man and separated his head from his body and drank directly from the man's open throat.

Even though the moonlight provided good light, Kasuo questioned what he was seeing. Kage was feeding from a headless body, careful not to get any blood on his clothing. After satisfying his thirst, he dropped the body.

Kasuo looked, but could not find the man's head.

"Stay here, Captain," Kage ordered, removing the tunic from the dead merchant. "I'll take this man's cart and enter the village. After I have questioned enough villagers, I'll report back here."

"O-Okay," Kasuo said, huddling behind a bush for warmth. "Good luck."

"There is no such thing as luck in this world, Captain," Kage said. "Only the willful actions of a few determined men."

And in the moonlight, Kasuo saw his eyes. They were solid black, as if his pupils had expanded to cover his entire eye socket.

Kage donned the man's robe and began rummaging through the cart. He tossed Kasuo a couple of pears.

"When I return, we will eat again."

"Thank you," Kasuo said weakly as Kage pushed the cart toward Sinanju.

CHAPTER SIXTEEN

The traditional second day of a Sinanju wedding called for a separation of the bride and groom. Chiun had no idea what purpose such a tradition could serve, other than to make him long for Eon even more.

Traditionally, a group of men would rush the groom as he left his house, and carry him to a predetermined place to isolate him from the bride, while women escorted the bride to another secret location in the village. They would remain with the bride and groom and speak of their past and future for the entire day.

But while the women quickly rushed Eon away to the east, the men of the village waited for Chiun to walk to the village center. When he arrived, they bowed and stood quietly, looking at each other, wondering what they were supposed to do.

Most just smiled.

"I suppose you should leave in a different direction," Kako, the fish monger said. "My wife said that Eon is going east, so perhaps you should go west."

"Yes, that is a good idea!" Liu, the butcher said. "We would normally escort you ourselves, but, uh…I have work to do."

"I understand," Chiun nodded.

These were the ordinary things that he missed about life in Sinanju. Even as Apprentice Master, he could not afford to be seen as weak, and regardless of the circumstances, he would not allow any of the men to force or escort him anywhere.

And they knew it.

"I appreciate the sentiment, gentlemen," Chiun said with a slight, but thoughtful bow. "And I shall return in the morning."

But instead of moping in the House of Many Woods for the rest of the day, Chiun left to meditate in the Caretaker's Forest. When he was younger, he had found a perfect meditation spot at the southwest corner of the forest, just behind Hae-Won's Scholar Tree. It was the only place in the village where you could see both the bay and the west beach.

Chiun lowered himself to the grass at the edge of the cliff in a lotus position and smiled. Despite the sun, the grass was shaded, and still cool to the touch. The spot he had chosen was the edge of the largest cliff in the village. The cliff's face was a stoic wall of weathered stone, carved by millennia of wind and sea spray. Below him, the waves softly crashed against the beach, sending small plumes of white foam into the air.

The west beach was not as well-known as the entry point in the bay, but it was clean and large enough to separate Sinanju from the inlets and islands that led west to China.

Chiun closed his eyes under the shade of the Scholar tree, and allowed nature to envelop him. It was after high noon and the sea was illuminated with a brilliant, shimmering light. The air was filled with the salty tang of the bay breeze, and in the distance, he could hear the faint cries of terns, egrets and herons.

The moment was expansive and alive. The simple, repetitive acts of the terns hunting fish, the rhythm of the waves, and the warmth of the sun combined to form a moment of serene harmony with the natural world.

Then a scream shattered his concentration and Chiun darted

past the forest toward the west beach. The woman who was screaming was Soo-Min, the leather maker's young daughter. She was struggling with someone who was dressed like Kyung, the peddler. Normally, Kyung arrived much earlier in the day, especially during holidays and celebrations to garner as many sales as possible.

As Chiun concentrated on the peddler, he could instantly tell something was wrong. Kyung had a slight limp and there was power in this man's gait. Chiun leapt from his place on the cliff. His feet were moving before he hit the beach, but it was too late. The peddler had exposed her neck and was gulping blood from her throat.

"Unhand her!" Chiun ordered.

Kage pulled back his hood and dropped Soo-Min onto the rocky area of the beach. His eyes were black and as wide as his eye sockets; his smile was stained with her fresh hot blood.

Chiun no longer detected life from Soo-Min.

"Heh," Kage chuckled defiantly, widely opening his mouth and then licking his lips. "Your woman was delicious."

Chiun charged Kage and struck. His hand pierced the air, led by an impossibly sharpened nail that could shave granite.

Kage sidestepped the attack, and Chiun only managed to slice a few strands of his hair. The momentum of his blow carried him past Kage, and into a log on the beach. Using his palm for balance, Chiun ignored the thin slimy shell of the mossy log and used it to bounce over Soo-Min's body.

He had no idea how this man was fast enough to evade his blow, but he instinctively read the situation. Instead of assuming he was facing an insane man who could possess a temporarily augmentation in strength, Chiun found something else as he studied Kage: near perfection. From movement to balance and muscle tone, and *almost* in breathing, the man before him could have been trained in a crude cousin art to Sinanju, if such a thing existed.

Kage did not wait for Chiun to attack again. He lunged forward, twisting his body at the waist in midair, and at the last moment, let the momentum of his arms spin him into Chiun. He made contact, striking Chiun's shoulder with his fingertips.

Chiun's eyes opened wide in confusion as his left arm fell uselessly to his side. The man had successfully landed a nerve blow. For the first time in his life, Chiun considered running away. But his trust in the superiority of Sinanju would not let him leave in defeat.

Without anticipating the pain he would incur, Chiun grabbed his left hand with his right and quickly pulled, twisting his shoulder out of, and back in socket. Pain shot through his neck and down his back, but he was able to wiggle his fingers. His left arm was numb and full of bee stings, but he could move it once again.

The men began pacing each other, studying the nuances of the other's movements.

"I remember this place," Kage said, glancing around. "Only by name, of course. I was asked to replace your shaman many centuries ago. Had I known it would be this interesting, I would have accepted."

Chiun ignored his taunts, focusing on the man's movements and breathing. As impossible as it seemed, everything within Chiun said that this man was as fast as he was, but much stronger.

Then Chiun suddenly detected movement from behind.

Soo-Min sluggishly and impossibly rose to her feet and Chiun could smell the tainted rust of her blood. Her panicked eyes were a dull gray, accented by bloody veins. Her lips were blue.

"Master Chiun!" she cried, staring at the alien pale of her own blanched flesh. "Help me!"

"Your woman is now my woman," Kage taunted, springing toward Chiun.

His fingernails were not as long or as strong as Chiun's, but they were enough to tear through Chiun's robe, drawing blood.

Chiun resisted wasting his breath on a scream of pain, but only barely. While he had been trained to absorb a punch, there was no training for the tearing of your skin. Chiun rolled with the impact, mustering all of the speed he could to minimize damage. He pushed Soo-Min back toward the beach, out of the way of the battle. Chiun dodged beneath Kage's next blow, shattering Kage's thigh bone and then followed through with a strike to his knee, twisting his leg at an abnormal angle and Kage fell to the sand.

"That actually hurt!" Kage shouted, and then began laughing.

Chiun watched, horrified, as Kage's shattered leg began to mend. Each bone snapped back in place with sickening crunches as his flesh began knitting itself together and Kage stood, wiggling his foot.

Before he could fully recover, Chiun launched a flurry of blows, each one a strike meant to disintegrate granite. But each strike was equally met with a block or parry. Disbelief morphed into steely resolve in Chiun's eyes. He was no longer there to disable Kage and press him for answers. He was there to destroy.

Chiun became a blur, circling Kage, searching for a weakness, but Kage had regained his strength and answered every one of Chiun's blows with a strike of his own. A single, predatory glint in Kage's eyes betrayed his focus, and Chiun made his move. He feinted left, then rocketed forward, aiming a nerve strike at Kage's exposed neck.

But Kage took advantage of Chiun's proximity and replied with a strike of his own. Chiun's strike landed first, but instead of Kage's body lifelessly collapsing to the ground, his weakened palm made contact, cracking Chiun's sternum, forcing the air out of his lungs.

Chiun stumbled back, gasping for breath. Every instinct

screamed at him to run. As he detected motion from behind him, Chiun felt a faint sense of confusion. Soo-Min was helplessly trying to get back to her feet. Using the last of his strength, Chiun feigned weakness, striking Kage in the chest as he approached, shattering ribs. Kage fell backward, blood coming from his mouth. But his ribs began crackling back into place and Kage returned to his feet.

'Who are you?" Chiun wondered.

His body ached, but Chiun filled his lungs, strengthening his center. His vision began to blur at the edges, and he felt like a child who had just learned to properly breathe.

"That's what I like to see," Kage said, grinning. "Weak prey."

He lunged toward Chiun and began wearing through Chiun's defenses, when he felt something pierce his back.

Soo-Min had stabbed him in the back with a branch. Kage howled in pain and landed a solid kick to Chiun's midsection, sending him sprawling back.

He landed in the sand and did not move.

"Until you learn better, you are still the enemy," Kage said, pulling the branch from his back.

Chiun lay dazed on the beach.

In the distance, he saw Kage once again drinking blood from her throat. Chiun tried to center again, but his lungs were on fire. Then, he sensed something else—movement from behind Kage.

It was his father.

Ignoring any pretense at stealth, legs that were capable of holding back an elephant pumped into the ground, propelling Nūk forward at the speed of a gazelle.

Within the two seconds that it took Kage to identify the sound and turn, Nūk reached him. He tore Soo-Min from Kage's grasp and hurled her far away. Confirming Chiun's safety in his periphery, Nūk struck with a greater speed than Chiun or Kage had ever seen.

Imagining that the blow was aimed at his face, Kage placed a fist up to block, only to realize at the last moment that Nūk had anticipated his move and was actually targeting his hand.

Kage's fist exploded from the impact, each bone splintering into a dozen places. His fist instantly swelled with the impact and even though it had already begun healing, Nūk was just getting started.

He grabbed Kage's other hand and twisted, tearing his arm from its socket, in a manner designed to cause as much pain as possible. Kage wailed as his tendons tore, one at a time. Tossing the arm aside, Nūk smashed his kneecaps into pulp, but knew that he only had a limited amount of time before Kage's body fully recovered.

"Talk!" Nūk ordered. "The only reason your tribe was allowed to live was by avoiding the rest of us."

"Tribe?" Kage asked, genuinely confused. "What are you talking about?"

"Where is your camp?" Nūk asked as Kage began struggling. He placed his thumb on Kage's sternum and pressed. "How many more are there?"

Kage groaned as his chest cage began to crack. "My master died hundreds of years before your birth."

"But why attack Sinanju?" Nūk asked. "We're the one tribe you should *know* not to attack."

"You talk when you should be fighting," Kage said. "When I am through with you, I will take…rawwwwrck!"

Nūk removed his jaw with a quick slap and Kage began to panic. The small buds of pulpy flesh of his arm had already sprouted tiny fingers and were wiggling, trying to reach anything. Nūk removed the rest of his head and tossed it away from his body.

As Kage's body collapsed into the bloody sand, Chiun was suddenly overwhelmed with the spiked scent of jasmine, chokingly sweet…but then, a thick, oily scent came through…

mustard oil, something he had once smelled in the shaman's apothecary, but this was far more pungent.

Soo-Min had stood and began walking to Chiun. Her steps were unsteady and she began to wobble. As she approached Chiun, she leaned down to him.

Chiun reached up to help steady her, when Nūk came up from behind and, with a flash of his deadly nails, removed her head.

A scream ripped through Chiun as the nightmare played out before his eyes. His knees buckled as the strength drained from his legs.

"No!" Chiun screamed as her body collapsed into the mud before him. "Why did you do that?"

"Tomorrow," Nūk said as he helped Chiun to his feet.

Chiun looked at his father in disbelief.

"She was trying to help me!"

"You don't understand," Nūk said.

"Who was that man? How was he as strong and as fast as we are?"

"I said, *tomorrow!*" Nūk shouted, with an edge to his voice that Chiun did not recognize.

"Take the cart to the village and see the shaman for your wounds," Nūk said in a more restrained tone. "And stay out of sight. You're still not allowed to be seen by Eon."

Chiun cast one last look at Soo-Min's lifeless body and then his father. For the first time in his life, he was angry at his father and confused. But Chiun dutifully returned the cart to the village and then quietly met with the shaman. He would wait until the next day, but he would get answers.

Nūk waited for Chiun to leave and brought Kage's body to the waste pile. He took a moment to say a silent farewell to Soo-Min before tossing her body in the pile as well before setting it on fire. Then he followed Jin's path back to its source.

There would be one more death today.

Kasuo had waited behind the small hill where Kage told him to stay. When he saw the Master of Sinanju return instead of Kage, his breath caught in his chest. He knew that meant his friend was not returning. Kasuo remained as still as possible, watching from a distance, but his heart pounded in his chest so loud that he thought it could be heard.

The master knelt by the body of the peddler that Kage had killed and Kasuo suddenly felt shame for what they had done.

"Kyung, you didn't deserve this," Nūk said to the headless corpse before him. "You weren't Sinanju, but you were a good man."

Nūk broke some branches from a nearby tree and covered Kyung to keep the birds away from his body. He would send for someone to return his body to his kin in Pyongyang after the ceremony ended.

Kasuo waited in silence, thinking he was safe, but as soon as Nūk was finished covering the body, he turned to look Kasuo in the eye.

"The Sinanju live in peace because we are feared," Nūk explained. "When someone violates our border and kills one of our own, we have to make an example."

Kasuo sat quietly, tears forming in his eyes as he watched Nūk through the leaves of the bush. Nūk did not move toward him, but the judgment in his eyes said everything that he knew to be true: behind the fancy suits and military titles, Kasuo was a coward and Nūk was going to stand there until he came out.

"I...I didn't do it," Kasuo pleaded, moving out from behind the bush with his hands held high. "Kage killed him."

"Don't start with the excuses," Nūk said. "You allowed your friend to enter our village under false pretenses and now we have lost two of our people."

"Two?" Kasuo asked, concerned. "Did he kill your son?"

"Of course not," Nūk said coldly. "What's left of your friend is burning in our waste pile."

Kasuo looked down, remembering how many times Kage had saved him. But he was gone now and Kasuo stood helplessly in front of the Master of Sinanju.

"You were conversing with Hirohito when he landed," Nūk remembered.

Kasuo's eyes opened wide with alarm as he realized Nūk's implication.

"No!" Kasuo almost shouted. "The emperor knows nothing of this! He would have had me killed if he realized we were spying on you!"

Kasuo tried to catch himself from saying anything else, but his entire life had been lived hiding behind others: a cowardly lie, lived without principle. In the final moments of his life came clarity. Kasuo decided to die with honor.

"This mission was orchestrated by the Privy Council," Kasuo said. "I am sure Hamaguchi was behind it."

"Thank you for the information," Nūk said. "But this does not absolve you of your crimes."

"I know," Kasuo said, looking up at the sky and trees as if seeing them for the first time. He began crying, but he felt relief. The lie he lived was over. He made eye contact with Nūk for the first time.

"Please believe that I never intended any of this."

"Your intentions don't matter," Nūk said. "You brought violence to my doorstep, and with it, the obligation of a harsh response."

Kasuo nodded slowly. His shoulders slumped, and silent sobs wracked his body as resignation began to set in.

"If my end will serve as a lesson, then let it be swift."

"It will be," Nūk promised.

With a motion that was lost beneath the roar of the waves, Nūk carried out his promise with more mercy than Kasuo deserved.

As Nūk returned to the village, the weight of his own decisions bore heavily upon him. He had seen the look of betrayal in Chiun's face and felt his unspoken accusations.

'*Intentions don't matter,*' he thought. '*Even my own.*'

Nūk's plea to the wind was more a whisper against the inevitability of the sea's chorus, seeking an absolution he knew would not come.

'*It's been a good life,*' Nūk thought.

CHAPTER SEVENTEEN

The most memorable day of a Sinanju wedding celebration was the third and final day. It officially began with the shaman's fireworks, brightly bursting in the early morning sky, loud enough to alert the few villagers who had not yet arrived. Vibrant tones of folk music filled the air to celebrate the reuniting of the bride and groom.

Brimming with joy, Eon squealed with happiness as she ran from her friend's house, where she had been taken the night before. Instead of the extravagant dress she had worn for the wedding ceremony, Eon emerged in a flowing, copper-toned robe. It was embroidered with the traditional Sinanju motifs of waves and dragons using thick silver threads, which caught the light as she walked. Her long, black hair was held back with a pair of ornate pearl combs, and around her neck she wore a necklace with a pendant bearing the village crest—a symbol of her new life with Chiun.

Her friends quickly followed behind, laughing and throwing dyed rice and small perfumed flowers, creating a colorful path on their way to the Gatchi. Built on the site of the blacksmith's original hut in the nineteenth century as a communal lodge, the

Gatchi was not specifically intended for wedding celebrations, but over the past hundred years, it had become the default site for such events.

Chiun watched everything from the top of the hill with mixed emotions. This should be the happiest day of his life, but he could not stop thinking about Soo-Min. His father had seemed more interested in taking care of the cart than a proper burial.

He stood resplendent in his own ceremonial robe, tailored from deep red silk and embroidered with gold thread. The ornate gold emblem on his chest was heavy enough to alter his internal balance and remind him of the importance of the day. A black and gold sash encircled his waist, from which hung a ceremonial dagger, an heirloom of Sinanju's ancient past.

There were far more people at Chiun and Eon's wedding than a standard wedding, so extra tables had to be set outside the Gatchi to accommodate the overflow. The tables featured vibrant banchan dishes that painted the culinary landscape in every hue—fiery red kimchi, bright green namul, and deep orange marinated crab. At the center of each table, plates of bulgogi and galbi emitted enticing aromas, their marinades caramelizing beautifully over gentle flames.

Eon waited for Chiun at the entrance of the Gatchi, happy, but shivering. Her laughter mingled with her replies to friends and family, but her eyes kept searching the crowd for Chiun.

Seeing her daughter's nervous glances, Eon's mother intervened, her voice cutting through the crowd.

"Clear a path for the groom!" she shouted, waving her arms. "Please, step aside!"

The crowd parted as Chiun approached from the north. A quiet smile played on his lips.

Eon's heart leapt. "My love!" she cried out.

Unable to contain her happiness, she rushed to his side. The couple embraced, taking the moment to enjoy a shared breath, followed by a modest kiss on the cheek.

Chiun walked Eon back to the protective wind shelter of the Gatchi and bowed slightly.

"Instead of singing the traditional poem by Yun Seon-do, I have chosen something different," Chiun began, gently holding Eon's hands.

"This poem is from Master Shang, the master who walked to the moon for his wife. It is not as well known, but it speaks truth to the eternal journey that I wish to take with you."

[Editor's Note: Chiun insisted that this poem was so important that it had to be published first in Korean before being pilfered by the inferior, English translation]

영원의 걸음

한 평생을 당신과 걷고 싶어요
행복의 길에서도, 슬픔의 순간에서도
당신의 손을 잡고 느리게 걸어가며
모든 계절을 함께 맞이하고 싶어요

우리의 사랑은 바다보다 깊어
그 어떤 폭풍도 우리를 흔들 수 없어요
마음속 깊은 곳에서 우러나오는 사랑으로
영원히 당신을 지키며 살겠어요

당신은 나의 봄날, 여름의 밤
가을의 노래, 겨울의 따스함이에요
사계절이 변해도 변하지 않는 것처럼
우리의 사랑도 영원할 거예요

당신과의 약속, 오늘 이 자리에서
세상이 끝날 때까지 소중히 간직할게요

RISING SON

당신과 함께라면, 어디든 천국이니까
평생을 당신과 함께하고 싶어요

Steps of Eternity

I wish to walk with you for a lifetime,
Through paths of happiness and moments of sorrow,
Holding your hand, slowly walking together,
Welcoming all seasons, side by side.

Our love is deeper than the ocean,
No storm can ever shake us.
With love springing from the depths of our hearts,
I will cherish and protect you forever.

You are my spring day, summer night,
The song of autumn, the warmth of winter.
Like the seasons that change yet remain the same,
Our love too will last forever.

The promises made with you today,
I will treasure until the end of time.
Anywhere with you is heaven,
I wish to spend my lifetime with you.

Chiun stood and for the first time, the couple kissed.

The cheer from the villagers fell to the wayside as their bodies leaned into each other. Chiun absorbed the softness of her lips and he grabbed an extra and unnecessary breath and quickly turned away, leading Eon inside the Gatchi.

THE FATHER of the groom typically enjoyed the day with his son, seated at the end of the table, but Nūk only had a limited amount of time to spend with Emperor Hirohito. After Chiun and Eon entered the Gatchi, Nūk turned to Hirohito.

"Heika, would you follow me? There is something I must show you before you leave."

"Of course, though it grieves me to leave your son's celebration…"

"We would not be able to see anything of interest at this point," Nūk said.

Hirohito followed Nūk as they descended from their viewpoint at the top of the hill.

"I would like to thank you for inviting me to your son's wedding," Hirohito said. "I had merely hoped to see the Horns of Welcome and perhaps a few buildings, but this…"

"The honor is mine," Nūk replied, his tone respectful yet somber. "I am glad we could finally share this experience."

"One thing. Over the past decade, I have had my chefs prepare many of the foods common to your people, but they taste bland compared to the real thing," Hirohito admitted. "Perhaps I can have your chef visit with ours so we may perfect the recipe."

Nūk chuckled.

"We don't have chefs. This food was cooked by a couple of the women in the village," Nūk said. With a wink, he added: "You probably don't want to dig too deep into their recipes."

They walked west, past the water pump, and past the shaman's morning holy spot. In the small area between the village and the beach, the morning wind was relatively calm, allowing the terns to dance above the waves, playfully darting at the spray.

They reached the large stones where the women washed their clothes and where Ji had died. Nūk took a glance at the stones to ensure that the moss had not grown back.

'Ji would have loved to have seen our boy wed,' Nūk thought sadly.

"These easels are majestic!" Hirohito declared after seeing the stones.

He walked over to them and began tracing his fingers over the smooth surface. "Is this where your painters practice their art?"

Nūk suppressed a grin.

"These are the stones our women use to wash clothes."

Hirohito looked at them and softly chuckled.

"Yes, that makes much more sense," he admitted.

As they turned north, out from behind the protection of the Caretaker's Forest, stone and grass turned to beach. Sand crunched softly under Hirohito's feet, mingling with the rhythmic whoosh of the surf rolling back and forth. The air was thick with the tang of salt and seaweed. Brisk winds tugged unceremoniously at Hirohito's robes, whipping strands of hair across his face.

"This is the west beach," Nūk said. "Unlike the beach below the Horns of Welcome, this is a private beach for the villagers."

"The sand is beautiful," Hirohito said. "But I do not think you brought me here for the beach."

"You are correct, Heika," Nūk said. "Even in this place of beauty, violence has left its mark."

Stopping beside a small dune with two covered forms, Nūk drew back the cloth to reveal two severed heads, their lifeless eyes staring blankly at the sky.

Hirohito's face, usually a regal mask of grandeur, twisted in shock. His eyes darted between the grisly trophies and Nūk's solemn expression.

"By the gods…" he whispered.

Hirohito's hand involuntarily reached to his mouth in a gesture of disbelief. His breath quickened as he tried to reconcile what he knew with what he saw.

"You recognize these men?"

"That is Kasuo, the captain of my Imperial Guard," Hirohito said, nodding to the first head. "The other man is his aide, Sgt. Kage. What befell them?"

"I did, Heika," Nūk said. "They attempted to infiltrate the village and killed two of my villagers."

Hirohito looked at Nūk with grave concern.

"The Empire had nothing to do with this!" he asserted.

"I know," Nūk said calmly, holding up both hands. "This was the work of traitors within your court. Before he died, the captain confessed that your Privy Council concocted this scheme, led by a man named Hamaguchi."

Hirohito paled, choking out the name "Hamaguchi!" like a curse.

"A man hungry for power," Nūk finished. "I do not have proof, but I believe he was trying to blame these murders on you, hoping that I would eliminate you, but he underestimated Sinanju."

"How could such a betrayal come from within my own ranks?" Hirohito whispered under his breath.

A heavy silence fell between the two men as Nūk gave him time to process the situation.

Hirohito stared past the sea, focusing on a lone seagull as it glided over the waves. One minute stretched into two and then Hirohito turned back to Nūk, his gaze hardened.

"This treachery will not stand," he said.

"There is something else you need to know," Nūk said, pointing to Kage's jawless head. "This man wasn't human."

"I do not understand," Hirohito said, confused.

"Are you familiar with the Jiang-shi?" Nūk asked. "The undead Chinese flesh-eaters?"

"I am aware of the fables," Hirohito said.

"They are not fables," Nūk said. "This Jiang-shi killed a

peddler and an innocent girl in our village. He tried to attack Chiun."

Hirohito's heart skipped a beat.

"They were reported as missing this morning," Hirohito said, embarrassed. "I had no idea…"

"Do not worry. Japan and Sinanju remain friends," Nūk said reassuringly. "I just wanted to make sure you know what happened, and, more importantly, *why*."

"I will have their profane bodies removed from your soil at once," Hirohito said, angered.

"You may take the bodies," Nūk said. "But my son will speak with you later about the heads."

∽

As the ceremony continued, Chiun checked off the list of each ritual, waiting for the time he and Eon could leave and start their new life together. The historical reading of their bloodlines had already taken twenty minutes and they were still fifteen generations away.

While Chiun's eyes appeared to be focused on the generational presentation at the front of the Gatchi, he was actually looking around the room. From his peripheral vision, he noticed Eon's father Joon standing quietly against the wall. He had surprised everyone by remaining sober for the entire celebration and had handled himself well with the emperor by merely not talking.

Twelve generations to go.

The shaman's presenting of the blessing pendant would be next, Chiun thought, glancing over to the pendant. Typically, it was a small token dedicated to the couple by the shaman, that represented their life together. Eon had chosen a blood red selenite crystal with a gold inlay Sinanju token in the center. Chiun imagined that it would be gaudy, but after seeing it, changed his mind. It was reminiscent of a tower jewel he had once seen in his visits overseas.

Ten generations to go.

Then Chiun saw Nogg, the father of Soo-Min, enter the Gatchi. Nūk had met with him earlier in the morning and explained what happened to his daughter. Chiun was not present at the meeting, but from the look of distress on Nogg's face, it had not gone well.

Nogg pushed through the crowd, walking to the serving table at the front where his wife Liu was serving. She was one of the three cooks who had spent the past week preparing food for the ceremonies. He quietly motioned for her to come from behind the serving table. She smiled and removed her apron.

Chiun could have overheard their conversation if he chose, but he already knew what was going to be said.

Liu's demeanor instantly changed from happiness to confusion. She shook her head and, ignoring her husband, began scanning the crowd for their daughter. Liu collapsed to her knees. The people inside the Gatchi fell silent when they heard her wail.

"No!" she cried. "Soo-Min!"

Her cry pierced Chiun's heart.

Eon turned to see what was wrong.

"What happened to Liu?" she asked.

"Soo-Min died last night," Chiun said.

"What?" Eon asked, turning to Chiun. "What happened?"

"I am not allowed to speak of the incident until I meet with my father after the feast," Chiun said, his voice tinged with guilt.

"You can tell me anything," Eon said.

Chiun closed his eyes and held up his hand.

"You are my heart, Eon, my very life, but there will be some things as master that I cannot share with you…not yet."

Eon's eyes narrowed, a flicker of hurt passing through them before she masked it with understanding.

"I am here whenever you are ready to share your burdens," she replied softly, her hand squeezing his.

In the following chaos, the shaman's table was dislodged and the pendant fell to the floor, the sound of its shattering hid by the commotion.

But Chiun heard it.

He looked down, between the rushing feet, seeing shards of red selenite. In the midst of the shattered remnants, the gold Sinanju token remained whole and untarnished. Chiun was not superstitious, but he felt a chill crawl up his spine.

Once Liu and Nogg were escorted out of the Gatchi, the ceremonies continued, but with a more muted atmosphere.

Nūk had escorted the emperor back to his ship. His escorts carried a long box with them. The villagers assumed it was samples of Sinanju cuisine and trinkets, but Chiun knew what was hidden beneath the sheets.

As the crier blew his hojeok, penetrating the village with its loud sound, the sky above the village burst into a cascade of colors, signaling the end of the ceremonies. These were far greater than the opening day's show, filling the sky with enough light and color to remember for years to come.

Eon and Chiun gathered at the center of the village as the elders sang the ancient songs of binding and blessing. Their voices echoed off the Gatchi's stone walls, encircling the heart of the village.

Chiun stood amidst the flurry of celebration, his mind a tumult of thoughts as he watched his father retreating to the House. The celebration ended with cheers and bows, smiles and small gifts. Chiun led Eon to her mother.

"My father wishes to speak with me," Chiun explained. "If you can watch my beautiful wife until then, please."

He smiled and kissed Eon's hand. She blushed.

"We are married," Chiun said with a wink. "It is allowed."

"I will be waiting here, my love," Eon said.

Chiun nodded, appreciating her strength and the sanctuary she offered. It would be needed in the coming days. Chiun nervously ascended the stone stairs that led to the House of Many Woods, his thoughts in turmoil. He felt that his father had betrayed him and everything he had been taught.

For the first time in his life, the House felt alien, an architectural jumble that made no sense.

Chiun slowly bowed as he entered.

"All hail the Master of Sinanju," he said quietly.

His father was sitting silently on his chair, his eyes closed in meditation. For some reason, he looked…old. There was a very subtle, yet noticeable hunch in his position. And in the dim lighting, the golden tiger that had once brightly wrapped around his green robes now appeared a tamed mustard on top of a field of worn moss, a faded highlight of past glories.

"My son, sit," Nūk said softly without opening his eyes.

Chiun sat in front of his father, modestly adjusting his robes. His father's tone was unexpectedly somber.

"We need to speak about yesterday," Nūk said, opening his eyes.

Looking at his eyes, Chiun wondered if he had been crying.

"I have many questions," Chiun began.

"You will first hear me out," Nūk said. "Yesterday, you faced an unknown enemy who almost cost you your life."

Chiun started to ask who he was, but his father held up his hand.

"Worse than bending your elbow, you held back!" Nūk said. "You committed the greatest error that can be made: underestimating your opponent. Now you may speak."

"What was I supposed to do, run?"

"Yes!" Nūk thundered. "If you are not familiar with a situation, run and learn what you can, so that you can return and attack with knowledge. Sinanju cannot afford to be lost because of your pride!"

"Who was that man?" Chiun asked." Why have I never heard of him before?"

"You *have* heard of him and his kind many times before, but until yesterday, you refused to even acknowledge their existence. The man you fought was a jiang-shi."

Chiun stared at his father in disbelief.

"A vampire?" he asked. "You are right. I do not believe in them."

"Several masters have dealt with their kind in the past, though this man was apparently from a different tribe."

"There are many other tribes with great abilities," Chiun said, trying to make sense of what he had seen. "Perhaps this man is from a tribe we have not yet met."

"For once in your life, set aside your presumptions," Nūk said firmly. "This is important."

Chiun could not believe that he was listening to a tale about vampires, but he respected his father and remained silent.

"Originally, there were twelve great tribes of man," Nūk said. "But only five of those tribes survive to this day. Do you remember why?"

"Because the others destroyed each other before the Masters' Trial."

"Yes…and no," Nūk said. "I have taught you about all but two tribes. One of those lost tribes was Thracys."

Chiun tilted his head in thought.

"I have never heard of Thracys," he admitted.

"Thracys was the fifth tribe that Sinanju encountered and it was nearly our last. It was ruled by a jiang-shi named Zalmoxis. As a boy, he was enslaved and sold to a royal house in ancient Kemet. Even as a slave, his talents were apparent. He eventually gained the favor of Pharoah Neferkare himself, and lived with the pharoah for many years.

"Such was his reputation, that when the pharoah selected those slaves that were to be buried with him, his first choice was

Zalmoxis. He was charged with protecting the pharoah's doctor, so that on the third day after burial, the doctor could begin the treatments to the pharoah's corpse which would grant him eternal life.

"As the last stone was put in place, and everyone was sealed inside, something within Zalmoxis snapped. He realized that he did not want to die, but it was too late. Others tried to calm him down, but Zalmoxis struck out at them. And instead of protecting the doctor, he threatened him, forcing him to give the eternal treatments to him instead of the Pharoah. For hours, he suffered under the doctor's eldritch care.

"The doctor tried to warn him that this treatment was only designed for the dead, but he would not listen. The doctor's magicks twisted within an unknown frame, warping his body while rebuilding it, and he changed. He did not transform into the god that Neferkare wished to be, but instead, became a monster.

"When he awoke from a fevered sleep the next day, his body gnawed at him in a hungered fury. He mindlessly killed everyone in a bloody frenzy. When things quieted, part of his mind returned and he wept. Confused, he tried to move the stones that sealed them in, but they were too heavy."

"If he was as strong as you say, why did he not just shatter the stones?" Chiun asked.

"He had not yet fed. Now, let me finish the story."

Nūk sat back and his voice returned to the stoic baritone he reserved for teaching.

"The candles inside the tomb were designed to last until the Pharoah awoke as a god. Before they flickered out, Zalmoxis found a hidden door that led to an upper chamber. Inside was a replica of Neferkare's throne, surrounded by a large bounty of food and gold. He pounced on the food, feasting on roasted mutton, beer and bread, onions and veal. He could smell and taste the food, but it did nothing to quench his hunger.

"Returning to the original chamber, he began looking for anything to satisfy his hunger. He became so desperate in his hunger that he began feeding on the corpses around him and found that human blood was what he had been craving all along. He felt a new strength coursing within him. His senses had widened, taking in the rusty scent of his meal and the scent of mustard oil which now ran through his veins.

"Mustard oil?" Chiun asked. "That is what I smelled from the man who attacked me."

"You must always remember this scent," Nūk said. "It exudes from every vampire's pores."

"Go on," Chiun said, truly listening now.

"A further search found a small hole and a ladder leading out of the tomb. Taking what gold he could place in the pouches of his robe, he escaped the tomb, returning to his home of Thracys. There, he dispatched the chieftain who had sold him and his family into slavery and he ruled for almost two thousand years.

"Master Ung was the first to face him in the Masters' Trial. He noted that Zalmoxis was almost as fast as Wang, but much stronger. Using all of his skills, Ung barely managed to kill him, only to be greeted by Zalmoxis once again the next morning to continue the challenge.

"This battle lasted for six days. Master Ung would kill Zalmoxis, yet he would be alive again for the challenge the next morning."

"How did he do it?" Chiun asked.

"Did you not hear me? Zalmoxis was a vampire," Nūk explained. "Master Ung only succeeded in killing him after removing his head. That is why I removed their heads—it was the only way to truly stop them."

"Soo-Min was not a vampire," Chiun explained, his temper rising. "She was trying to help!"

"Was she?" Nūk asked, producing a leather bag that smelt of death.

He unwrapped the bag, revealing Soo-Min's head. The anger within Chiun began to boil over until he noticed that in the moment of her death, she had opened her mouth wide, revealing long, inhuman teeth.

"Father?" Chiun asked, worry creeping into his voice as the realization of what had really happened came to light. "Is this... is this all *real?*"

"What is real is the choice I made. Yesterday, I killed a villager, and today I will pay for my crime."

"What?" Chiun asked. "You're the Master. Your word is law."

"That might have been true in the past," Nūk said, as he remembered the world of his youth, when everything was a clearly-defined black and white. Nostalgia played with the time it was granted and Nūk returned his worried gaze to his son.

"The old ways are disappearing. Chiun, you will discover in your coming travels that this is a strange new world, one far different than any master has ever encountered."

"You were protecting the village!"

Nūk silenced Chiun with a shameful glare.

"What am I hearing? And where does this weakness come from?" Nūk thundered.

Chiun's gaze fell to the floor.

"Perhaps I have sheltered you too much," Nūk said in a low, disappointed tone. "You saw me kill the girl yourself. *You* are now the Master of Sinanju and you will need to be strong. For my crimes, you will banish me."

Nūk removed his outer robe and cast it into the fireplace, revealing a modest tunic beneath.

Chiun watched his father's robe as it caught fire. The robe's ornate tiger, once so powerful in Chiun's memory, now darkened to ash as it surrendered to the flames.

"Father?" Chiun asked, his mind numb.

"Do not choose this moment to fail me," Nūk said.

A lifetime of tradition clashed with Chiun's love for his father. The moment seemed to freeze as one stage in Chiun's life slowly died to the next.

"I refuse!" Chiun said defiantly, standing to his feet, matching his father eye-to-eye for the first time in his life.

"Good, good," Nūk said. "You will need this fire in the coming days."

Chiun paused and the air seemed to leave his body as the situation began to become clear. There had to be a way for him to fix this.

"Then I will declare a new law: killing a villager is only acceptable in defense of other villagers or the village itself."

"That is a very good law," Nūk admitted. "But it still does not absolve me."

"No," Chiun said. "I will not banish you."

"Then it is decided," Nūk said.

He knelt before Chiun and looked up, exposing his throat.

"The only sentence other than banishment is death. Kill me quickly, but do not shame me by bending your elbow."

Chiun stared helplessly at his father and took one last breath of innocence as the moment forced itself upon him. He regained his composure and slowly sat in his father's chair. He properly adjusted the wings of his sleeves before returning his gaze to his father.

"Nūk…former Master of Sinanju," Chiun said with the slightest quiver in his voice, "You have violated the most sacred of Sinanju laws and the trust of your village. For that, you shall wander the Earth as a vagrant, a man without a nation. You shall not use your skills except for self-defense."

Nūk smiled and bowed deeply to his son.

"You have learned well," Nūk said, his voice thick with pride. "All hail the Master of Sinanju."

Chiun sat numbly in his father's chair as he watched the man who had once been his entire life shut the door behind him.

There would be no honeymoon this night.

CHAPTER EIGHTEEN

In the heart of the village, the lingering joy of the final evening of Chiun's wedding unfolded under a canopy of lanterns which cast warm, dancing lights across the gathered faces. Laughter and music filled the air as the villagers continued their festivities, anticipating the couple's imminent departure for their honeymoon.

As they danced, Eon's mother leaned in close, her voice mixing with the music,

"I am so happy for you," she said.

Eon had never seen her smile like this and it brought tears to her eyes.

"Mama," she said, and grabbed her mother, giving her a large hug.

Eon's eyes were wide and smiling as she stepped back.

"Where do you plan to honeymoon?" her mother asked.

"Jeju Island! They say its beauty is unmatched, a perfect place for new beginnings."

Her mother smiled, her eyes crinkling with affection.

"It will be a wonderful journey for you both, a time to cherish and remember."

As the dance concluded, Eon's laughter filled the air, her heart light with the promise of the days to come. But the mood shifted suddenly, like a cloud passing in front of the sun, when Chiun walked solemnly down from the House of Many Woods.

His figure was resolute, his steps deliberate as he moved through the crowd. His eyes met Eon's for a fleeting moment. There was a profound sadness in his gaze, a silent message that something was amiss.

Eon's smile faded as she read the sorrow in his eyes. Her heart tightened, sensing the weight of what was to come. Without a word, Chiun passed by, his silence casting a shadow that dimmed the festive lights.

He ascended the small podium in the center of the village square, his figure solitary against the backdrop of the celebration. The villagers gradually noticed the change in the air, their conversations faltering as they turned their attention toward him. Eon stood still among them feeling a growing sense of foreboding.

Before he spoke, Chiun allowed himself a fleeting moment of introspection. The joyful cries of the village seemed distant as he contemplated the weight now resting on his shoulders. In such situations in the past, he had always been able to lean on his father's advice. Now, only a looming silence echoed in his heart. The traditions that he fought would be the very things he now depended on. They were all that remained.

Chiun raised his hands for quiet, and the music slowly faded, replaced by a hush of curiosity and growing concern.

"Beloved friends and family of Sinanju, thank you for joining Eon and myself to celebrate our wedding. My heart is full of gratitude for the love you have shown us. However, it is with a heavy, but hopeful spirit that I must address a matter that affects us all."

He paused, looking over the faces of the people he had

grown up with—his people. He tried to avoid direct eye contact so that his raw emotions would not show.

"Many of you have heard about the death of Soo-Min. I was present when she died."

The crowd began murmuring and Chiun did not want to think about how many new tales would result from the Widow's Hut.

"Yesterday, the village was under attack by a jiang-shi…a vampire. This ancient demon had already killed Jin, our peddler, and then attacked Soo-Min as she carried waste to the pit.

"Master Nuk dispatched the vampire, but believed that he had sensed something change within Soo-Min herself. He believed that she had become infected by the vampire. In order to save the village, he made a decision and slew Soo-Min. In doing so, he committed a grave sin against Sinanju. As such, Master…*former* Master Nuk was banished from the village. I stand here today before you as a new husband and as the new Master of Sinanju."

As Chiun's words settled over the crowd, the reactions varied as widely as the leaves in the wind. Murmurs of surprise and whispers of confusion rippled through the crowd. The news was as confusing as it was shocking, coming on the heels of such jubilation.

Some nodded in solemn agreement, understanding the harsh necessities of leadership. Others whispered in hushed tones, eyes darting with uncertainty and fear, not just of the vampire but of the new era suddenly thrust upon them.

A few of the older villagers exchanged looks that spoke of old memories, knowing too well the costs of such encounters with the supernatural.

The shaman and his wife looked upon Chiun with pity.

Chiun looked toward Eon, whose face mirrored the shock of the other villagers.

"My journey with Eon begins the same day that my journey as master begins with you. I promise to write a new chapter in our lives, relying on the traditions of Sinanju.

"Let us not dwell on the nature of my father's departure, but rather remember the many things he taught us: vigilance and integrity are the guardians of our way of life. We must protect them as diligently as we tend our fields, or educate our young."

With a final, respectful bow, Chiun stepped down from the podium. As the crowd dispersed under the night's deepening shade, Chiun felt Eon's hand slip into his. Her touch was both a comfort and a reminder of the life they planned to build together.

"Whatever comes, we face it together," Eon whispered, her words threading through the turmoil in his heart like a soothing balm.

They stood there, hand in hand, the lanterns flickering above, casting light on a new path that lay uncharted before them.

"We have many things to discuss," Chiun said. "Tomorrow, I have to make a small trip."

"I will always be here for you," Eon said.

With that, Chiun took Eon's hand, leading her up the stone steps to her new home.

CHAPTER NINETEEN

The next meeting of the Privy Council was called by the emperor himself. Fresh from his return to the wedding celebration in Sinanju, the members had all breathed a huge sigh of relief. It appeared that the wedding went off without a problem and they could return to their normal routines.

Each member took his seat, noting that an extra chair had been added to the table. The leather of their chairs creaked uneasily as they took their positions. Somewhere, a clock ticked a relentless rhythm.

A male servant entered the room, bringing a small tray of drinks. Unlike the members of the council, he was dressed in a pristine Western suit. The sharp black and white marked him as a servant. Most of the members favored black tea, with the exception of Yamamoto, who required a few drops of soju to be added to his tea.

"Any word from Kasuo?" Hamaguchi's voice cut through the quiet hum of the room. "I haven't heard from him since the emperor's return."

"He's probably celebrating with the getakko," Yamamoto said.

The other members softly laughed. Despite his high societal rank, Kasuo was known for trawling the lower east end brothels.

"Was anyone told what this meeting is about?" Kido asked. "Who is the extra chair for?"

"Something to do with Sinanju, no doubt," Yamamoto said, yawning. "I don't know what the emperor sees in those flea-bitten rat eaters. The Master has to be what, seventy by now? Totally useless for anything other than past war stories and pity."

"Perhaps the emperor has found the gateway to the Celestial Palace there," Hamaguchi said, snorting.

"You are correct," a voice as cold as winter steel said from the back.

The council members had not heard him enter, but when they turned around, they saw a young Korean man in bright white robes.

"My shoes have already been shined today, dear boy," Hamaguchi drawled, barely glancing at Chiun before flicking an invisible speck off his immaculate sleeve.

"What are you doing here?" Yamamoto demanded. "This is a private meeting!"

Chiun remained calm with a pleasant look on his face. His fingers tightened on the leather bag he carried as he gave a small, but polite bow.

"You must leave! The emperor will be here soon!" Kido said, embarrassed. "Where are the guards?"

But it was too late.

Large chimes at the front of the room were struck precisely five times, each note hanging in the air before the next sounded. Silence descended, broken only by the rustle of silk as the men uneasily shifted to face the throne at front.

In this room, where the atmosphere was usually thick with private political maneuvering, the arrival of an unexpected guest was not merely unusual—it was a breach of centuries-old protocol.

"His Majesty, the emperor!" a hidden voice cried out.

Sunlight glinted off the Imperial crest as the emperor entered, his face a mask of practiced serenity. The men scrambled to their feet, but Yamamoto hesitated, his jaw clenched. Kido bowed lower than the rest in a typical sycophantic gesture.

Hamaguchi tried to shoo Chiun away before the emperor could see him, but Chiun remained standing where he was.

The members of the council tried to read the emperor's face, but it was as staid and uninterested as normal. The only difference the council could see was that he was wearing a robe very similar to the young Korean man. Both were white with ornamental patterns running up their sleeves.

This caused a particular fear in Yamamoto, who did not believe in coincidences.

"I am glad that you are all in attendance," the emperor said.

"What can we do for your majesty?" Kido asked. "We await your guidance."

"Today's wisdom comes not from me, but from my esteemed guest. Please welcome Chiun, reigning Master of the House of Sinanju."

The council began to politely clap as they turned to face the young boy who sat in the extra chair.

Chiun stood, softly, like a ghost. The gold phoenix on his back, a symbol of rebirth and fiery ascent, arose from the folds of his robe.

"Forgive me, but I thought the Master of Sinanju was an older fellow," Kido interrupted.

"Yes, but never was he 'useless,'" Chiun said. "Your majesty, may I?"

"The Chrysanthemum Throne observes the Master of

Sinanju," the emperor said, nodding with a respectful bow of his head.

Chiun stood and performed a deep, respectful bow.

"I wanted to personally thank the emperor for his appearance at my wedding," Chiun said, smiling. "My bride and I are forever honored."

"Congratulations," Yamamoto said. "My apologies about earlier..."

"It is of no concern," Chiun said. "I only have one question for the members of this austere council: whose plan was it to spy on my village and kill two of my villagers?"

Chiun held the duffel bag above his head.

He flamboyantly untied the bag and the severed heads of Kasuo and Kage bounced onto the table. The councilmen scrambled to get out of the way of the resulting seepage. Whatever had kept the smell trapped inside the bag now surrendered its stench to the entire room. Even the emperor tucked his nose into the folds of his robe.

"I ask once more, with the weight of these lives between us: who among you dared to threaten Sinanju?" Chiun asked, making eye contact with each council member. "Speak now, for I consider silence as damning as the deed itself."

The other members of the council quickly pointed fingers at Hamaguchi.

"What?" he coughed in defiance. "It wasn't... wasn't just me!"

Seeing guilt behind the anger in his eyes, Chiun walked over to Hamaguchi and softly placed one fingernail over his heart. He tapped twice and Hamaguchi began squirming in place as the nerves connected to his heart began to misfire. The first tap had forced adrenaline into his heart, and the next denied the heart the ability to slow.

Hamaguchi saw the hand approaching his chest, but oddly felt no fear. It was so slow. And when he felt the long fingernail tap his chest, he was confused...until the second tap. It felt like a sledgehammer, knocking the wind out of him. He desperately reached out to the other councilmembers, fear painfully warping his face.

They refused to even look at him.

"Someone...help me!" he screamed, seeking the faces of his former allies. "Your majesty, please!"

The emperor looked away in embarrassment. One never honored a coward's death with eye contact.

Hamaguchi's heart beat faster and faster and harder and harder, until it exploded in his chest. His lifeless body twitched one last time after collapsing to the floor.

The emperor then stood and despite what they had just seen, everyone instinctively turned to face him, most still holding their noses.

"We must *all* provide an apology to the great Master Chiun and his father, Master Nūk. Our indirect actions have caused a wound in the hearts of our friends, the Sinanju. Japan profusely and grievously apologizes to the Master and House of Sinanju. This shall *never* happen again!"

Each member began bowing to Chiun and loudly apologizing. Kido bent over only to come face to face with Kage's jawless head and collapsed in a puddle of his own vomit.

Chiun returned with a slight bow of gratitude to each member.

"The House of Sinanju accepts the emperor's apology and appreciates his sympathy. Our fates are entwined, our heart is now restored," Chiun said in a flowery Japanese tone and left the chamber.

As he exited, the emperor snapped at each councilmember, denigrating them because Japan had been embarrassed in front of the world. Each council member was ordered to beg the throne for forgiveness.

Chiun waited for a few minutes outside the chamber door. After he heard enough groveling, he left, smiling.

CHAPTER TWENTY

Chiun's first two years as Master were spent studying the scrolls. While his father had properly trained him in the art, something in Chiun would not allow himself to feel worthy of the title 'Master.' The villagers had reluctantly accepted Chiun after his father's banishment, though Minji, the eldest gossip in the village, had "good evidence" that Chiun had secretly killed his father to become master.

Chiun could have done something, but he knew that to fight a gossip was to deliver their message.

At first, Chiun had suspected that his new caretaker Pullyang had been passing along tales, but the boy was a dullard who had only inherited the position after the death of his father the prior year.

There was hardly any depth of personality in him, but he was trustworthy. He was also very slow, but thorough. Chiun was satisfied that he would adequately fulfill the position until it was his time to grow in the Caretaker's Forest.

It wasn't until his third year when Chiun became comfortable with the title 'Master.' The year started on a good note. Minji died (*of natural causes, of course*) and Chiun did not correct the other gossips when he overhead them whispering that Minji must have been right about all of her tales, and that Chiun had silenced her.

Of course, her death could not possibly have anything to do with her 74-year-old, 258-pound frame, or her tendency of sneaking sweets into the many pockets of her custom-sewn hanbok.

After hearing their whispered tales, Chiun would often go out of his way to pass the Widow's hut. On the times that he noticed the women peeking from behind the curtains, he would simply smile and wave, making sure to give honor to the new elder, Sunja. The first time he had called her name out, he heard a scream and a thud as she attempted to get away from the window and fell to the floor.

After passing the hut, if he still felt their stares, Chiun made sure to stop, turn around and give a serious backward glance, which was answered by the rustled wave of hastily-shut curtains.

No, it was a month later when Eon gave him the news he had longed to hear: she was expecting a baby. His father had been correct. Chiun had to carefully study the practices and diet that would ensure a son. It was definitely not the same pleasurable sensation that he normally enjoyed with his wife, but with only two exceptions in Sinanju history, one of which was in question, this practice had always produced a male heir.

Chiun took time away to allow Eon to announce the good news. His father had taught him the path to a good marriage: "Weddings and births are for the wife. Marriage and a son belong to the Master."

So, while Eon prepared to celebrate with the other wives in a small feast, Chiun would travel to Seoul for a minor attitude correction. Chiun had once met Governor-General Saitō Makoto while accompanying his father. The man seemed to respect his father, though he kept referring to Chiun as boy. But after Chiun became Master, he had traveled to Seoul to announce that he was now Master. But Makoto was still condescending, calling Chiun by the ragged Japanese tongue as a 'nanjok' (*savage*).

Chiun was well aware of what he said, and let it pass. It was apparent that Makoto did not hold Chiun with the same esteem as he had his father. Indeed, his actions spoke louder than his words. The governor-general's tribute to Sinanju had not been paid in the past two months.

Then a messenger from the Governor-General's office posted a letter at the edge of the village. It introduced the new Governor-General, Kenji Tanaka in the worst way possible.

TO THE VILLAGE OF SINANJU

I, General Kenji Tanaka, newly appointed Governor-General of Korea, pen this letter with a weighty sense of responsibility and an undeniable conviction of Japan's superior governance.

You should consider yourselves most fortunate, for under my judicious rule, the Divine and Esteemed principles that guide the Empire of Japan will soon grace your humble lives.

I have been entrusted with the monumental task of administering and modernizing Korea. Know that I shall be visiting your village shortly to observe and evaluate the potential of your compliance with the new order.

Failure to show the utmost respect and obedience to my person and Imperial rule will be considered not just an affront to me, but to the Emperor himself, under whose Divine grace you now subsist.

Prepare for my visit. Let it be a lesson in the benevolent force of Japan's embrace! Do not squander this opportunity!

**Yours in assured Authority,
田中健二大将
General Kenji Tanaka
Governor-General of Korea**

The villager who found it brought the sign to Chiun.

Chiun thanked the villager, and after reading the note, understood why the tribute had stopped. A new Governor-General had arrived without notifying Sinanju. Chiun would have to return to Seoul to inform the new Governor-General about his limitations.

As dawn broke, Chiun sent a boy to call for the carriage and informed Eon of his journey.

"Your first trip to Seoul as the Master of Sinanju!" Eon said proudly. "Could I attend with you?"

"Unfortunately, no, my love. There is a new Governor General," Chiun said. "He may need to be taught a lesson and while you understand what I do, I would rather you not have to see it."

"Perhaps we can spend time in Seoul another time?"

"Why confine a trip to Seoul?" Chiun asked. "We can travel to Kyoto, or Shanghai, or visit the beauty of Siam!"

"I would love that," Eon replied with anticipation. "We can discuss it after your return. Good fortune, love."

"Sinanju *is* fortune," Chiun said, pulling her to him.

They kissed softly and passionately, a puzzle formerly separated, finally complete. After a moment of hesitation, Chiun spoke.

"My heart is here," he said.

Chiun smiled as he exited, but his inner thoughts were troubled. Eon was right: this would be his first political test as

Master. No one would have dared posting such a sign during his father's time as Master. While the thought of beheading the Governor-General was tempting, Chiun knew that they would just send another bureaucrat to fill his position.

The cold sky blushed with the first light of day, casting a soft glow over the village as Chiun awaited his carriage. Used mostly for diplomatic reasons, the carriage was easy to see as it turned the corner. The entire carriage assembly had been designed to be a moving tribute to the House of Sinanju, a visible declaration of the village's enduring legacy and the esteem in which its Masters were held.

As a child, the carriage was a fun way to travel. But as he aged, Chiun began to notice the masterwork of its craftsmanship. Its dark, polished wood frame gleamed against the morning light, only surpassed by the intricate gold carvings on each side that bore the symbol for the House of Sinanju. The large, sturdy wheels, bound by iron and etched with delicate patterns, cut through the dirt road with a quiet dignity that defied its size.

Leading the carriage were two majestic horses, their coats a deep chestnut that rippled like velvet with each powerful stride. They wore bridles that bore small gold crown bits, designed to catch the light with a regal brilliance that had once graced the hoses of the Sultan of Morocco. Like the side of the carriage, the gold trapezoid symbol of the House of Sinanju was embossed on each side of the blankets.

As a child, all he could think about was riding the carriage. He thought that once he became master, he would ride around forever with the beautiful horses, but his father quickly disabused him of the notion, noting that the less people saw of the carriage, the more important it became.

He looked at the approaching carriage and realized that the horses he played with as a youth had died long ago and had been replaced. Though the new horses looked just as strong,

Chiun knew they were not the same, which somewhat diminished them in his esteem.

As the carriage pulled to a stop before Chiun, the coachman, dressed in the traditional dark attire of his station, gave a respectful nod to Chiun and descended from his seat.

Some past tradition prevented the Coachman from speaking directly to the Master. Four hundred years after that, the tradition had somehow evolved to the master not acknowledging the Coachman. It was another tradition likely decided by the whim of a past Master, something not even important enough to be registered in the scrolls. It was vocally reinforced, which meant that it fell into the category of tradition.

TRADITION.

Chiun was *drowning* in tradition, but nodded to the Coachman as he entered the carriage. The Coachman bowed and silently shut the door upon Chiun's entrance. He had often thought that the Coachman's job was the easiest in the village. The man rarely worked more than once a year, but Chiun noticed that he took immense pride in his job. The Coachman kept his hands steady on the reins, guiding the horses with an ease that spoke of years of dedicated service.

The soft creak of the carriage's axles, and the gentle jingle of the horses' adornments filled the air, merging into a rhythm that seemed to beat in time with the Earth's own pulse. Hooves clacked against ancient stone, a relic of Roman tribute to the House of Sinanju. It was more than just a path of stones, it was a historical artery that had sustained countless travelers across millennia.

Chiun disappeared into his thoughts between each rest stop.

The landscape unfurled like a painted scroll filled with verdant hues, dotted by the occasional village and punctuated by the rhythmic chants of farmers tending to their fields. Most stopped and bowed as they saw the carriage approach. Others quickly grabbed their children to explain how special the carriage was.

Despite tradition, Chiun allowed himself to nod in recognition to the people throughout his journey, especially the children, who marveled with large eyes and gaping mouths. He continued acknowledging the people even after the sun had set.

Perhaps this would become a new tradition, Chiun thought, drifting into sleep.

CHAPTER TWENTY-ONE

At dawn the next day, Chiun awoke in the back of his carriage and looked out the window. The orange and pink skies played with the horizon before the breaking of daylight. The carriage was nearing Seoul, and the landscape quickly began to change. The simplicity of rural lands slowly gave way to the outskirts of the Korean capital. Here, the last breaths of the historic past meshed with the pulse of a city growing into its modern skin.

Chiun's arrival was not heralded by either the fanfare or spectacle he had read about in the scrolls. Rather, it was a quiet assertion of a change in the road and the soft clatter of the carriage's wheels. The carriage slowed as it approached the Government Building and the horses' muscles quivered as they flexed to recover from the long journey.

Chiun had met the first Japanese General during a trip with his father. The Government Building was almost complete and Chiun thought that it looked ugly. But looking at the completed structure, he realized that he had been too kind. It was a lard-colored cube with windows, clearly designed by someone with no budget, one eye and half a brain.

Chiun's robe was instantly recognized as he stepped out of the carriage, the guards immediately stepped away from the door, surrendering any pretense at guarding the entrance. Once he entered, many soldiers tried to escort him to the Governor-General's office. Chiun dodged their clumsy attempts to grab him and walked directly there himself. The soldiers outside the office quickly stepped aside, and the doors opened as if he had been expected.

Four large soldiers were stationed inside the room, two on each side of the door. They held their rifles at attention as Chiun entered. The only other man in the office other than the Governor-General stared nervously from a plush couch.

Governor-General Tanaka did not look up when Chiun entered and pretended to be writing.

"One moment," he said, holding up a condescending finger.

Chiun noticed that unlike the guards outside, none of the men inside the building were Korean. They were all very large men of Eastern European origin who reeked of pork and cheese. The soldiers in the office did not display concern when Chiun entered. Their hearts pumped normally, and their breathing did not betray the slightest concern.

"Greetings," the Governor-General said in broken English, smiling a politician's smile.

Tanaka was a large man in an expensive suit. His eyes were insincere and he smelled of elderberries.

Chiun returned with his own diplomatic smile and gave the slightest of bows.

"Governor-General, there seems to be a misunderstanding," Chiun replied in proper English, placing the posted sign on his desk. "The village has not received a shipment in over two months."

Tanaka ignored the sign and glared at Chiun.

"My predecessor agreed to your father's terms, and those terms ended when he left," Tanaka said, as if he was speaking to a five-year-old. "There is no misunderstanding. I personally ordered the shipments to be halted."

"Then we shall arrange for a new agreement," Chiun insisted.

Tanaka chuckled.

"The only reason we approved your father's pact is because of his reputation," Tanaka said in a patronizing tone. "There is no such political pressure with a young and an unknown entity like yourself."

"Sinanju does not bow to transient powers," Chiun said. "Our agreement is with Japan."

"Look around you, boy," Tanaka said scornfully. "I am Japan."

Chiun had been taught many levels of diplomacy and the first thing he learned was that even the worst of enemies held their private tongue. Though aggressive, diplomacy was an elaborate dance of compliments and lies, each searching for soft spots.

But Tanaka displayed no attempt at diplomacy.

"Your father was some kind of regional warlord," he said. "Many in our own military had respect for him. Our generals considered it wise to keep him at bay by supplying his...your village with trinkets and dog food. But after you announced that you had become Master, I asked around and I was surprised when no one had ever heard of you."

"*Every* Korean knows of the Master of Sinanju."

"Perhaps they have heard of the title, but no one has heard of *you*. No one is aware of a Master Chiun in any region I could find. No one admitted having a pact with you and, more importantly, none of them said that they would defend you. Instead, they pledged allegiance to the emperor, and said that if you declared war on us, it would be a village of fishermen facing the might of the Japanese Army...as well as your own neighbors."

"You have no honor," Chiun said.

Tanaka returned to his desk and motioned. The four guards

immediately stepped forward, placing their rifles against their shoulders, aiming at Chiun's back.

Then Tanaka revealed an honest smile. It was both condescending and poisonous.

"Return to your village, nameless fisherman," Tanaka sneered, returning to his papers. "And be thankful that I have spared your life."

Chiun took a moment to allow a tiny smile of his own and whispered to Tanaka.

"Behold your mistake."

Chiun did a backward flip and everything seemed to freeze in place.

Chiun had made sure to allow the soldiers time to pull their triggers. The smell of their condescending breath combined with gunpowder, filling the air with the thunderous barrage of noise that reverberated against the walls.

But their bullets were already irrelevant.

Chiun had caught each one before landing behind the men, tossing the bullet into one of the many hidden pockets of his robes. The trails of compressed air from the rifles continued futilely forward without their charge, expanding in a fiery breach exiting the barrels.

Chiun looked at the guards. No doubt 'highly trained' specifically to combat Sinanju, their height and muscles did nothing more than make them large flesh targets, uselessly staring down the sights of their rifles.

Chiun brandished his fingernails, ten of the longest and strongest nails in existence. Stronger and sharper than any steel, his father called the fingernails of a Master of Sinanju the "Knives of Eternity." Chiun silently slashed the steel barrels into metallic shavings, so effectively that the soldiers did not feel the disturbance—at least, not until he shattered the rifle grips they held. The wood burst into splinters, peppering the men with their sharp bite.

In the tiny fraction of a second that it took to happen, the soldier's pupils began to dilate, widening in an attempt to gain as much visual information as possible, but it was not fast enough to send the information to their brains, much less process what was happening.

Fingernails thrashing, Chiun disassembled the men into random body parts and they seemed to collapse simultaneously, staining the governor's polished floor.

Tanaka saw Chiun standing in front of him and his guards firing their rifles. Then the guards collapsed to the floor in sectioned, bloody pieces. Chiun remained standing in the same spot. Frightened beyond belief, he aimed his pistol directly at Chiun's chest. His mind could not understand what he had just seen and his hands would not stop shaking.

"Don't come near me!" he shouted, reverting to Japanese, pulling the trigger over and over until his bullets were gone. "Stop!"

The dervish of red robes in front of him disappeared. Though he felt the recoil of each round as it exited the barrel of his pistol, each bullet had vanished from the air.

When Chiun appeared in front of him unharmed, Tanaka screamed.

"Yaaaaaaah!"

Chiun glared into Tanaka's eyes, showing him a handful of useless rounds in the palm of his hand. Without looking, he glared into Tanaka's fearful eyes and removed two of the rounds. He hurled them at the guards approaching from the hallway with enough force to take them off their feet. He removed all but one of the rounds and squeezed. The high-pitched squeal drilled into Tanaka's ears. Chiun opened his hand and dropped a solid piece of lead to the floor.

He placed the last round between Tanaka's eyes. The front of the round dug softly into Tanaka's forehead.

"This last man," Chiun said, nodding to the cowering man on the couch. "Who is he?"

"Ugaki Kazushige! He...he's my second-in-command!" Tanaka answered, wondering why the Korean was holding a spent round against his forehead. The Korean was insane! The mere thought of it helped him calm down and regrow his spine.

Tanaka smiled and took a deep, cleansing breath.

"But he won't help you," Tanaka said with a growing confidence. "He only answers to me and the emperor!"

"Good," Chiun said and flicked the round through Tanaka's forehead with a force greater than when it was fired from the rifle.

Ugaki shrieked and passed out on the couch.

When he awoke, he was seated in Tanaka's chair. Chiun stood politely in front of the desk, smiling.

It took Ugaki a moment to focus, but when he finally did, he wished that he hadn't. Outside the shattered door behind Chiun was a large pile of dead soldiers. He would have passed out again, but Chiun reached a long fingernail across the desk and pricked the back of his hand. Before the pain even reached his brain, Ugaki was suddenly more awake than he had ever been in his life.

"Greetings, Governor-General," Chiun said with a formal bow. "It is good to meet you."

Realizing everything that just happened, Ugaki dropped to the floor in front of Chiun, and began crying.

"We will never again miss a delivery!" he shouted between sobs.

"As for the 'dog food' you have been sending?" Chiun asked.

"Your village shall be sent what my own family eats!"

"Excellent," Chiun said, turning for the door. "This is a good start for our new relationship and I do not wish to return. You may convey to the emperor that the House of Sinanju is pleased with your service."

Ugaki, unable to pass out again, slumped to the floor, emotionally spent.

Chiun returned to the village the next day with a large convoy of food and goods and the villagers cheered his arrival. Chiun took the moment in, realizing that this was why the Master of Sinanju existed.

CHAPTER TWENTY-TWO

On the day of his son's delivery, Chiun waited anxiously in the House of Many Woods, sitting in what he would always consider his father's chair. Eon was gathering a few things to take with her to the delivery room in the small house behind the shaman's hut.

Hye-Sook, the Life-Giver, remained in the greeting room with Chiun. She was a matronly woman in her mid-fifties who dutifully wore modest apparel and had a penchant for the color yellow. She had delivered all of the children of Sinanju for the past four decades, including Chiun himself.

Like all Sinanju mid-wives in the past, Hye was married to the shaman. She was trained in the ways of medicines and herbs, and was nearly as knowledgeable about them as the shaman, especially when it came to treating the women of the village.

Chiun trusted her, and even though he personally felt the strength of his son's heartbeat within Eon's womb, he also felt apprehensive. Part of it was Hye's behavior. As a child, she had always made time to give him a soft greeting or a warm smile.

Now, she stood quietly near the door, unable to make eye contact as if fearful of an impending attack.

"The House thanks you for your service," Chiun said, in an attempt at small talk.

"Your son shall be delivered safely, Master," Hye said, looking at the floor.

"Is this your first time in the House of Many Woods?" Chiun asked.

"No," Hye said softly.

"Boo-in, for just a moment, speak to me openly the way you would have spoken to the boy you once knew," Chiun said. "I must know a truth."

Hye looked up. Chiun's face was stronger and he was much taller, but she still saw the little boy within his concerned eyes. Her body relaxed and she turned toward him.

"My first time to the House of Many Woods was when I brought you to your father," Hye said. "You were small. Your father worried that you would not live."

"I…did not know that," Chiun admitted. "The shaman cared for me?"

"My husband would not allow your mother to wean you until you were three, which delayed your training."

Chiun was transfixed as he heard these things for the first time.

"What else do you remember?" Chiun asked.

"Nothing of consequence," Hye said. "You wore straps on your legs when you first began walking. It took both my husband and your father many months to strengthen your legs."

'I was a sickly baby?' Chiun thought. 'And my father did not discard me.'

Chiun was even more impressed that his father had never even spoken about it.

"When you were older and I saw you running around with

the other children, it reminded me of the great progress you had made and the fun you almost didn't experience."

Chiun paused, thinking about how to ask her the question that had bothered him since she arrived.

"Why do you now fear me?" he asked, softly.

Hye's stance softened even more.

"I do not fear you, Master Chiun. I remember who you were," she said softly, a thin smile gracing her memories. "…a kind and energetic little boy, full of curiosity and wonder, a boy who protected children from bullies and watched out for the small things, like a bird you once saw being tortured. You filled my heart with your presence every time I saw you. Your father saw it as a weakness that should be driven out."

"Then why do you avoid me?" Chiun asked.

Hye paused and glanced to the floor.

"Because I also know who you *are*," Hye explained, sadly. "You are the bringer of death."

"You think me as an evil?" Chiun asked.

"No, Master, I do not," Hye said, shocked at the question. "You are no more evil than an earthquake or a monsoon, but your nature is to bring death. Yes, it is how you feed our village and protect us. My family is eternally grateful for the Masters of Sinanju, but by the end of your time in this world, you will have killed many times the number of our village, so we are saved only by the involuntary sacrifice of others. We walk opposing paths, Master Chiun."

Chiun began to reply, but heard Eon's footsteps approaching. She opened the door and Chiun smiled.

Eon was wearing the traditional layered brown and gray rag cloths of a birthing mother, carrying a pouch with a book and a few personal items. She was clearly exhausted and already given to the pangs, ready to give birth, but still held a twinkle for him in her tired eyes.

"Consider his name wisely, love," Eon said, giving Chiun a

soft kiss. "I know you miss your father, but Kwan just named his newborn Nūk."

Chiun smiled as he held her. He understood her concerns. The wife of a Master was the first to hear the child's name after the Life-Giver, but not until then. This explained Master Ak-Chwi's name, which translated as 'smelly.' Chiun's father tried to explain it away as a word that was spelled differently at an earlier time, but as a child, Chiun privately remembered him as 'Master Poop.'

"Just return to me in good health, my love," he said to Eon.

"I remember the story of Master Ti-Sung," Eon said, grabbing a deep breath.

Eon had no problem learning about past masters of Sinanju. She loved reading, but she had no idea that Chiun had so many stories! And Chiun took every one of them personally, as if every story he had learned in the scrolls would happen to him or someone close to him. So, when she found out that she was pregnant, she recalled how Ti-Sung's first son had died, and knew that Chiun was going to be overly protective.

Hye smiled as she saw Eon, and relaxed her posture.

"It is time for us to leave, Manim," Hye said respectfully, opening the door.

Eon wrapped herself with the snowbear fur that Chiun had provided on their wedding night. She forced a smile to him as another wave of pain pulsed through her body.

"May your son please you," she said, attempting a bow.

Both Chiun and Hye jerked forward. She was not supposed to bow.

Eon returned upright with a slightly irritated look. She knew that Chiun meant well, but she was tired of being treated like an invalid.

"Be well, my love," Chiun said with concerned eyes.

Hye led Eon out the door. As she returned to close the door, her smile disappeared.

His father had tried to explain to Chiun about the effect that being a Master would have on others, but Chiun was a child, and some things can only be truly learned through experience. The people of Sinanju were a proud people, his father said, far prouder than they had a right to be, and their fear of the Master was partially a manifestation of their guilt.

Chiun learned that fear firsthand shortly after becoming Master. The smiles he now saw were more likely to be from people he was close to before becoming Master. They were... formal, displaying no real emotion.

It felt like a form of betrayal, but his father insisted that there had to be distance between the Master and the village. It did not take Chiun long to realize that no matter what he did, that fear, born from thousands of years of tradition, would never change.

Pullyang waited until everyone had left before he brought Chiun a tightly wrapped package. The contents had been masked with spiced meat and cinnamon, but Chiun could tell that whatever was inside had the smell of death.

Pullyang moved with the speed of his late father—like porridge dripping from a frozen bowl. Sometimes Chiun did not know if Pullyang was really that slow, or it was a side-effect of his accelerated perception of time.

Chiun unwrapped the package, revealing a heart. At first it appeared human, but this heart had eight chambers—the heart of a Jiang-shi. A small drawing inside the wrapping showed twelve figures crossed out, and a crown on top of the heart inside the package.

It only took Chiun a moment to understand its meanings. The knots that were used in binding the package were his father's. And even though his father's name did not appear anywhere on the package, the message was clear: he had found a camp of twelve Jiang-shi and killed them all. The heart had belonged to their chieftain, demonstrating that all were slain.

Chiun silently thanked his father.

His younger self would have still found some way to disagree with his father, but as Chiun got older, he began to appreciate the wisdom of his father. At one point, when he first learned of the speed and killing power of a full master, his mind was filled with fanciful notions that he got from reading a book his father had brought back from London. The characters were large and their actions were even larger. That made Chiun very excited about becoming Master.

He was seven years old, and during breaks in his training, he daydreamed about being the Master of Sinanju. He was walking into a large palace. A king would hand him a bag of gold and tell him to do something stupid. And it was always about making the king more powerful. Even though he succeeded, the king would recognize that no matter how much power he obtained, he would never be more powerful than Sinanju.

So, the king planned on ending Sinanju.

Young Chiun would try to leave the palace with the gold and hiding a grin, passing the guards who did not realize how dangerous he was. And, of course, the king would wait until Chiun was in the middle of them. He would rise from his throne and yell KILL HIM! in an attempt to get his gold back. Chiun released his grin and tore through the guards, sometimes five or six at a time! and then the king would send his greatest warrior.

The man always looked like a ten-foot-tall gorilla wearing human skin and a long, twisted beard like the savages of Norway. His axe weighed more than the fat king and Chiun started laughing at him.

The gorilla guard led with his axe and that was when Chiun knew that he was strong, but stupid. The axe hit the floor and Chiun ran up the handle and placed the palm of his hand on the gorilla guard's nose. The bone shattered through the back of his skull, carrying brain and blood, through the air, piercing the wicked king's heart.

Young Chiun picked up the bag of gold and left for another adventure.

Chiun caught himself smiling. The world of his youth was so simple. Solutions were easy, and Sinanju always won. But, he realized, surrendering his smile, that world never existed. Was that the meaning of maturity? Remembering your youth and applying current wisdom to the past? Using that wisdom to smear the black and white, just to see how many levels of gray existed?

When Chiun was imagining being master, he was perhaps fifty or sixty years old, not thirty, and his father was still there for advice. Now he was left only with the memories of his father, and five thousand years of recorded history.

The scroll room...another thing that Chiun needed to work on was entering events in the scrolls. His father, like most Masters, numbly listed dry facts as an entry and provided nothing more. Others whined, or listed personal information that was awkward to read, much less teach. Three masters only wrote a single entry just to prove that they had completed at least one large job. And then there was the fire of 404 A.D. It destroyed many of the scrolls before Wang and a few after. Not so ironically, no one explained what had happened.

Chiun's initial tendency was to provide less, not more, but since he wanted to be known as not just a teacher, but a great teacher, he compromised. His entries would contain all of the necessary information as well as a bit of embellishment to make the story 'easier to read.'

His first entry in becoming a master was written carefully on the silk parchments reserved for important events with the flowing and artistic strokes of an artist. It was longer than he had intended, consuming four pieces of silk parchment, written on both sides.

And yet, even within that volume, he did not mention the specific details of his father's departure. Chiun did not lie, but he did not provide the complete story. He said that his father left to promote Sinanju during a time of great need, propelling Chiun to Master ahead of his time.

He might also have mentioned that his father had inadvertently caused the Great War, but even that was better than what really happened. Besides, everyone in the future would be aware of the War to End All Wars, so surely, they would understand the need to transition.

Chiun looked down at the blank canvas and paused. What did he have to write? The babe had not yet been born, much less officially named. He returned his parchment to the pristine stacks of new parchment at the back of the room, ignoring his momentary apprehension.

The day had come and gone and Hye had not returned with the child. Chiun had enough mental discipline to set aside his paternal worry. He looked around the greeting room where he sat, remembering what he said about changing everything in his youth.

The greeting room was the first room in the labyrinth that was the House of Many Woods. In fact, it was the entirety of the original house that was first mentioned by Master Mangko, built from Hwanjangsil, a tree that no longer existed. With the thousands of years' worth of fireplace smoke, its formally white bone boards had long ago faded into a light mustard.

One of the initial chores of a new caretaker was "Prepare the greeting room", which was a fancy way of saying to apply a cream-like substance developed thousands of years earlier by Egyptian Heka to the walls. This supposedly gave the wood immortality.

But as he traced the oddities mounted on the wall, each artifact whispered stories of his father, providing comfort. Chiun had even kept the odd jar on the mantle that he hated and had kept it filled with his father's favorite Chrysanthemum paste.

No, after all was said and done, Chiun had decided that if he could not protect his father's legacy, he would protect his memory.

Chiun heard Hye's steady footsteps as she approached the door.

Pullyang opened the door, bowed to Hye and then left the room. What came next was not for his ears.

"All hail the Master of Sinanju," Hye said with a deep bow.

Chiun forced himself from staring at the bundle in her arms.

"You have brought new life into the village," Chiun said with the traditional greeting.

Sinanju tradition dictated that everyone, whether fisherman or the master himself, waited at their home for the Life-Giver to return with their newborn. Only after reaching the father's house could the babe be named. Chiun assumed that was because a sickly babe would not survive the trip.

"His name will be…?" Hye asked, handing the child to Chiun.

Tradition could not prepare Chiun for the feelings that flooded his heart as he looked at the tiny body wrapped in cloth. The babe had already been cleaned and his mother had been given time to bond and provide his first meal. Chiun was amazed that this tiny helpless thing held the promise of carrying forth the legacy of Sinanju to all future generations.

As the village celebrated the birth of the new heir in the town square below, Chiun could not help but envision the child's future. He would follow in Chiun's footsteps, but that would have to wait. Traditionally, the rigorous training of Sinanju began after weaning. Until then, a son of Sinanju belonged to the mother.

Chiun accepted the small bundle into his arms and smiled. The babe was wrapped tightly to protect him from the biting icy winds. He pulled back the wool to look at his son's face and, in the weight of his son's gaze, Chiun felt a bridge, stretching back through Sinanju history. Had his father felt this same blend of awe and vulnerability when he first held Chiun?

Chiun knew that in this silent communion between father and son, that a cycle continued — and Sinanju endured for another generation.

"His name shall be Song-Mira," Chiun said, very carefully.

His wish to include two names was not unheard of in Masters of Sinanju. To call his son "Great Master" was perhaps presumptuous. And, while using 'Song' as an abbreviation of both 'Seon' and 'Saeng' was usually reserved for past Masters who had already accomplished great things, Chiun had already determined that his son would surpass all masters, with the possible exception of Wang himself.

As Chiun brought his newborn to the village center, a sudden shift in the air caught his attention and he instinctively drew his child closer to his chest. A distant, yet focused gaze pierced through the crowd, unsettling him. It wasn't threatening, yet unmistakably directed towards him. Someone was looking at him from a distance.

Chiun was confused.

He could clearly feel the focus, but no threat. It was mixed in with the hundreds of eyes watching him approach the village center, like someone was focusing on him and yet not focusing on him. Chiun stopped and concentrated on the feeling. Turning toward the direction of the focus, he could barely make out the outline of the stranger. His presence was a silent whisper just beyond the village's boundary, a mere sliver of a silhouette against the light of the setting sun.

Sinanju training had many aspects of focus detection, but Chiun was puzzled with this feeling. He had never felt anything like this before, both familiar and unknown.

It was just there.

Then he realized that the stranger was not looking at Chiun, but rather his newborn. And in that moment, Chiun recognized the feeling.

It was his father.

He had allowed Chiun the dignity of knowing that he was at the village border without violating his exile. Chiun smiled and turned toward his father and held Song up for a better view, and the villagers hushed in the moment. Even the children fell silent, seemingly understanding the significance of the moment.

"His name is Song!" Chiun said boldly. "For he is your future Master and mine!"

The crowd cheered with genuine joy, as the future of their village had once again been preserved.

Chiun looked back to the tree line, but the silhouette was gone. The feeling of focus, the last tangible connection between Chiun and his father vanished and, standing in the midst of the entire village, Chiun felt incredibly alone.

CHAPTER TWENTY-THREE

Four years after assuming his role as Master, Chiun had finally settled into the rhythms of leadership. The villagers, once skeptical, now nodded respectfully as he passed, their trust earned through his quiet strength and recent successes, including a small job that helped motivate European forces to leave Asia.

One of Chiun's favorite things to do as master was his monthly walk through the village, allowing him to observe the day-to-day life that pulsed through the heart of Sinanju.

He started his walk north to the village's small mill. The sky was filled with strong winds and clouds that threatened rain. Even before he reached the mill, the sound of the Haneulgang river became a steady roar in the distance, followed by the rhythmic churn of the mill—a sound that, to Chiun, was as comforting as it was familiar.

The mill was perched neatly by the riverbank, utilizing its steady, strong current. It was built from the same rough stones that dotted the landscape. Chiun stepped inside, the cool air rushing past his skin.

It was a simple building: a large, wooden water wheel was

mounted inside a sturdy barn. The wheel turned with the flow of the river, grinding the millet and corn against a stone base. Today, Chiun did not find the old miller inside, but his son Tang, a young man with strong hands and a keen eye for the craft.

As Tang noticed Chiun's approach, he stopped to provide a respectful bow.

"How does the mill fare, Tang?" Chiun asked

"The river's been generous this season, Master. The harvest is good," the young man replied nervously.

His respect for Chiun was palpable, and his smile was vindication for the trip.

"And your father?"

"He has finally retired, Master," Tang said, a hint of pride mingling with the responsibility now resting on his broad shoulders. "The mill is now mine."

"The village is fortunate to have such skilled hands guiding the mill."

Chiun's approval lit up Tang's face, his simple acknowledgment worth more than any accolade.

Chiun left and headed west. The farmers were busy in the field, the largest family in Sinanju, an army of relatives each performing their own duties, so Chiun did not disturb them.

As he walked past the aging banyan tree just north of the west beach, Chiun's thoughts drifted to his early days as a novice under his father's stern gaze. Each gnarled root seemed to hold a memory of Chiun practicing crawls and rapid ascensions. He pondered how he might use the tree to foster the same resilience in his son without the harshness that had shaped his own childhood.

Chiun quickly passed the west beach, which had still not recovered from Soo-Min's death. Sadly, families no longer visited the stretch of fine sand as they perceived it to be celebrating her death. It would likely be another generation before the beach was used by families again.

The path wound past the village center. Passing the blacksmith's forge, Chiun felt the heat radiate into the cool air. The clang of hammer on anvil was a steady beat that spoke of hard work and determination.

The butcher's shop was silent and the drapes were drawn, but Chiun knew what was transpiring inside and chose to pass. He walked until he reached the small marketplace, where the air was thick with the aroma of roasting fish and sweet myrtle. Colorful stalls flaunted a tapestry of foods and goods. Women who were known for being the humblest in the village vigorously bartered over fresh vegetables and eggs, their voices a melody of haggling and bartering. Their children playfully darted between the stalls, furtive blurs of laughter and energy.

More than once, Chiun had considered making a purchase, but he quickly found out that his choices resulted in tales of favoritism and promotion.

Chiun's steps next took him past the shaman's hut, and through the archway of blossoming cherry trees that led to the villagers' huts. The archway was a stark contrast to the bare, frost-covered branches he had walked under just a few months earlier. The beckoning soft pinks and whites spoke of renewal to Chiun, and he was glad when they were in bloom.

He walked past a small dwelling, its doorway adorned with vibrant cloths, a telltale sign of a recent birth. The echo of joyful cries drifted from within, causing Chiun to smile. Not wanting his walk to become intrusive, he turned to the section of new huts that had been built over the past year. For the first time in over a century, Sinanju was growing.

His path led south and he stopped to watch a spider reconstructing its web, broken in the previous night's storm. What lesson did this creature wish to teach him?

"Even the smallest creatures face and overcome disruptions," he mused as he pondered his own lesson. "Is resilience learned, or is it innate? Must I teach Song resilience, or merely provide the storms that will reveal it?"

Near the docks, Old Man Cho limped towards him, leaning on a battered cane. He attempted a small bow, which only resulted in his head lowering, but Chiun gladly received the gesture.

"Master Chiun," Cho greeted with a voice as rough as the sea. "The nets are full this season, thanks to your…suggestions to the fishermen. Even Joon-Hu is productive these days!"

Chiun clasped the old man's shoulder, feeling the weight of his years. Chiun momentarily frowned as he felt the life rhythms in the old man's bones.

He did not have long to live.

"The sea provides, Cho. We just need to listen," Chiun replied.

By the time he reached the fishermen's quarters, the sun cast long shadows across the familiar paths of the village. The smell of salt and fish welcomed him, a stark contrast to the earthy tones the rest of the village was known for.

The community that the fishermen had built within the village was unique. It thrived in its own unique rhythm, unencumbered by the traditions that guided the rest of the village. These men and women, who drew their life from the sea, shared a bond that was both enviable and at times, confusing.

It was the ultimate dichotomy: until recently, the fishermen generally failed at their job, which threatened the survival of their families, yet they succeeded with the time they spent with their families. They were not the people you would choose to protect your valuables, but, with a few obvious exceptions, they were the most family-oriented people in Sinanju, and Chiun had grown to respect that.

They would often have their own communal meals and collective family activities separate from the village. This was especially difficult because the area they shared was not protected by the walls that had been constructed to protect the rest of the village. Yet, when asked, they refused such shelter, insisting that such an accommodation would hurt their ability to work in the frozen rain.

Chiun paused, watching a group of children help their fathers mend nets, their small hands quick and sure. A sense of peace settled over him, a quiet affirmation of his role not just as Master, but as guardian of these simple, precious moments.

As the sun dipped low, Chiun paused by the riverside, watching the water ripple as it emptied into the bay. The steady current, relentless and enduring, reminded him of his own journey—from a wary novice under his father's strict gaze to a master now shaping the future of his village. Each step and every decision bore the weight of tradition and innovation. The chill of the evening breeze, carried whispers of smoke and the laughter of gathering families, hinting not just at the shifts within Sinanju, but those stirring within his own home as well.

CHAPTER TWENTY-FOUR

One day, shortly before Song turned two, Chiun returned home early from his walk up the north coast. He greeted Eon with a tender kiss and immediately turned toward their little boy. Song had been playing all day and had collapsed onto a thick rug.

"How was your walk?" Eon asked.

"I have thoughts I would like to share," Chiun said. "I am trying to see the advantages of each area in the village and perhaps consolidate them for the benefit of all."

"You're going to have a fight on your hands," Eon said. "There are five families I can think of who don't want to associate with anyone."

"Prepare some tea and we can talk," Chiun said, smiling at Song. "I will hold my son."

"Be careful…he just fell asleep," Eon said.

Chiun carefully picked up Song, placing his little round head against his shoulder and began softly singing.

The bay wind whispers, whoosh! whoosh! whoosh!

> *Stars are twinkling bright, tiny specks of light*
> *Oh, colorful butterfly, spread your wings and fly*
> *Follow the starlight to dreamland*

EON SMILED. Chiun's mother had died when he was young, and with his father's exile, family had become very important. Even before Song was born, Chiun had told her that he was going to be close to his son, and provide him a strong family foundation.

"Why, listen to you!" Eon teased as Chiun continued to sing. "If you were not the Master of Sinanju, you could lead the Seoul Troupe in Gukak performances!"

Chiun grinned and shook his head at the suggestion. Masters of Sinanju had absolute control of their body, which allowed for dynamic singing ranges. But Chiun also knew that if he sang too much, it could make it into the scrolls. Song would perhaps write favorably about his father's powerful singing voice once or twice, and then in three generations, he would be remembered as "Chiun the Great Singer."

Chiun's smile disappeared as he began paying attention to his little boy. He rubbed his hand on Song's back and though undeveloped, his body was in rhythm, something that did not normally happen until after someone had mastered proper breathing.

For the past few months, he had been teaching Song the basics of Ung poetry. It was customary for all masters to do so, though normally not this young. Ung poetry was created to stretch the lungs in preparation for the harsh breathing lessons that would come. But mastery usually did not come about until the child was closer to four.

Chiun cast a quick glance at his wife. She was still gathering leaves for his tea. Chiun looked at the serene smile on his baby's face and slid his long fingernails to the center of Song's spine. He touched the boy's nervous system and immediately pulled his fingers back. Proper breathing, though basic, was already there.

Song's eyes popped open.

When he locked eyes with his father his face wrinkled in joy.

"Papa!" Song cried and tried to squirm down to the floor.

As he started wiggling, Chiun felt something so strange that, for a moment, it startled him. Song's body was balanced…even. When he awoke, his body's rhythms synched as if he had been breathing properly for many years.

His little feet hit the floor running. Eon set the tea cup down and followed Song, but he was too fast. Chiun leaned down as he passed by and swooped the boy back into his arms, noticing that Song was holding the horseshoe that had been placed above the doorway.

It was bent.

"Your tea is nearly ready, love. Please hold him," Eon said, and Chiun began lightly tickling Song's feet.

Eon placed the cup on the table before Chiun. She had already added perilla leaves and a pinch of dried ulgim powder.

"Our boy has plenty of energy today," she said, adding a drop of honey.

She slowly began pouring hot water over the leaves until the cup was half full.

"The perilla leaves are fresh," she said proudly. "I gathered them this morning."

Chiun closed his eyes and allowed the aroma to fill his senses. Tea was always better with fresh leaves.

To most of East Asia, tea was a heralded part of the day. But in Sinanju, if done properly, tea was a celebration of nature. Every master had their own favorite blend. It was the one area where masters were encouraged to find new flavor combinations.

Chiun's father preferred strong mugwort tea with ground almonds, but Chiun could never get past mugwort's bitter taste, no matter how many almonds were added. He even tried a pinch of cinnamon in an attempt to sweeten it, but the mugwort was just too strong.

"Did you take the horse shoe down from the door?" Chiun asked.

"No," Eon said, puzzled. "Why?"

Chiun held up the twisted horseshoe.

"I did not do this," he said. "Song brought it to me like this."

Eon looked at the naked area above the door and then examined the horseshoe. The stress marks in the iron blended seamlessly into the metal as if it had been crafted in that shape. Handing it back to Song, they watched as he tried to bite it. He became frustrated and twisted it even further.

A small cry of surprise escaped from Eon.

The tea pot began to whistle, tearing her attention away. The leaves had started to gently unfurl, so she finished filling Chiun's cup.

He was excited about both Song and his tea.

"The scrolls have never mentioned progress like this at such an early stage," Chiun said, handing Song to Eon. He took a sip of his tea, reveling in the experience.

"Perfection," he said.

As she took her son to feed him, something felt different. The balance in his little body shifted, as if he was compensating for the differences in his own weight.

Song quieted as he rested in his mother's embrace, but he refused to nurse. In fact, he never fed from his mother again after that.

He was weaned.

"What did you do?" Eon asked.

"I did nothing," Chiun said.

"What does that mean?" Eon asked, her brow bent in worry

because a child began training once they were weaned. "I'm not ready to give up my little boy yet."

"What mother is?" Chiun asked. "The child has always been the one to provide the timetable for training. Song has chosen his."

"He is still too young," Eon said, worried.

"His body is not yet fully balanced," Chiun admitted. "Perhaps two more weeks with you will give him time to adapt."

"This is happening so fast," Eon said, feeling unheard.

IN THE COMING weeks and months, Eon watched as Chiun took Song out for his first lessons. Chiun outlined his training—a regimen meant for students twice Song's age.

"This is too much, too soon," she protested one evening, her voice barely a whisper against Chiun's relentless enthusiasm. "He has so many bruises."

"This is the time when his bones have to be toughened," Chiun explained. "His body will learn this as a normal part of his life and harden. When my father first began training my bones, he had to take me away for a few months because of the cuts and bruises."

"I am your wife," Eon said earnestly. "But I am also his mother."

"My love, I expect nothing less," Chiun said, softening his tone. "But there will be many things about Song's training that you will likely never understand. This boy of ours, one day, he will become one of the great masters, and I have to ensure he is properly trained."

"What did Master Kik say in the scrolls?" Eon asked, referencing something she had once heard Chiun say. *'The greatest rivers are carved over time, not in the rush of one storm'?"*

"He was referring to an actual river," Chiun said. "Besides, Song is not like other children, even other Sinanju children."

"But as his mother, I see the *other* side of his training," Eon explained. "I see the tears that he won't show you. I feel the desperate hugs he gives before leaving to train. Chiun, it breaks my heart."

Chiun paused.

He remembered going through the same thing. One day, after an especially hard day training, he had returned bruised and crying. His mother refused to let him train the next day.

"Perhaps I am rushing things," Chiun admitted. "I will watch the boy closely, but you have to take this more seriously. The more pain he feels now, the less he will feel later when he faces threats in the real world."

WHEN SONG REACHED the age of four, it became evident that he possessed an innate talent and extraordinary abilities. Chiun watched in awe as his son absorbed the techniques and wisdom of their ancestors with astounding ease.

Song's progress surpassed even the most accomplished students in Sinanju history, achieving feats that, according to the scrolls, were typically attained years later in one's training.

The village elders marveled at the young prodigy, recognizing that within him lay the potential to usher in a new era of Sinanju. The ancient scrolls had spoken of such rare talents in the history of their lineage, and Song seemed destined to be among the greatest.

Song playfully darted through the muddy pathways of the fishing village, his cherubic face radiating pure joy and curiosity. He often accompanied Chiun with his monthly walks, his presence was like a ray of sunshine that brightened the villagers' lives. They began to view Song not just as the Master's son, but as a beacon of what Sinanju would become under his guidance.

In the heart of the village, a master in the making filled the air with laughter, and the legacy of Sinanju sparkled with brilliance. With each nimble step and playful gesture, Song carried the promise of a future that would see Sinanju's name resounding across the lands once more.

Sinanju had found its new heir.

CHAPTER TWENTY-FIVE

     *E*on awoke at dawn as the sun pierced the stained-glass panel at the top of the bedroom's east wall. The room filled with multiple colors, softly at first and then brightly scattering off the polished domed ceiling.

In her first day touring the House of Many Woods, there were so many things to explore that she had forgotten to ask Chiun about the beautiful stained-glass panel in their bedroom. It was eight feet long and over three feet high, separated into multiple-colored panels, representing the four elements: the deep blues of water, red shards of fire, white wisps of cloud, and rich, earthy browns. In the center of the panel, the bright golden symbol for Sinanju connected them all.

Chiun had no need for the panel. His internal clock allowed him to choose what time he wished to wake. And on those rare mornings that he chose to sleep in past dawn, the bright lights did nothing but increase his snoring, which Eon discovered was an alarm clock unto itself.

This morning, she awoke to the sight of Chiun standing at the end of their bed, with a small tray containing biscuits and tea. He had already bathed and donned the new day's robe, a turquoise blue kimono featuring a peacock. It was only one of two blue robes that he possessed, so she knew that he had travel on his mind.

"Good morning, my love," he said, bringing her breakfast in bed. "My tea may not be as delightful as yours, but perhaps it will start your morning on a good note."

Eon smiled and sat up in bed, accepting the small tray with a nod.

"Thank you, love. This is so sweet," she said with a soft smile, yawning. "I think the sun rose too early this morning."

Chiun sat by her side and gave her a soft kiss.

"You're wearing your peacock robes," Eon noted. "Where are you going?"

"I must make a small trip to Pyongyang to meet the new administrator."

"Going to Pyongyang, eh?" Eon asked. "It's not the bureaucrats you need to watch out for—it's those girls in the skimpy dresses on the street."

Her tone was teasing, but carried a small twinge of jealousy that made Chiun pause and turn.

"The only beauty that captures my attention has already won my heart," he replied, his voice filled with warmth. Taking her hand, he gently kissed it.

"Good," Eon teased. "Because I would have to go to Pyongyang and show those girls some Sinanju moves of my own!"

"They would definitely be wise to fear your wrath," Chiun said, holding his hands up in mock surrender.

Eon laughed and took a sip of tea. Her husband was a master of many things, but making tea was not one of his skills. Whether he based the tea on his own subdued tastes, or just forgot to add cinnamon and honey, his tea tended to taste like warm water.

Eon smiled and took a bite of one of the biscuits. They were much better.

"Chiun, when you were young," she wondered, chewing her biscuit. "Did you expect so much of your time would be dedicated to bureaucracy?"

"Not at all," Chiun admitted. "I imagined my life would be a constant battle against raging monsters and entire kingdoms."

"And now, evil bureaucrats," Eon said. "Your peacock robe makes sense now."

"I would much rather face raging monsters," Chiun said, leaning in for one last kiss before leaving. "I have taken your advice into consideration, my love. Yesterday was a very hard day for Song, so after breakfast and his morning chores, please let him know that he will have the rest of the day to himself."

"Awww," Eon said. "He's going to love that."

"Okay, now pay close attention," Chiun taunted with a grin, standing completely still at the end of the bed. "Are you ready?"

Last week, Eon asked Chiun how he disappeared. Did he distract people or was it a form of hypnotism? Chiun told her that he moved so fast in one direction that the eyes were involuntarily pulled in that direction, so when he dashed away in the opposite direction, the eyes were left with no image of him at all. To anyone watching, it looked like he simply disappeared.

Every day for the past week, Eon had tried her best to see him leave.

"I am going to watch very closely," she said with a steely gaze. "And I won't blink this time."

Chiun smiled and his eyes twinkled.

"Goodbye, my love," he said and disappeared.

"Oh, you!" Eon shouted in feigned disgust, taking another bite of her biscuit. "It's a good thing you make such good biscuits!"

CHAPTER TWENTY-SIX

Song normally slept in each morning until Eon woke him. On most days, it was an hour or two after dawn. She was of the opinion that, for the intense training he was receiving, he needed good sleep and good food. His digestion had not yet changed to the strict diet of the masters, so to prepare him for a full day of training, he typically ate rice porridge, beef and eggs with scallions.

Chiun watched his meals, carefully making suggestions so Eon could maximize his protein.

Today was a special day, so Eon made his favorite breakfast of rice pancakes with honey drippings. It was not long before the sweet scent filled the family rooms. Eon stood at the doorway to Song's room, watching him sleep.

Despite the fact that children lived in the House of Many Woods, none of the rooms were built for them. The four bedrooms that existed apart from the Master's bedroom were the same size and design.

Song's room had belonged to Chiun before he was married and it was decorated in the same manner it had been since Chiun moved into the room after he was weaned. Windows only existed on the south side, and the sunlight that entered was filtered through paper screens, casting subtle patterns across the room's straw-matted floor.

Song slept comfortably on his yo, a thick, quilted mattress. He had his father's eyes, but clearly his mother's delicate nose and mouth. While sleeping, his face was relaxed and Eon could still see the little round face that he possessed as an infant.

Eon sat next to the low wooden table beneath the window and began to softly whistle the Korean song 'Arirang'. Song began to stir, but his eyes remained closed, so she purposely whistled a note off-key.

"No, Mama!" Song said, his eyes still closed. "Do it right!"

"It is time to rise, my little bear," Eon said gently, brushing his hair with her fingers.

Song opened one sleepy eye and his nose crinkled as he detected a familiar scent.

"What's that smell?" he asked, bouncing into his mother's arms. He leaned his head on her shoulder, and for a moment, Eon thought he was going back to sleep.

"Today is a special day," Eon said, gently rocking him. "Your father had to leave for business, so after breakfast and chores, the day belongs to you. I made you some rice pancakes to celebrate."

Song opened his other eye and smiled.

"Really?" he asked, his voice still scratchy from sleep. "Thank you, Mama!"

Song gave his mother a big hug.

Eon relished the embrace. She knew that it would not be long before hugging his mother would be considered embarrassing.

Song dropped to the floor and ran to the dining area. He took a moment and looked at his father's empty seat.

"Did Papa get some pancakes, too?" he asked, before remembering Chiun's diet. "I mean, I *wish* he could eat pancakes."

"I am sure he does, too," Eon replied. "The path of a master is not without sacrifice."

Eon placed a small plate before him. The pancakes were soft, round and toasted white. Tendrils of left over pancake, covered with honey, were spread over the top. She brought a small cup of water, some porridge and a stick of beef, sitting them to the side of the pancakes.

"What do you think you'll do today?" Eon asked.

Song looked up in thought, grabbing a quick bite of beef.

"I think that I will pretend to be a master," Song said between bites. "Yes! I will take Papa's walk around the village."

"That's a long walk for a little boy," Eon warned.

"But I will be invisible, like Papa's stealth walk! No one will ever see me!"

"Even so, there's no need to go north and bother the farmers," Eon said sternly. "Stay within the village and behave. People are busy and have work to do."

Song smiled and quickly nodded, grabbing a spoonful of porridge.

"You're a good cook, Mama," he said.

"And you are a good son," Eon replied, kissing him on the forehead. "When you are finished eating, take the rugs out to the line and sweep the greeting room."

"Ahmuh wam," Song mumbled, his mouth full of food.

Eon raised both of her eyebrows and held up a finger.

"Masters of Sinanju do not speak with a full mouth," she said.

Song smiled and remained silent until he was finished eating.

It took Song less than twenty minutes to finish his chores. He pulled the rugs from each of the bedrooms, one at a time and placed them into a pile outside. After throwing each rug over the line, he began hitting them with a wire beater.

Song had fun beating the rugs. Dust exploded with each

strike. He stopped a few minutes later when his arms got tired. He left the rugs on the line and grabbed a broom before running to the greeting room.

He had been there a few times, mostly with his father. Song considered the modest room as something sacred. This is where every Master of Sinanju had sat! He smiled as he stepped onto the portico and began sweeping the leaves. He loved the bright seashells that had been tacked to the outside door.

As he entered, a wave leaves flew in with him. He tried to shut the door quickly, but the floor already seemed carpeted by them.

"Oh no!" he cried, racing to pick up each leaf.

After emptying the leaves into the fireplace, Song swept the floor and brushed off his grandpapa's old chair with his hands. The chair did not need cleaning, and was not even on his list of chores. Song just wanted an excuse to sit on it.

It looked like a huge square of wood with a seat carved out of the center. There was a faded red pillow on the back and the seat. What Song thought was best about the chair was that someone put jewels all over its sides!

Listening to ensure he was alone, Song climbed up onto the chair. As he set back, he realized just how big it was. He turned his head and moved the cushion to look at the carving on the back. It was a man, sitting in the lotus position. Around him were various shapes that Song did not recognize.

Returning the cushion to its original position, Song leaned back and looked at the room as his father saw it. A small fireplace was to his right and a pot of water sat beside it. A fine gold chain dangled near the chair and Song was tempted to pull it, but quickly changed his mind. It might release a dragon and he was not ready to fight dragons.

A large carved log had been mounted above the fireplace. Song had to stand on the chair to see what was on top. There was a sky-blue bowl in the middle of the mantle, with small wisps of incense escaping from the top. To the right and left were small, colorful trinkets that he wished he could reach. When he was master, he would be tall enough to play with all of them.

He sat back down and wondered what a Master of Sinanju did while in the chair.

"I am the Master of Sinanju!" he shouted, raising his hand in declaration. "This evil man will perish and Sinanju will win!"

"May I help you with something?" a calm baritone asked from behind.

Startled, Song turned around to see Pullyang, the caretaker for the House of Many Woods. He was a thin man in his early twenties, with a taught, bony face that gave him a strict look. Despite his youth, to Song he looked really old…and creepy. His hair was black, but slicked back so tightly that you could see the shape of his skull.

"No, sir," Song said sheepishly, hopping down. "I was just cleaning Grandpapa's chair."

"I see," Pullyang said. "And you felt that you had to sit in his chair to do so?"

"I'm sorry," Song said and bolted out the front door, mindful to not let more leaves in.

It was his first decision of the day, and he was already in trouble. Song hoped that Pullyang wouldn't tell his mother. He still had a full day of fun ahead of him!

After watching to make sure Pullyang was not following him, Song continued his walk. He had followed his father a few times, but while Chiun had always started north to visit the mill and farmers, he remembered his mother's instructions and turned west, entering the Caretaker Forest.

Each of the trees in the two-acre section represented a caretaker like Pullyang. Once a caretaker died, they were buried in the forest sitting up and their favorite tree was planted in the small mound.

At night, it was a spooky ghost forest, thick enough to block the moon and maybe even hide wildebeests and spike worms. During the day, it was a colorful variety of trees, and one of his mother's favorite places to picnic.

Song searched until he found the Stewartia tree for Pullyang's father Kong. It was the most recent tree and, though he had died years before Song was born, the base of the tree remained swollen with Kong's remains. Song's small hands brushed against the bark of the tree. The trunk was broad and sturdy, its surface a rippling tapestry of grays and browns that peeled away in thin, curling layers.

Song tilted his head, looking up through the branches that clawed at the sky with wooden fingers, whispering secrets to each other. He could barely see the clouds but he could see the frantic movement and hear the chatter of the birds that filled the forest. It reminded Song that after he learned the ancient languages of Sumaria and the Indus, he wanted to learn the language of the birds next.

His gaze dropped to the bulging base where the earth rose in a soft mound, the final resting place of Kong. For a moment, he felt sad for Kong being trapped in there for so long.

"Are you in there, Kong?" Song whispered.

His fingers hovered over the cool mottled bark, listening for an answer.

A rustling from behind made him jump, but it was only a squirrel darting through the underbrush. Song giggled at the squirrel and turned back to the tree, his curiosity deepening.

"I hope I didn't wake you up," Song continued. "Does it hurt to become a tree? Do you become just the roots, or the leaves, or everything?"

He imagined Kong's spirit living in the tree, maybe watching over the forest or dreaming tree dreams. Placing both palms against the tree, Song closed his eyes, trying to feel something, *anything* that might suggest life other than his own. He leaned his cheek close against the bark to listen and the scent of earth and old leaves filled his nose.

"If I were a tree," he whispered, "I'd want to be tall, with lots of flowers, so Mama could see me every spring."

Song had recently been taught about life and death, the cycle that bound everyone, whether king or pauper, but it was different when it was right in front of you, forever silent and cold. Song wondered if Kong's bones were still inside, or if the tree was using them to grow taller.

Maybe that's why Pullyang is always so serious, Song thought. *I would be sad if I lost my Papa.*

Walking deeper into the forest, Song began to hear the sound of seagulls and caught the scent of sea spray. He began to walk to the beach, but stopped. He had promised his mother that he would stay within the village, so he skipped south instead to the blacksmith's hut.

Grabbing a deep breath, Song concentrated and felt a tingle fill his body with power. He could only center for a few minutes at a time, but he was determined that he would walk to the blacksmith's hut without being detected.

Po was the largest man in the village. The vest he wore was large enough for a tent, Song thought. When he was younger, he asked Po if he could beat up his father. Po's laugh confused him.

"No one beats your Papa," he said with a hearty chuckle. "And if you learn like you're supposed to, no one will beat you, either!"

"Not even you?"

"Not even me and Tae combined," Po said, nodding to the leather maker next door.

"But he's so skinny," Song laughed.

"Don't let that fool you," Po said. "I've seen that man take down a wolf!"

Po was working on something on the other side of the hut. Song inched closer, remaining as close to the foundation wall as he could, walking with his feet sideways, like his father did. Looking down, he did not see any foot prints in the frozen ground.

It's working! He thought.

His steps were measured and quiet and as he approached the end of the wall, he looked for his next opportunity to move. The end of the blacksmith's hut was close to the wall, and would mask his movements, but Po had returned to this side of the hut. Song would have to hold his concentration to its maximum if he hoped to achieve stealth.

The rhythmic clang of the hammer against the anvil was usually a source of comfort for Po, but today, each resounding blow echoed his growing frustration. Smoke curled lazily from the forge, showcasing his mood.

He had woken up to a dull ache in his lower back, a stubborn souvenir from a lifting mishap the week before. The first commission of the day was a simple horseshoe. It had warped under the heat resulting in a misshapen banana. Po tossed it into the quench vat with a growl, the hiss of hot metal turning into a frustrated sigh.

"You and me both," he said.

Turning around, he bumped into his buckets of charcoal, scattering them all over the ground.

"Gods!" he cursed.

He bent over, picking up the precious pieces of coal, when a searing pain shot through his back and his tongs clattered to the floor. He stumbled to a nearby stool, the air thick with the smell of singed cloth and his own despair.

Then he caught something move out of the corner of his eye. It was small and dark and at first, he thought it might be a squirrel or weasel, but as he looked more closely, he saw that it was the Master's boy, Song, tip-toeing from behind the foundation wall.

Po smiled. Maybe he just needed a small distraction.

"Ooooh," he moaned, casting his tongs behind a large anvil. "I've lost my tongs!"

He fell to one knee, appearing to search the ground.

Noticing his distress, Song rushed to his side.

"How can I help, Po?" he asked, his eyes wide in concern.

"My tongs," Po cried. "Song, I've lost my tongs!"

"I'll help you find them," Song said, getting on the ground with Po.

The pair walked on their knees for a few minutes when Song turned behind the anvil.

"I found them!" he said, holding the tongs high in the air.

Po grabbed the tongs and held them to his chest, smiling.

"I don't know what I would've done without you, Song!" Po said. "Thank you!"

"It is my job to help," Song said proudly.

"What are you doing out here?" Po asked. "Where's your father?"

Song leaned in and whispered.

"He's burrow…burrowcatting, so I'm practicing stealth walking," Song explained. "I wanted to see if I could move without being seen or heard."

Po nodded in understanding.

"You were certainly invisible to me!"

"Thanks! Now I will see who else I can help!" Song said, skipping to the butcher's shop, but it was closed. He tilted his head sideways, looking through the doorway. They did not normally close until sundown. Song walked to the door and knocked, but there was no answer.

That's odd, he thought, and continued to the marketplace.

There was no chance of him being stealthy in the most crowded place in the village, so he began helping the vendors set up their booths. He stopped at the fruit stand and helped arrange the vibrant array of fruits, his small hands carefully placing each apple and pear in a row. The fruit vendor, was an elderly woman with a kind smile. Song did not remember her name, but she thanked him with a ripe persimmon.

Song helped the other merchants as he could. His laughter and chatter brought a lively atmosphere to the market. After everything was finally set up, a few villagers started walking in, thumping melons and warily eyeing the prices.

Even though they were yelling at each other, it appeared that the adults were having fun bartering and haggling over prices. Song had tried to learn the foreign codes the merchants were using, but he had not yet learned about any form of money other than gold.

The sun was reaching higher into the sky as morning turned to afternoon. Song was hungry and, for a moment, thought he should return for lunch, but then he remembered: today he was a Master. Song chose to ignore his belly and survive the entire day on his own.

As he approached the shaman's hut, Song attempted his stealthiest approach yet. The shaman was the scariest man in the village. Other kids swore that they had seen him turn into a dragon and steal eggs from chicken coops!

"Here he comes," the shaman said, sipping his morning tea. "Luckily, he didn't find out what was going on in the butcher's shop."

"Did Po bite his head off??" Hye asked.

"He actually made the old man smile," the shaman chuckled. "I don't think I have enough wart powder to cast that strong of a spell!"

"Why is he wandering around by himself?" Hye asked with some concern.

"I suspect young Master Song is on an adventure. He will be fine."

As he silently ascended the steps, Song looked at the talismans and symbols mounted around the door. His father had taught him not to play with such things, but the shapes were so different than anything he had ever seen. Some were normal shapes, like a triangle with an eye in the middle, but others were shapes within shapes and he could swear that some of them were glowing.

Inside, the shaman and his wife quietly watched Song's bravery as he carefully and slowly ascended the steps. Then the shaman saw something odd—a brown haze surrounding Song's body.

"What's wrong?" Hye asked.

"Nothing I can't fix," he said, going to his closet.

Song looked carefully at the talismans and started to touch one when the window curtain moved. Song dashed down the steps and hid behind a tree. His breathing became fast and shallow and he could feel his heart beating fast. The door slowly creaked open and he closed his eyes in another attempt at stealth.

"I thought I heard someone out here," the shaman said dramatically. "Perhaps it was just…a *ghost!*"

Song looked around the tree for a ghost, only to find the shaman standing directly behind him. He was wearing his regal robes, multiple layers of long, trailing crimson and a strange mask. It had six sets of eyes, and all of them were focused on Song.

"Aaaah!" Song cried.

"Do not fear, child," the shaman said in an overly-dramatic voice. "I am here to protect you!"

The shaman snapped his fingers and a small necklace appeared in his hand. As the shaman handed it to Song, his voice dropped to a mystic whisper.

"The spirits have told me of your great quest this morning, young master," the shaman said. "This blue pendant was carved from a piece of the sky itself! It will protect you whenever you are on a journey. Wear it in peace, young master."

Song, still frozen by the unnatural sight of the shaman's

costume, nodded quickly and followed the shaman's instructions, placing the amulet around his neck and then ran away, hiding behind some rocks.

He waited and looked behind him. The shaman had disappeared, so Song took his first real look at the amulet. At the end of the twine rope was a bright blue sapphire, set into an old stone.

Satisfied that he had been given his first reward in his quest, Song's attention was captured by the glimmer of dragonflies hovering over an overgrown fence. Their iridescent wings sparkled in the sunlight, drawing him like a magnet. He watched them for a moment, marveling at their graceful dance.

Then, with the tenacity only a child possesses, he began to chase the dragonflies, laughing as he leapt and twirled, trying to match their aerial acrobatics. The dragonflies, as if playing along, darted just out of his reach, leading Song on a merry chase through the villagers' huts.

When he tired of chasing dragonflies, he returned to the overgrown fence, to what he called the 'Bug Kingdom.' Song smiled as he looked at the insects crawling and flying and building. Though his mother refused to allow him to bring even one into the home, Song often played with them as if he was Master of the Bug Kingdom.

Looking closely, he spotted a grasshopper on a leaf, and sat next to it.

"Do you see this amulet?" he asked the grasshopper, twisting the sapphire until the sun reflected in the grasshopper's face. "It's the most powerful amulet in Sinanju!"

Unimpressed, the grasshopper bent its leg and carefully swept it over its head and body. Song giggled, imagining it was trying to tidy up its little green suit.

"I have been told that you are the most powerful warrior in your world, grasshopper," Song said solemnly. "You are the king of the insect world and all the insects in it!"

Song slowly reached for the grasshopper and it crouched perfectly still on his finger. Feeling no threat, its head twitched, as it studied Song with its compound eyes.

"But you still need Sinanju, o, king grasshopper! I tell you that there is another in your realm far greater than you. He flies above your kingdom looking down on you in pity."

Song slowly brought his right hand out, shaping it like a dragonfly. His pinky and thumb began flapping and he drew it near the grasshopper. It leapt off Song's finger and disappeared into the grass.

"No, no," Song said, shaming his fist-dragonfly. "You were not paid to kill this grasshopper!"

His hand flattened, as if the dragonfly was embarrassed.

"Your prey was notified by your bent elbow and has fled into another part of the kingdom where he will gather troops against you!"

Satisfied with the end of his little play, Song looked at the rest of the village. He had not even covered half and it was already afternoon. The sun was hot and his stomach was growling. Perhaps he would finish this walk another day, when his father had returned.

Song bounded home, leaping over rocks and sticks, up the stone steps that had been placed there by the...by the old guys with helmets and red capes. He passed the entrance to the greeting room and entered the residential door around the east side of the building.

He burst through the door in victory.

"I did it, Mama!" Song cried. "I did it!"

Eon came into the kitchen and picked him up.

"When you didn't return for lunch, I became so worried," she said, swinging him around in circles. "Let me get you some soup. You look tired."

"Oh, Mama, I had such an adventure!" Song cried, telling her how he solved the blacksmith's mystery and was awarded a noble blue necklace from the shaman and flew among the dragonflies, trying to teach them not to bend their elbows.

"It sounds like you had a very big day," Eon said, setting the bowl of soup in front of him.

Song tried to continue his story, but as he filled his belly, his eyes became heavy. His head surrendered to the table and Eon moved the bowl out of the way. She slowly picked him up, his limp body providing no resistance. She softly patted him on the back while carrying him to his room and gently laid him on his yo.

As she left, she turned back and this time saw a boy, not the baby she had seen earlier, and a part of her worry dissolved. Perhaps she should reconsider her worries and trust Chiun more with his training.

As she shut the door, Song's arm twinged as he fell deeper asleep. The world around him was so big, with talking trees that touched the sky and wizards and armor-making blacksmiths.

Song raised his arm and called for his flying steed, a majestic dragonfly with shiny purple armor. He mounted the dragonfly and together, they flew off for yet another adventure.

CHAPTER TWENTY-SEVEN

As the years passed and Song's training continued, the bruises became smaller and the injuries fewer. Eon no longer felt reluctance from Song when he left for training, but a hunger. He even began venturing out on his own from time to time.

Today, he stood inside the kitchen holding the head of a bear. Eon recoiled, her hands flying in the air.

"Song, by all the gods! What is that?"

"I stopped the bear that was harassing the farmers," he said proudly.

The bear's head was larger than Song's torso, and three times as heavy, but he held it out in front of him as if it was a doll's head.

"Chiun!" Eon yelled to the living quarters, her voice tight with fear. "Come in here! And you," she said to Song. "Take that thing outside!"

Eon was very protective of the kitchen. It was the only place in the living quarters with a tile floor, an expensive gift from a past client.

Confused by his mother's reaction, Song nonetheless stepped outside.

Chiun entered the kitchen with a smile on his face.

"Impressive for an eight-year-old, wouldn't you say?"

Eon's eyes opened wide in confusion.

"Perhaps you need to keep me updated on his training," she suggested. "I thought he was attacking tree stumps and perfecting his breathing."

Chiun looked to the floor, slightly embarrassed.

"He stopped doing that at four, love."

"Mama!" Song called from outside. "I'm going to take it down to the leather maker and see if he'll stuff it for me!"

Eon watched her son skip down the stairs as the bear head bobbed weightlessly in his hand, her motherly fear warring with a strange sense of awe.

Chiun squeezed her hand in reassurance.

"Chiun, I don't know if I'm ready for this."

"Song is shattering stones with his fists, and he can already outrun a horse," Chiun said, his voice a blend of wonder and pride. He reached out, placing a reassuring hand on Eon's shoulder.

"Believe me, when he faced that bear, he was as safe as if he were facing one of his stuffed toys."

"And that's *normal*?" Eon asked, trying to place herself into Chiun's shoes.

Chiun's smile widened with confidence.

"Our son will become the greatest Master of this age. The things he will accomplish will eclipse anything that any master has ever done. When you see the man he becomes, you will understand what it took to get there. If you trust Sinanju, trust me."

Eon looked down, her motherly instincts trying to filter his words.

"I love you, Chiun, and I *do* trust you. But I am the mother of an eight-year-old boy and it is difficult to reconcile the two."

"Come, let us sit," Chiun said.

The couple left the kitchen and entered the family room. It was the largest room in the personal quarters and Eon's favorite room in the House. There were eight doors in the octagon-shaped room: an entrance from the kitchen, four doors to each of the personal rooms and hallways that led to the Greeting Room, the Master's Chambers, and an exit to the courtyard behind the House.

Though constructed like a sterile Roman theater, it was softened by paintings and silk curtains.

"Before all of this happened, you said that you wanted to see me," Chiun said.

Eon hesitated. She had forgotten about her own request after seeing the bear head. She wiped her eyes with a cloth before looking up.

"I'd like to speak with you about having another child," she said, grinning hopefully.

"We do not need another son," Chiun said, puzzled.

"Yes, I know. I would like you to perhaps consider a daughter, someone that *I* can raise."

Chiun grinned. While girls were useless when it came to Sinanju, it would be nice to have someone help his wife in her duties.

"Yes," Chiun said. "I would like that."

Eon smiled. "I was so afraid to ask you," she said.

"The full moon begins next week," Chiun said. "I shall begin eating jujubes and pine nuts immediately."

"Could I name her?" she asked with her cutest grin.

Chiun balked.

The naming of a child belonged to the husband, but looking at the desire in his wife's eyes, he did not feel that he could just tell her no.

"We can think about that," he said.

Eon rushed from her seat and sat in Chiun's lap, hugging him.

"Thank you love," she said.

They sat together for long minutes in a hug. Eon's eyes remained closed in bliss.

"I was afraid to ask you," she admitted. "And after Song came home with that bear head!"

"Your…apprehension about Song's safety is my fault. I obviously need to keep you up to date," Chiun said, then his eyes widened. "I have an idea. Follow me. And bring a large candle."

Eon grabbed the largest candle she could find, lit it and followed her husband down the hallway that led to the Greeting Room. She had been in the room many times, but had never visited any rooms other than that.

Chiun said nothing as he passed Pullyang, who, upon seeing Eon, raised a curious but silent eyebrow.

Chiun waited for Eon as he traveled the small hallway that led down to the more private areas of the House of Many Woods. There were many rooms below ground for security and safety reasons.

The one Chiun was leading her to was the Scroll Room. A room carved out of stone, with pockets chiseled out of granite for shelving, the room was only protected by a small curtain that was older than anyone cared to remember. Whatever pattern had once decorated its majestic front had long faded away.

Chiun held the curtain open and motioned for Eon to enter.

"Be careful, love," he warned.

Eon carefully held the candle above her head and it was enough to show her how many scrolls there were. Chiun was not exaggerating. The scrolls were so tightly packed together that it looked like a solid wall of cotton wads. Only the north wall had a couple of empty shelves.

"This is the scroll room?" she asked, excited.

"The very room where I spent a third of my childhood," Chiun replied, nodding to a small stool. "That is where I studied."

"I never knew…" she said, speechless.

Reading was one of her favorite things to do, but there was so much to read that she felt overwhelmed.

"You've read all of these?" she asked.

"No, but I should be finished reading everything before I turn forty," Chiun said.

"No wonder you have so many stories."

"I have brought you here for a very special story," Chiun said, looking on a shelf near the floor. "Ah, Master Balmung," he said, slowly pulling the ancient leather scroll from its shelf.

"Pullyang needs to lather the scrolls on this shelf," Chiun said, inspecting the scroll. "I see a small crack."

"I have never heard of Master Balmung," Eon said.

"Except for one thing, he remains unknown to most of us," Chiun said, untying the leather that bound it.

"What was that?"

"His son was enormously talented and learned Sinanju instinctively," Chiun said. "He was much more talented than his father, who did not know how to properly train him."

Eon looked over Chiun's shoulder, careful to keep the candle at bay.

"How do you even see down here?" she asked.

Chiun pointed to his eyes and smiled.

"Is there anything you can't do?" Eon asked.

"Obviously my skills at making tea need work," Chiun said. "Ah, here it is."

Eon smiled. She could tell that Chiun was going to try to lower his voice into the baritone that his father had used, but his voice was a natural tenor.

It took Chiun fifteen minutes to read the story, and then he abruptly stopped.

"That's it?" Eon asked. "You were getting to the good part."

"As I said, Master Balmung was not prepared to teach such a talented pupil."

"Did his son become a good master or one of those who was known for being weak?"

"His son died," Chiun admitted. "Master Balmung had to train his second son, Master Sam, who then gave up one of Sinanju's secrets to an emperor. He was worse than a failure. He was an example to all future masters."

"How did his son die?" Eon asked weakly.

Chiun hesitated to carefully choose his words.

"There are three training stages in Sinanju. The first is preparation. The risks are small and managed. You've seen the bruising and minor injuries. Some masters even broke bones at this stage, but I have shielded Song from anything substantial."

"Is Song at risk?" Eon asked.

"He soon will be," Chiun admitted.

"What kind of risk?"

"He has already begun the second stage of training. Normally the second stage begins between twelve and fifteen, depending on the pupil and it is at this stage that involves *external* risk, dangers that would prove fatal for anyone not trained in Sinanju. This is the time where fears are purged."

"Like a fear of bears?" Eon asked.

"Exactly. You can't succeed in Sinanju if someone decides to attack you with their pet bear...or elephant, as I found out most recently."

"You killed an elephant?" Eon asked.

"Of course not," Chiun said. "I merely caused it to fall asleep and then killed its rider."

He could tell that Eon was still worried.

"On the other hand, this part of the training is the best time.

Anything that Song fears, from heights, to animals to specific situations are all addressed to show the pupil that fear is nothing more than a feeling. You feel hot, you feel cold, you feel angry, you feel afraid. Fear can never kill you, but panicking around things you are afraid of most certainly will."

"Will you be shooting at him?" Eon asked, worried.

"Oh, we've already been playing around with boom sticks... that's what Song likes to call them."

"You shot our son?" Eon asked in shock.

"I didn't *hit* him," Chiun explained. "The boy can already dodge three bullets!"

"Part of me wants to know what is going on but when I hear things like this," Eon said, burying her face in her hands. "I don't know which is worse."

Song entered the scroll room, his eyes alight with excitement. He had overheard their conversation, and with a tender smile, stood before his mother, and held her hand.

"Mama," he said, his voice brimming with confidence, "Don't worry. I'm always careful!"

Eon's heart skipped a beat as she looked into his eyes. They were shining with pride and determination. In that moment, she saw not just a child, but a soul who had already embraced the path that destiny had laid before him. Her fears softened and her breathing relaxed.

"Listen to your father," she said. "And be careful!"

"I will," Song promised. "Can I go play now?"

Chiun and Eon silently watched as their son returned to his room, humming the sounds of his imaginary play—a stark reminder that he was still just a boy.

CHAPTER TWENTY-EIGHT

*E*ven before the mysterious chimes rang to awaken the shaman, a sense of anticipation filled the House of Many Woods. The night air, pregnant with warmth of the coming dawn, carried the morning call of the first birds as Song mentally prepared himself. Today was the day they would embark on his perilous mountain ascent up Mount Paektu.

Paektu was the largest mountain in Korea—a majestic, dormant volcano crowned with a large crater called Heaven Lake. Despite thirty years of dormancy, occasional rumblings had been reported, stirring unease among the mountaineers Chiun had spoken with the previous month. He had to reassure Eon almost every day since that they would cancel the training if the mountain showed signs of activity.

As they left and the door began to shut behind them, Eon rushed forward. Reaching Song, she gently cupped his face with both hands, searching for the same fierce spark in his eyes that both comforted and worried her. With a soft trembling smile, she kissed his forehead and whispered a silent prayer against his skin.

"Be careful, my heart," she said, her voice choked with emotion.

"I will, Mama," Song replied, reassuring her. "Please don't worry!"

"Expect us back in ten days' time, love, or perhaps a little longer if the mountain spirits demand it," Chiun added with a reassuring grin. "The boy will be fine. He might even enjoy himself."

After a final, nervous kiss, Eon stepped back silently, allowing them to begin their journey. As they walked away, her eyes remained fixed on Song as her little boy grew smaller and smaller in the distance, before finally slipping from view.

The Sinanju carriage awaited them at the edge of the road. The coach driver was silently standing by the open doors. Song sat on the wrong side and only moved after seeing Chiun's raised eyebrow.

For the first few days, the trip was uneventful. The days were long and they camped each day after sundown. Each night, Chiun shared stories of ancient masters, each tale a lesson in perseverance and wisdom. Song listened, his eyes wide, absorbing every word as the fire crackled and the shadows danced.

Chiun took the opportunity to teach Song not just about Sinanju, but about the world and life. He addressed everything they passed and everything they saw: the stars, the wind, the behavior of animals. Each lesson was woven into the fabric of their goal, letting Song know that he was not just a part of Sinanju, but of life.

As the landscape grew wilder and the path less defined, the carriage struggled over rough terrain. The coach driver skillfully navigated around larger rocks and through narrow passes, but the going was slow.

At one point, a wheel caught in a deep rut, and Chiun allowed Song to free it, cautiously warning him to not damage the wheel. It was a minor delay, but it served as a reminder of the mountain's remoteness and the unpredictability of their quest.

Just before sundown as they neared their destination, a thick fog enveloped the ground. The mountain, veiled in its ghostly curtain, seemed like a slumbering giant.

"We are close," Chiun said. "Tonight, there will be no stories, only sleep."

Song laid down on his straw mat, which provided little comfort from the rocks and sticks below him. He watched as the sun faded behind the mountain, only to be replaced by stars. Then he fell asleep and the mountain claimed his dreams.

It was after three the next day before the carriage brought them as close as it could. Song felt as though he had already traveled through multiple worlds, each with its own lessons and trials. He looked at the summit, already large, but shrouded in mist.

"We shall return later this evening. We will pitch tent here before returning home," Chiun advised the coach driver, who nodded silently before making camp.

Chiun and Song walked the last half mile in silence, arriving at the foot of the towering mountain. Song looked up in amazement to the top of Mt. Paektu. It was one thing to hear about how tall the mountain was, but quite another to see it stretching upward, its summit touching the sky, mingling with the clouds. The mountain seemed to call to him, a silent challenge hanging in the cool air.

"As you begin your ascent, remember that the mountain changes with each step," Chiun warned. "This mountain is a collection of its past, a tapestry of fire and earth woven together. Some parts are strong like granite, while others may be soft, like charcoal."

Song placed his hands on the nearby rock, experimenting with the texture of its surface.

"Carefully observe how the rocks vary in color and texture. These will be the only clues the mountain will provide. Heed them, and they will guide your hands and feet," Chiun advised. "And remember, you must always respect the mountain. Challenge it with your skills, but do not underestimate its power to teach harsh lessons."

Song nodded, taking in every word.

"Is there anything else that I need to know, Papa?"

"Do not concern yourself with any sounds you might make. This is not a test of stealth, but of strength and agility," Chiun cautioned. "Your primary concern is safety. I do not wish to explain to your mother why you have returned with a broken arm."

"I'm ready, Papa," Song said, his voice determined.

Chiun nodded and they shared a confident smile.

Song turned to face the mountain.

There were no pre-carved handholds or easy footholds. He would have to create them himself. His small hands struck the rugged surface, grabbing onto every ledge he could find. Where he could not find a handhold, he made one. Steely fingers chipped into the rock only long enough to lift his body higher, using his handhold for a foothold. His wiry muscles rippled with each strike.

The cold wind whipped against his face, carrying the faint scent of pine and earth. Song's eyes traced the path ahead. Each step was deliberate, every movement a testament to his training.

Chiun's voice echoed in his mind, "Focus. The mountain respects those who respect it."

As he ascended, Song felt the rough texture of the rock beneath his fingertips, and he smiled. Each crevice and ridge was a small victory. The sky above shifted from a deep blue to a lighter hue, hinting at the approaching afternoon. He listened to the distant call of a hawk, a solitary sound in the vast silence.

Unlike his father, Song could only center for a limited time.

He found a narrow ledge and paused to rest, breathing deeply and taking in the view. He had never been this high before. His mother had worried that he might panic because of the height, but his father had already chased the fear of heights from his body.

The landscape below stretched out in a patchwork of greens and browns, a testament to the distance he had already covered. A sudden rustle to his right caught his attention. He looked in time to see a small lizard scurrying across a nearby rock. The sight brought a brief smile to his face, a reminder of the life that thrived even in such harsh conditions. He watched the lizard disappear into a crevice, marveling at its agility.

Centering once more, the climb continued, and with each step, Song felt a deeper connection to the mountain. The challenges it presented were not just physical but mental as well. He encountered sections where the rock was smooth and offered little grip, forcing him to think creatively and use his body's full range of motion. At times, he had to leap from one precarious hold to another, his heart pounding with the thrill of the experience.

He reached a particularly difficult section and had to pause to catch his breath. The altitude was higher now, the air thinner and colder. He felt the pressure in his lungs, but he did not waver. This was his test, his rite of passage. He slowed down just enough to refresh his lungs.

With renewed resolve, he began to scale the challenging section. His fingers found purchase on a small outcropping, and he pulled himself up, feeling the strain in his muscles. The rocks were cold against his skin, but his determination burned hotter.

Midway around the mountain, Song found a small cave. He decided to take another rest, away from the biting wind. The cave was cool and dark, a welcome respite from the exposure outside. He sat down and allowed himself a moment of reflection. He thought of his mother, her gentle smile and encouraging words. She had always believed in him, and he was determined to make her proud. After this, she would have nothing to fear.

As he sat there, he noticed a small, delicate plant growing in a crevice, its leaves a vibrant green. It was a testament to resilience, thriving in a place where most would struggle. Song reached out and touched one of the leaves, feeling a kinship with the tenacious plant.

The rest was brief, and soon he was back on the mountain, his body and mind recharged. He encountered a section where the handhold disintegrated as soon as he grabbed it, forcing him to find another. He began searching for alternate handholds, and had to descend to find the next one.

The climb was relentless, each moment a test of his endurance and willpower. Song's lungs began to ache but he continued. He was on the other side of the mountain when he felt a deep rumble beneath his feet. At first, it was a low, grumbling gulp, but it quickly grew into a never-ending roar that shook his bones.

Song's heart, steadfast moments earlier, stuttered in fear as the tremor intensified. He had never heard anything so loud and he resisted the urge to land on an outcropping and cover his ears. The rocks above him, shaken loose by the mountain's wrath, began pelting him, first with pebbles, but then larger stones became dislodged.

He had no room or time to dodge the rockslide, so he leapt to the side in an effort to avoid it. His hands moved with the practiced strength and speed of his training, but the mountain was indifferent and cruel. As the first rocks struck him, he lost his grip and plummeted eight feet, landing on his back, almost knocking the wind out of him.

He leapt to his feet and hugged the side of the mountain, reeling from the pain of a broken rib. He grabbed a breath to center as a pain shot up his back.

. . .

When he felt the first tremor, Chiun leapt up the mountain, crisscrossing to where Song should be. He ignored the panic building in his heart, and destroyed everything in his way, carving a diagonal path up the mountain with a speed borne of desperation.

When he reached the rockslide, he had to leap between the boulders, twisting his body to curve around and through the granite storm. His body instinctively took over. Foot grabbed stone, flipping his body toward the mountain in an impossible cartwheel that carried him to his destination.

Song's back was on fire as he leapt to a nearby ledge, moments before the foothold he was using crumbled, falling two hundred feet below. He began crying as he chiseled new handholds, and his fingers began to feel the strength of the mountain wall.

While in mid-leap, the sharp edge of a large stone struck him in the back. Overwhelmed, his little body lost its center. He was semi-conscious when he bounced off the side of the mountain and that was when he saw his father. Despite his fear, he smiled, reaching out for him.

As Chiun rounded the bend, his eyes met Song's. Chiun's heart clenched in his chest as he pushed his body faster, possessed by a force beyond himself. He paid no heed to the terrain that tore at both cloth and skin.

But the mountain was faster.

In the final moment, there was a silent exchange, a frozen moment between father and son, with hope and despair balanced on a razor's edge. Then Song's small body hit the ground.

In less than a heartbeat, Chiun was at Song's side, shielding him from the incoming rubble. Chiun winced as rocks tore into the meat of his back, but he gathered Song and leapt from the ground to a stone outcropping and from the outcropping to a large tree, rolling out into a small clearing.

He pulled Song close to inspect him, but his face was swollen and his eyes mindlessly reflected the sky above. Chiun listened as his breathing became shallow and fleeting. His mind taunted him with the memory of his father's failure to save his mother and for just a moment, Chiun almost surrendered to the remaining boulders that continued their way. Grabbing Song and dashing away, Chiun only stopped when he was far enough from the mountain's threat.

Satisfied with its show of strength, the mountain fell silent.

Chiun held Song close, feeling the broken hiccup in his son's heart. He began prodding Song's back, searching for something in his body that he could fix. Each raspy breath that Song took was a reminder of every laugh, every cry, every moment that had led them to this mountain.

Chiun plied his fingernails to the nerves in Song's back, but only managed to provoke more pain in his son's body.

"Stay with me, Song," Chiun pleaded, willing his son to fight the shadow encroaching upon them both.

With the last of his strength, Song squeezed his father's hand and Chiun began to cry.

Song's eyes, once vibrant with the spirit of adventure, now mirrored the infinite expanse above, capturing the fading twilight in his eyes.

Chiun saw the reflections of the fiery sunsets they had chased and the starlit nights they had navigated, the essence of a young soul who had danced with the winds and still dreamt of playing with toys.

As Song's grip gently loosened, Chiun felt his strength bleed into the cold terrain.

CHAPTER TWENTY-NINE

Chiun gently lifted Song's lifeless body from the carriage, holding him tightly against his chest. The coachman stepped aside and bowed before Chiun.

"My heart weeps with you, Master," he said, breaking his vow of silence.

Chiun nodded, trying to hold back the river of emotion that was smashing against the dam he had built during the trip home.

"Thank you," Chiun said weakly, ignoring the coachman's transgression.

With each step, the weight of grief and guilt pressed heavily upon him. Chiun entered the village from the north, his face a mask of sorrow. Wordlessly, he walked to the residential portion of the House of Many Woods.

Eon quickly opened the door as she saw movement from the other side. But something was wrong. She recognized Chiun and that he was holding something, but she could not process that it was her son.

She looked at Song's face. It was swollen, blue and lifeless, and then she looked back to Chiun.

It took a moment for reality to sink in, but in that moment, her emotions overwhelmed her and heartbreak transformed into a seething sense of betrayal. She tore Song from Chiun's grip and clutched him close, as if trying to breathe life back into his tiny body.

"I warned you!" she screamed. "But you wouldn't listen!"

As the waves of grief crashed over her, something snapped. She knew Chiun was impervious to her attack, but the surge of emotions overpowered her reasoning. Gently setting Song's body down, her eyes bulged with an insane rage, and she unleashed her fury upon Chiun, slapping and punching him with all her might.

Initially, Chiun instinctively dodged her attacks, but then, understanding the depth of her pain and her anger, closed his eyes and let her vent her rage upon him.

When her adrenaline was spent, Eon collapsed to the floor, a puddle of grief, gasping for breath. Her hands were bruised as she crawled back to the body of her little boy, hugging him close and wailing with a pain that Chiun had never witnessed before.

Unable to bear the weight of the grief he had caused his wife, Chiun retreated into the bowels of the House of Many Woods. He sealed himself off from the world, allowing the darkness to envelop him as he grappled with his own guilt and grief.

News of Song's death sent shockwaves through the village, and the newly-thriving streets fell silent as grief enveloped those who had known him. Once unified under the promise of Song's vast potential, the villagers now felt the loss of their future.

The shaman hurried preparations to accommodate the burial plans. Sinanju funerals were always held at sundown, to help the departed soul pass peacefully into the Void.

Po, the blacksmith and Tae, the leather maker, took it upon themselves to ensure that the Hallows was a fitting resting place. They left for the sacred ground as soon as they heard about the planned funeral.

The Hallows had not been attended since the last funeral there, hundreds of years earlier. Large swatches of weeds had overgrown the graves. Branches from nearby trees were strewn everywhere and the stones that outlined the tiny cemetery had long ago surrendered to tall, dry grass.

Po's large hands were more accustomed to the heat of the forge than the cool dampness of the earth, but they were strong. He took up a shovel and began to dig. Each strike of the blade into the soil seemed as loud as if he was striking his anvil.

Tae worked alongside his friend, clearing the rubble and branches that sullied the sanctity of the place.

"We really need to take better care of this place," Tae said, noticing the disarray.

Po looked pitifully at his skinny friend as he struggled to pull the large tufts of grass from the ground.

"Tae, you know you don't have to be out here, right?"

"I know what it's like to lose a child," Tae replied coldly, as he piled the grass into a pile. "Damn me if I wasn't out here."

"No one has seen the Master since we heard the news," Po noted.

"I know why," Tae said coldly. "That man is replaying every single moment of the last few days trying to think about what he could have done differently to save his child."

Po finished digging the grave and set his shovel down.

"I imagine you're right," he said.

As the sun began to dip into the west, the villagers gathered in a solemn procession. The air resonated with a heavy silence, broken only by the soft rustle of footsteps and hushed whispers.

The absence of Chiun was palpable, a void that seemed to deepen the collective anguish of the community.

The shaman led the procession. His hands cradled Song's lifeless body, wrapped in a shroud as white as the clouds overhead.

Eon numbly followed behind in a matching white shroud. Her face, once vibrant, was now a canvas of pain. The villagers, united in their sorrow, formed a silent procession behind her. They moved as one, their footsteps echoing the rhythm of a mournful dirge.

As they reached the Hallows, the villagers formed a hushed semicircle, their faces a mosaic of sorrow under the fading light. The ground, still damp from an earlier drizzle, seemed ready to embrace Song into its fold.

The shaman gently lowered Song's body into the freshly dug grave and began his invocation, his voice a deep, resonant thread weaving through the still air.

"Today, we lay to rest a child of Sinanju, whose laughter once filled our hearts and whose spirit brought light to our lives," he began. "Though his time with us was brief, his memory will endure with each of us."

Among the villagers, hushed sobs broke the silence, a mournful chorus echoing the shaman's anguish. A young mother clutched her child tighter, her eyes filled with a fear that mirrored Eon's own. Po hid his tears from the crowd, finding solace in his wife's embrace.

The shaman continued, his voice finding strength in the very words he spoke.

"Song brought joy into our lives. His spirit was a testament to the enduring power of hope. May his soul find peace in the embrace of the Void, and may his legacy live on through the love and hope he inspired in all of us."

Eon stood at the foot of the grave, numbly staring at the shrouded body at the bottom of the grave. It was still hard to believe that Song was wrapped beneath it. As the shaman's chants rose and fell, she reached down and placed Song's favorite toy, a small duck carved from wood, gently on his chest, her movements careful and precise.

She made sure to pose it just right.

The villagers, moved by the ceremony and the depth of Eon's despair, began to step forward. One by one, they placed a stone inside Song's grave at his feet. With each stone came a memory of the young boy. It was not long before the stones began to cover his feet.

As the ceremony drew to a close, the shaman waved a long incense bowl over the grave, its smokey aroma mingling with the damp smell of the freshly turned earth.

"We consecrate Song's journey to the Void, and release him to the peace beyond."

The villagers each passed the grave one more time. Some placed their hands on Eon's back in sympathy, while those close to her shared grieving hugs.

Even after the villagers had returned to their homes, Eon remained, whispering her last goodbyes to her little boy. The night closed in, its darkness a chilling reflection of the void within her soul. In the distance, a mournful howl echoed through the forest; whether it was a wolf or her own fractured spirit, she could not tell and did not care.

Chiun had watched the ceremony unfold, hidden amongst the copse of ginkgo trees in the courtyard. His figure was a silhouette of torment, aching with a pain that no amount of breathing could repair. The weight of his guilt pressed down upon him, and with a final, anguished glance at the pain in his wife's eyes and the fresh grave of his son, Chiun surrendered to his grief, disappearing into the night.

As autumn crept into Sinanju, the village was still cloaked in a pall of sorrow. The villagers spoke in hushed tones, their smiles as rare as the warm sun, as they tried to process the events that had led to Song's mysterious death. They had even begun to wonder if Chiun had exiled himself as they struggled to come to terms with Sinanju's future.

Two months after Song's burial, Chiun silently returned to the residential quarters. Eon sat motionless in the living room.

"This is your fault," she said, her voice barely above a whisper.

She refused to make eye contact as if the sight of Chiun sharpened her pain.

Chiun felt a stab of guilt pierce through him.

"I know," he admitted, the weight of his own words suffocating him. "I loved our boy."

Eon's eyes finally met his, flashing with a pain so raw that it seemed to bleed into the air between them.

"Do not say that!" she hissed, her body trembling as if the effort of containing her grief demanded her entire being.

Silence filled the room, thick and oppressive, as Chiun struggled for words that could bridge the chasm of grief between them.

"I do not know what to say," he admitted.

"This is the house of your fathers," Eon said. "I will stay the night at my parents and move out tomorrow. I only ask that you provide a small hut and provisions for me."

Chiun sat humbly on the floor at her feet and tried to make eye contact.

"Eon, you are my heart and my love. Losing Song was devastating," Chiun admitted. "You once said that you would be there whenever I needed you. I *need* you, Eon."

"Song needed you!" Eon shouted, rising from her seat. "Where were you when *he* needed you?"

"I did everything I could," Chiun said, his voice trembling as he replayed the last memories of his son.

Eon sat back down, refusing to break into tears.

"I come to you about another matter," Chiun said. "I know that we once spoke of a daughter, but Sinanju needs a son."

Eon's face began quivering with rage.

"Why do you think I would ever consider giving you another child to kill?"

Chiun looked at Eon, his eyes pleading for a forgiveness he knew he did not deserve.

"I know...I failed Song...but..." his voice broke. "I have a duty..."

"You *failed* at your duty to Song...and to me!" Eon said, with a growing hatred in her eyes.

As Eon prepared to leave, her steps were slow, heavy with the weight of unresolved grief. There was a long, suffocating silence, filled with the words neither could bring themselves to say.

"There is nothing left for us here, not after this," Eon said, her voice steadier, as if each word she spoke affirmed her decision. "I will return at dawn to retrieve my things. Do not ever speak to me again."

Chiun stood motionless, unable to find the words that might halt her departure—words that perhaps no longer existed.

Eon paused at the door as the night air brushed against her face, carrying whispers of the past, echoes of laughter and moments of joy that now seemed worlds away. She turned briefly, her eyes scanning the shadows of the home she could no longer bear, each corner a burst of memories she needed to escape.

Eon stepped out into the night, indifferently leaving the door open to the cold wind.

CHAPTER THIRTY

*I*n the fading light of the Korean dusk, Chiun stood numbly amidst the trees of the Caretakers' Forest, overlooking the village he had sworn to protect. His gaze swept across the familiar huts and hovels laid out below. Once, viewing the village at dusk had provided Chiun with a sense of solace and purpose. To feel the sigh of an evening breeze as it flowed through the forest, to swell with the joy of villagers' faint laughter, had allowed him a connection with both the village and the villagers.

But every rustle was now a hiss of accusation, each lamp a beacon of his shame. Smoke rose from tiny hearths, each plume a choking reminder of his failure. Where Chiun once would have smiled, his face now puckered into a sneer.

A man who could not protect his own son, could not possibly protect an entire village. Chiun searched his soul, reaching out for any connection to keep him attached to the people or village, but it had been shattered by his own hand. Soaking in one last glance, Chiun turned from the village of his ancestors and ran. As fast as he could, he ran, whipping through the thickets, quickly passing the line of trees and brush that separated Sinanju from the rest of the world.

Faster than a gazelle, he ran down a muddy highway, so fast that if anyone had seen him, they would have thought they had seen a mountain god—correctly so, as the translation of 'Sinan-ju' was literally 'god-inside-village.' Most Koreans simply said: "A god resides here."

"A god?" he internally scoffed. *"Sinanju is a noose of traditions; it is a sea where all drown!"*

He ran.

He ran from the village. From his wife. Even from Sinanju itself, he ran.

With each step, he shed a portion of his being, forsaking everything that he once was and would become in an attempt to free himself from the suffocating chains of tradition. His heart hammered an unfamiliar beat and as his emotions began taking control, his running became erratic.

The corner of his robe caught on a small thicket, shredding the edges. Mud began clinging to the soles of his feet and small cracks of broken branches were heard. The grass beneath him began carrying the sounds of footfalls and splashes, the sound of mortal feet, growing heavier with each stride. Chiun ran until he reached a small clearing overlooking a valley to the north.

As a child, the valley had often put everything in perspective. The vast expanse of nature lay before him. A small rabbit ran along the hedges seeking food, a bird above enjoyed the lift of a rare, warm breeze. Everything fed around a stream that ran the length of the valley, providing audience and life to all. In nature, everything had a place, and everything had a purpose.

But Chiun could no longer find a place for himself in nature.

The expanse of whispering grasses seemed to hold its breath, participating in his sorrow. Chiun's gaze was distant, lost in the realm of memories where he once felt the warm embrace of a loving wife, and the laughter of a child had filled his days. The memories were both a balm and a torment, soothing the jagged edges of his loss while reminding him of how much had been irrevocably lost.

His emotions began rising in his throat, and Chiun once again felt the weight of tradition bearing down upon him. It shamed him, demanding discipline, and unyielding willpower. But in this quiet moment, far away from the eyes of the village and the haunted whispers of judgment, Chiun…the man…cast away the chains of tradition.

"I am not worthy," he whispered in realization.

For the first time in his life, Chiun tried to allow his breath to relax and uncenter, but no matter what he tried, his body resisted. He tried violently coughing and taking intermittent short and long breaths, as deeply as he could to break his center. He hurled his body at a tree, only to instinctively twist around it. The rage inside his heart built until he could hold it in no more. He collapsed to his knees, unable to cope with the emotions building inside.

A soul-wrenching wail erupted from Chiun's throat.

With every ounce of his body, he screamed. And in that scream, he packed every pain, regret and sorrow until he had no breath left. And when his breath left him, so did Sinanju, and his center finally cracked. So powerful was his cry that birds fled their evening nests and beasts retreated deeper into the forest.

Chiun became enveloped in a headache so strong that it would not allow him the dignity to remain upright. His senses dulled and a dizzy rush of despair filled his body. The surrounding area seemed to shrink around him until he was only aware of the constant buzzing in his ears and the smell of cold mud clinging to his body.

As the world around him began to spin, his lungs collapsed and he fell backward into the mud. Unable to bring in the air his body desperately craved, Chiun began to hyperventilate. Short and shrill gasps of air tried to feed a body that was once fueled by the lung capacity of a horse. Wheezy screams tore through his throat in an attempt to grab as much air as he could.

It took several minutes before Chiun managed to steady his breathing, but even then, his breathing was a rapid and thin substitute of his former self. And in that moment, he felt the corruption of every man's body. He was hungry and thirsty and sleepy and frail and, for the first time in his life, Chiun feared for his own existence.

What had he done?

Stripped of the artificial enhancements that Sinanju had granted him, Chiun struggled with his own body weight as he tried to right himself. This is who he really was: Chiun the Weak, Chiun the Failure.

He once had everything. Eon was to be his great and eternal love…and his little boy…Song! Chiun remembered his precious smile and silly faces. Song was beautiful and funny and confident. He would have made a great master. But he had failed him. Now Song was dead.

Chiun's hands, once instruments of lethal devastation, now trembled, betraying his inner turmoil. The hands that had held his son at birth could not protect him. In the solitude of the cold field, Chiun allowed the last part of stoic mask to slip, revealing the raw pain of a father who had lost a part of his soul.

"Song!" He screamed into the growing darkness. "My *son!*"

Unbidden tears traced a path down his cheeks. In the embrace of the approaching night, Chiun's heart ached. His strength spent, he whispered his son's name over and over. It whispered through the grass, carried by a gentle breeze.

"Song…"

Chiun surrendered to the mud, a useless man without a future and without hope. He did not notice that the breeze around him had congealed into a fog that engulfed the area.

Then a light, soft and ethereal, pierced the gloom.

"There is always hope," a voice said from behind.

Chiun had not detected anyone approach him or he would not have allowed himself to become so vulnerable. Whoever was behind him had just surrendered their life.

Chiun stood, twisted and instinctively struck with the four fingers of his right hand. It was a devastating blow called 'Stone Burst,' and was intended to pulverize granite walls. But without his center, his hand wildly flailed, throwing his shoulder out of its socket. Off-balance, Chiun once again landed in the mud.

"That wasn't very smart," the ghostly figure said, amused. "Though, I have always wondered what a Sinanju move would look like if a person was not centered."

The man was Chiun's height, but had to weigh two hundred pounds. He wore an older, more traditional robe, with muted orange figures that had once represented seagulls. It was something Chiun had not seen outside the sketches in some of the oldest scrolls. But there was something odd about the man apart from his perpetual grin—an internal glow caused his body to seem slightly transparent.

"I am Wang," the fat man said with a slight bow.

"What?" Chiun asked, wincing in pain. He curled his shoulder back in an attempt to relieve the pain.

The friendly smile remained on Wang's face.

"It is nice to finally meet Chiun the Great Teacher. I will forgive your clumsy attempt to harm me."

Chiun had read in the scrolls about moments like this, where a master was supposedly visited by Wang or one of the other masters in times of great change. He had never considered them as real experiences.

"I have gone mad," Chiun said to himself.

"You are in great pain, young Master," Wang said, his smile fading. "I know this pain."

"If you are Wang, then you are not great!" Chiun screamed. "This world of power you have created is strangled by tradition!"

Wang cocked his head in disbelief.

"What you refer to as 'tradition' is the accumulated wisdom from the life experiences of past Masters. Do you think any of us had it better?"

Wang gently glided toward Chiun, dragging the fog with him. Chiun felt a breeze pass his shoulder as Wang touched it, and his shoulder returned to its socket.

"You have lost a son. I understand this pain," Wang said. "I lost my first two sons in training and would have killed many more if my third son Ung had not discovered a way to properly teach someone how to breathe. But his poems are so boring."

"Ung is the Master of Poetry!" Chiun said in defence. "His rhythm knows no equal!"

"Does it?" Wang asked and his smile returned.

Wang began to softly whistle, and the air thickened around them until Chiun saw a little boy in a hut, being taught by a shrouded figure. As he approached, he could make out the boy's features.

Chiun was looking at his three-year-old self. He was sitting at the feet of his father Nūk. Seeing his father caused Chiun's face to relax for the first time in days.

"The sun sees the buuuuuutterfly," little Chiun sang in a tiny voice that had not been heard in decades. "The butterfly seeeeeeees the FLOWWWWWWER!"

"No," Nūk said sternly. "You have to hold the syllables out while increasing volume. You have to stretch those lungs, boy!"

"I hate Ung!" little Chiun said, stomping his feet.

Neither of the Chiuns saw Nūk's hand move, but young Chiun bounced against the far wooden wall, knocking the wind out of him. After taking a moment to re-orient himself, little Chiun returned saddened, but he did not cry.

He bowed deeply.

"I am sorry, father," Little Chiun said.

Nūk nodded and motioned for Chiun to return to his seat.

"Second Quatrain," Nūk repeated even louder. "Again!"

The air evaporated, losing its internal glow.

"It doesn't look like you thought much of Ung at the time," Wang said as the vision vanished.

"Is this a joke to you?" Chuin wailed. "I lost my son! I am not worthy to be Master! I am not even worthy of being a man!"

"Did you somehow think that Song would have lived forever?" Wang asked. "We all have our time. This was his, and you will record it in the scrolls to honor his memory. He traded a few years of his life to be with you. Do you not think that time was worth something to him? Or is this only about you?"

"You don't know me," Chiun said, his voice trembling.

"Hanuel, Duri," Wang said.

Chiun grew silent and looked up at Wang. Those were the names of Wang's two eldest sons who had also died in training.

"I am called the 'Great' Wang, and yet I could not train my own sons," he said sadly. "Like you, I watched them die. I had to carry both of their bodies home to my wife."

"How...old were they?" Chiun asked.

The fog around Wang curdled with the change of his emotions.

"Hanuel was seven. Duri was four," Wang answered. "Had they been trained to breathe correctly they would have been able to handle what was tasked to them. I joined my ancestors believing that I had been a failure. I had been given the greatest of all gifts and failed my first two sons. My failures lie in the small cemetery where their bones rest to this day."

Chiun paused. "The Hallows," he quietly said.

"Each body buried there represents a failed master. How many dozen graves sit behind your house uncelebrated and unmourned? My sons meant no less to me than Song did to you."

"The Scrolls acknowledge that your two eldest sons failed to learn to breathe properly," Chiun said. "As a lesson to us all. This should not happen after Ung."

"My sons became just another story in the scrolls, but they were loved and I cried as I dug each of their graves. But me? I became a legend, failures and all. Being on this side of the Void allows objectivity, something you do not possess."

"It no longer matters," Chiun whispered. "Sinanju is dead."

Wang laughed so hard that his belly shook beneath his robes.

"Sinanju does not belong to any one master!" Wang said. "I say to you that your pupil shall become the greatest master of all."

"I have no pupil," Chiun said. "And I do not wish to be responsible for any more."

"Do you think the 'Great Wang' would reveal a splinter of your future if it were not so?"

"It does not matter," Chiun said. "I can no longer center my being. I have abandoned Sinanju."

"Have you?" Wang asked.

He placed his ghostly hand through Chiun's chest and Chiun gasped. His lungs properly filled, and his headache disappeared. With the absence of the headache came some clarity. Though his heart was still pained, Chiun understood.

"The path of a Master was never promised to be an easy one," Wang said. "With great power comes...well, that's a different story."

"Thank you," Chiun said humbly, bowing.

"Farewell, Great Teacher."

"Wait!" Chiun said. "I have so many questions!"

But Wang laughed and he was gone.

Chiun could find no more tears, but closed his eyes in sorrow. When he heard the small familiar whoosh that had accompanied Wang's arrival. He turned to see a Korean man his age, wearing formal blue robes. The man was smiling, but it was clearly not Wang.

"Why is everyone so happy about being dead?" Chiun asked. "Have you come to mock me, as well?"

The man walked toward Chiun silently. His smile not only continued, it grew larger.

"No, father, I am here to honor you," Song said, bowing deeply.

Chiun looked more closely. The eyes…it was Song! But he was a man, at least Chiun's age. That was when Chiun noticed that he was not alone. Several men stood behind Song, and Chiun instinctively knew that each of these men had died while in training. But there was no shame on their faces, only pride. The men bowed deeply to Chiun in unison.

"All hail the Master of Sinanju!" they cried, their voices a thunderous chorus.

"How cruel is time, that it grants us the peace we seek, but only in dreams from which we must awake?" Song pondered.

"My son!" Chiun cried in joy. "How is this possible?"

Song's lips curved as he smiled, reminding Chiun of one of his mother's best features.

"You just spoke with the apparition of a two-thousand-year-old master, and yet you ask me how this is possible?" Song asked.

Chiun's gaze lingered on the ghostly figure he had only known as a boy, now standing before him in the fullness of manhood—a vision of what might have been. He rushed and tried to hug him, but his arms passed through Song's misty body.

Song's eyebrows raised in sorrow.

"While you spoke with Wang, I visited Mother," he said. "But her heart was hardened and she could not see or hear me."

"Your death has changed her," Chiun said.

"Remember her sorrow, father and please care for her," Song said, worry crossing his ethereal face. "She has many painful years ahead."

"Your mother is my heart, but I fear that this may have been too much."

"You both feel great grief, but I want you to know that this failure was not yours," Song said. "It was my own. I failed to heed your instructions and look closely enough ahead."

"No, you were given an impossible task for your age, my son," Chiun said.

"I saw you," Song said softly. "Tearing through stone like a wind god, moving so fast that I thought you had destroyed the mountain to reach me. It was the last thing I saw and it was good."

Unable to contain his sorrow, Chiun's eyes filled with tears.

Song hovered closer to comfort his father, but as he approached, the air around Chiun began to grow hazy. Song was filled with sadness as he was shown glimpses of his father's future. He saw the treacherous end at his second attempt at a pupil. He saw a father so broken that he began selling things so the village could survive.

But then, the images faded and a great light erupted, filling his vision. Song saw a man with thick wrists. His eyes were deep set, but round, like Chiun's mother, Ji. Though the man appeared to be white, Song saw the strong heart of a Sinanju Master beat inside his chest.

The man returned Song's gaze, power radiating from the bold lines of his smile to the unwavering conviction in his eyes. A ripple of joy touched Song's face, revealing a flicker of something like triumph. It was the spirit of Sinanju reborn, Song realized, poised to usher in an era eclipsing even that of the Great Wang.

"Do not worry, father," Song whispered with a tearful smile. "There are great trials awaiting you, but your story has just begun," Song said. He wished he could say more, but time would answer Chiun's questions. "I want to tell you...what an *honor* it was to be your son."

Song bowed again, looking his father lovingly in the eye. "All hail the Master of Sinanju," he said proudly and disappeared into the mist.

In the distance, Chiun heard chimes.

The fog lifted and Chiun dropped to his knees at the top of the valley. His tears fell freely to his robe, each filling a small piece of his broken heart. Chiun closed his eyes and embraced the image of his son, savoring the sound of his words.

When he opened his eyes, the sun was beginning to rise in the east. Chiun stood, a changed man. He gave one last look over the valley, once again feeling the connection to the river's flow, the path of the swan and the heartbeat of the hare. He had once again found his place in the world.

Spotting a few trails of morning smoke curling up from his village in the distance, Chiun gathered up his torn and muddy robes, beginning the slow walk home.

There would be many rough times in the days ahead with both his wife and the village, but he also knew that there was a future. He smiled.

Sinanju *is* forever.

ABOUT THE AUTHOR

JERRY & CHRISTINA WELCH

Jerry is author of the *Legacy* series as well as *The Last Witness* series. He has written 18 books, including *War in Heaven, Ung: Poet and Master,* and has two other books planned for this trilogy.

He lost his eldest son Justin when he was only 28.

ALSO BY GERALD WELCH

LEGACY, BOOK 1: FORGOTTEN SON

Will Stone and Freya, the lethal brother-sister duo, be enough to help their new boss Benjamin Cole stop the Great Mexican Ninja Army from invading the southwestern United States?

Also available as an audiobook!

LEGACY, BOOK 2: THE KILLING FIELDS

Her name is 14. All she really wants is a new best friend…but it's hard to make friends with someone you're trying to kill. Stone and Freya must face off against a bionic killer while inside a nuclear death trap!

LEGACY, BOOK 3: OVERLOAD

A figure from Sunny Joe's past seeks revenge by hiring Stone and Freya for a video game where there are no cheat codes…and death is for real!

Made in the USA
Columbia, SC
25 April 2025

57151561R00146